In A Year's Time

by

Cheryl M. Robinson

Credits
How Great Thou Art
Stuart K. Hine

Amazing Grace
John Newton

www.xulonpress.com

ACKNOWLEDGEMENTS

---

*I*N A YEAR'S TIME is a sequel to my debut novel, And, Not Only That. Both works were written in gratitude to God whose love, though showered on us daily, continues to amaze and humble me. To each of us He has given a gift. I am honored to share my gift with many. It is my hope, my prayerful mission, that all who read books written by me are encouraged, inspired and blessed.

The passion I have for writing would have remained dormant—or severely arrested—if not acknowledged and nurtured. I am indebted to all who encouraged, taught, corrected, inspired, advocated, and instilled in me the importance of realizing an important purpose for my life.

The reception of And, Not Only That exceeded my expectations and is a source of great pride and excitement because of the overwhelming response I received from many. Thank you to all who read the book and shared in my excitement. To the many individuals, book club members and organizers of other literary events who enthusiastically supported my debut writing endeavor, I sincerely thank you.

There are three exceptional women to whom I owe more than I can possibly repay: Ritchie Carroll, Jearil Stokes, and Patricia Stith Watkins. For excitedly sharing the journey of And, Not Only That, thank you. For critiquing the various drafts of In a Year's Time and sharing your insight, thank you. For demonstrating God's love and grace throughout the years, thank you. For the friendship we share, thank you.

Doug James is one of the most creative and talented persons I know. As a graphic designer, he has once again demonstrated his creative genius. I'm proud and honored to share the journey with you, Doug. You are indeed blessed with an incredible gift. Again, I thank you for going above and beyond.

Throughout this writing endeavor, I consulted with several persons. Special recognition is given to Gerald Jackson, II and Spencer Cochran who advised regarding general FBI and police protocol, respectively.

To Wendy Mills, professional editor and author: Thank you for sharing your invaluable expertise. It was my good fortune to have met you. I'm humbled and grateful for the important role you played in this literary effort.

To my entire village of family and friends, I continued a trend in this book that began with And, Not Only That. You may recognize familiar names throughout. In fact, you may find your own first, middle or last name. It is my way of thanking you and acknowledging your importance in my life. Please do not connect the character with your name. There is no connection. It gave me great joy to include the names of several persons in my book—living and deceased—who impacted my life journey. It is meant as a tribute and an expression of my sincere gratitude.

How does one thank her parents? I'm at a loss for adequate words to express my appreciation to the two individuals who loved me unconditionally, sacrificed for me, nurtured me, set expectations for me and taught me about the Creator of love. Neither death nor illness lessen the depth of our love, your influence, or the treasured memories.

To our children, their significant others and our grandchildren: You are priceless gifts. Because of you, we're rich indeed! I love you more than words can express.

To my husband and best friend: Will, I'm grateful for the blessing of you. You are my biggest fan whether I'm playing tennis, writing, trying a new recipe or a new hairstyle. I don't claim—or aspire—to be the wisest person but I'm wise enough to know that the love we share is exceptional.

DEDICATION

This book is dedicated to
those who suffer from a debilitating or terminal illness.

It is also written in loving memory of
Alice Corrine Allen Daugherty
and
Colonel (Retired) Donald Franklin Miles

———————✳———————

"Above all else, guard your heart,
for everything you do flows from it."
Proverbs 4:23

Prologue

───────────✳───────────

For 50-year old Janole, her home was her haven and her hell. Everywhere she looked there were constant reminders of Wallace and their life: photos, knickknacks from their travels, furniture they selected together, his clothes, favorite mug, tennis gear and other personal possessions. She could see him sitting in his recliner, legs stretched out, mouth slightly open as he "watched" his favorite sporting events. She could feel him, smell him. At times, she relished in this and, at other times, she was tortured.

Weeks passed and nothing had changed for Janole. Surprisingly, there was no news about or from Wallace. Nothing. It was as if he had vanished from the face of the earth. Meanwhile, her life was in shambles and the stress had taken a toll on her, physically and emotionally. She was a woman who seldom smiled and looked as if she had aged ten years. Because she only ate when she reminded herself, she had lost twenty pounds. She even avoided tennis, her one lifelong passion.

One evening, as she sat alone on the deck, staring at nothing, she decided to get away for a few days. She needed to go to a place where she was unknown, where she could think free from distractions or, better yet, not think. She was tired, just plain tired. She decided to go somewhere warm with water. She chose the Bahamas.

"Maybe, I'll try to play a little tennis while there," she said to herself.

After making arrangements and informing her family, she began packing. Finding no unopened cans of tennis balls in her bag, she looked in Wallace's tennis bag which was such a mess that she decided to clean it. Janole was about to close the bag when she noticed a small compartment oddly situated near the bag's bottom. Inside the small compartment she found a key and small piece of yellow paper. In Wallace's handwriting were the words, "It's not what it seems."

"Oh my God! Wallace left a message for me," Janole said out loud, recognizing his familiar signature. She held the note close to her heart as if it were the most precious thing in the world. So many thoughts ran through her mind. What is he trying to tell me, she wondered. Sitting on the floor, she had almost forgotten about the small key. As she scrutinized it closely, she was positive she hadn't seen it before. Wallace was trying to tell her something. Of that she was certain.

For the first time in months, Janole felt something that had become foreign to her. It was called hope. She returned the key and note to Wallace's bag, just as she'd found them, for safe keeping. That night she prayed for help, wisdom and insight. She thanked God for the encouraging findings and asked Him to show her what to do and who to trust. She asked God to send help to her. And with renewed vigor, she prayed for Wallace's safety and protection.

Janole spent most of the next day searching the house for a container that could possibly be unlocked by the small key she had discovered, but her attempts were futile. She looked under beds and in boxes, cabinets and closets. No room was left untouched including the attic and garage. Then, exhausted and disappointed, she decided to check her personal emails before going to bed. There was one from an address she didn't recognize. She opened it and began reading.

Hi Janole,

Ran into your brother and he gave me your email address. I recently relocated to Northern Va. and am still getting accustomed to the traffic. WHEW! It would be great to see you. Perhaps we could have lunch one day? I'm including my cell number. If interested, give me a call.

Hope all is well.
Nate

What a surprise. She hadn't thought of Nate in years; the only other man who had captured her heart. He was a good man, an honest and trustworthy man. Maybe he was the answer to her prayer. She had to trust someone. Janole decided to phone him and, after a brief conversation, they agreed to meet for lunch the next day at Bailey's in Tyson's Corner.

Nate hadn't changed much over the years. He'd picked up some weight which Janole thought was becoming and his hair was mixed with gray. He had a confident and assured persona balanced by a friendly and engaging smile. He was still a handsome man. Janole wasn't sure how she would respond when she saw him for she had loved him deeply at one time.

Wow, Nate thought, as Janole approached the table. *She is gorgeous!* Nate gazed at his former girlfriend with appreciation and told her how beautiful she looked still. They talked and laughed as they reminisced about old times.

A recent divorcee, he had three adult children. He spoke of his legal career with various governmental agencies and his current job as a consultant for the FBI. It had been a long time since Janole truly enjoyed another man's company. Their companionship was so easy, it always had been. She could have listened to him talk for hours but she had a dilemma on her hands and couldn't afford the luxury of idle conversation, no matter how enjoyable.

"Nate, I need to talk to you in confidence. I feel as though I can trust you but, I warn you, this is heavy stuff and it's way out of my league. I really need your help. But it has to stay between the two of us."

Nate sensed that Janole was deeply troubled.

"This sounds serious." Then, half-jokingly, he said, "If you retain me as your attorney, confidentiality is guaranteed."

"Okay. What's the retainer fee?" Janole asked without hesitation.

"One dollar," Nate responded.

"Really? One dollar? That's all you're charging? That's a little concerning. They say you get what you pay for." She half-heartedly laughed at her own joke as she slid a dollar across the table.

He looked at her with concern. "What is it, Janole? You can trust me. I know the type of person you are. If I can help, I will."

She took a deep breath and told him everything over lunch and two cups of coffee. She told him about Wallace the man, Wallace the husband, Wallace the father, Wallace the professional and all of the details related to his disappearance. Her voice quivered at times but she didn't cry.

Nate listened attentively and asked questions.

When she was finally done, she asked, "Well, what do you think?"

"It certainly is baffling. Do you have the letter he left you?"

She nodded and gave him a copy. The original was in her Bible at home. He pulled glasses out of his pocket and, after reading the letter, said nothing. He seemed deep in thought.

Impatient, Janole asked, "What?"

Removing the glasses, he said, "I think something is off. Neither you nor your boys have heard from him since you received this letter? That doesn't sound like the man you described. He hasn't come to collect any of his things? He is willing to completely walk away from you? And with nothing? He said in the letter that he was found out. By whom I wonder? What was the nature of his research? You have no idea who this woman is from his past?"

Janole answered all questions.

"Very strange. It's been several months," Nate said.

He sat thinking for a few minutes. "I wonder why he mentioned having an affair in his letter. And why did he specifically refer to her as a woman from his past? Interesting choice of words. I can understand why he felt compelled to tell you about the fraudulent aspect of his work since that was going to be exposed. But, usually affairs aren't newsworthy. Was there any mention of his involvement with this woman in the news?"

"No, thankfully. The only people who know about that are the ones who read the letter and the ones I've told. My best friend, Jenn—you remember Jenn, right? She lives in Seattle. My sons, Marlo, mom, my pastor and, of course, the police."

"Again, that doesn't sound like the man you described," Nate said.

"I think that's why I was so devastated and shocked," Janole explained. "It's been a tough and I mean tough ordeal. I'm still struggling. This all seemed so out of character for Wallace. But the evidence was there."

She paused.

"At first, I thought maybe he committed suicide and this may sound crazy but I would know if he was dead. I would be able to feel that. He's alive, I'm sure," Janole said, passionately.

"It doesn't sound crazy, Janole. Not at all."

Nate excused himself to use the restroom and when he returned Janole said, "There's one other thing, Nate. Two days ago, I found a note in Wallace's tennis bag in a very small compartment that I believe he created. The note, addressed to me, contained the words 'it's not what it seems.'"

She watched Nate's face as he processed this information.

"Will you help me?" Janole asked in desperation.

Six Months Later

Janole and Wallace

Chapter One

————————— ✳ —————————

A sinister presence was lurking; yet, Janole could neither identify it nor it's hiding place. She could feel it, however, and knew that it was near and threatening. Afraid, she quietly walked throughout her house looking into each room. She heard noises and saw shadows of movement, but when she investigated, there was nothing. *I'm not crazy,* she said to herself though not everyone agreed with her. For some time, she'd desperately tried to convince family and friends of the unusual occurrences but no one believed her because they saw and felt nothing out of order in her home. Their concerned expressions conveyed doubts and, more importantly, their beliefs that she was the problem...that something was wrong with her...that she, perhaps, was becoming mentally unstable. *I'm not crazy.*

Janole continued to walk throughout this beloved dwelling she called home; her surroundings both familiar and unfamiliar. She didn't feel safe. There was a charged atmosphere—a foreboding—of danger. As a result, she had been living in perpetual fear and unrest for some time. She felt so vulnerable and exposed that she was now sleeping with a gun under her pillow.

At this moment, her fear intensified. She knew that this sinister presence was real and that it intended to harm her soon. Every fiber of her being warned of impending danger. Looking over her shoulder, she ran to her bedroom, locked the door and searched for a hiding place. Nate was sitting in a chair reading the paper. *Why is Nate in my bedroom?* He didn't look up when she entered the room and there was no time to question him. She heard a distinct sound that gave her chills. This thing was coming for her and began calling her name as if it were singing a chant.

"Ja – nole, Ja – nole, Ja – nole."

The voice sounded like her father's and that terrified her even more because her father had been dead for years. She was in a state of helpless panic, not knowing what to do. Trembling and with a pounding heart, she frantically considered her options but saw no escape. Fear grabbed her so tightly that she couldn't move or speak. She stood in the center of her bedroom and watched, petrified, as the door knob turned ever so slowly. With little effort, it—he opened the locked door. As the door opened wider, Janole covered her mouth to stifle a scream. He continued to chant her name though his image was hidden from her view.

"Ja – nole, Ja – nole, Ja – nole." Again, it was her father's voice.

Finally, it—he stood in full view and, in horror, Janole stared at the image in the doorway. She shook her head to clear her vision. *Wallace? My husband? It can't be!* But it was Wallace. She was overcome with relief and exhaled loudly.

"Wallace, what are you doing? You scared me to death," Janole said as she lowered herself to the bed.

Oddly, Wallace didn't move or answer. Janole stared at him waiting for a response but he said nothing. Terror gripped her again as it became shockingly clear that he was not the Wallace she knew. He continued to leer at her with eyes that conveyed evil intentions. Janole clutched the side of the bed, her fear so great that she began to hyperventilate.

Meanwhile, the adjourning restroom door opened. *Who else could possibly be here?* Forcing her eyes away from Wallace, she stared as Wallace—another Wallace—walked out of the restroom and, seeing her fear, asked her what was wrong.

"What is going on?" Janole shouted looking from one Wallace to the other. She shook her head unable to accept what she was seeing.

She turned to Nate for help but he was gone. Then the two Wallaces made eye contact and smiled as if they knew each other and were part of a conspiracy. It became disturbingly clear to Janole that they were not surprised to see each other. Slowly, as if obeying an unspoken agreement, they both focused their attention on her and smirked. She gazed from one to the other, rendered completely speechless. In unison, they began walking towards her, still smirking. Janole had never been more frightened. *Which Wallace is real? Which one can I trust? Are they both going to hurt me? Which one is my husband?*

"Wallace!" she screamed just before she awakened.

With overwhelming relief, she realized that it was only a dream—a horrible, horrible nightmare—but it took quite some time for Janole to overcome her fear. In fact, thoughts of the nightmare persisted throughout the day causing her to feel jumpy and uneasy, especially in Wallace's presence.

Her accelerated heart rate slowly returned to normal. The sheet was damp from her perspiration but she refused to move because of her lingering fear. Thanks to tonight's full moon there was a soft cascading glow throughout their bedroom. She must not have thrashed about this time because Wallace, her husband of twenty-five years, was sleeping soundly beside her as if he didn't have a care in the world. Seeing the rhythmic rise and fall of Wallace's chest, she envied his ability to sleep so deeply and peacefully. There was a time when she enjoyed watching him sleep and, inevitably, when nothing else worked, she could lie in his arms and enjoy total peace and contentment.

His arms no longer comforted her. Janole couldn't remember the last time she had slept through the night. When she did manage to doze off, she was jolted out of her sleep just a short while later by the nightmare. She was exhausted physically, mentally, and emotionally yet wide awake.

Again, thoughts constantly raced through her mind and her body was in a permanent state of unyielding tension. She forced herself to relax by inhaling deeply and exhaling slowly—in through the nose and out through the mouth—and, after repeating this ritual several times her body released some of its tension but not enough to stop the racing thoughts or offset her insomnia. She longed for a dreamless sleep to overtake her so that she'd feel refreshed and energized—more like herself.

She continued staring at the man lying beside her with whom she'd shared half of her life. There were so many memories. She remembered the first time she saw him as if it were yesterday. He was a gorgeous man—tall with broad shoulders, long muscular legs, pecan brown skin, brown eyes and a neatly shaped fade—with the physique of a professional athlete. Her attraction to him was immediate but she entertained no expectations of a relationship with him—in spite of her attraction to him—since she was an unwed pregnant woman trying to make a way for her unborn child and herself. And, he was her boss; the one responsible for her having a job that she desperately needed.

Surprisingly though, they developed a friendship and through that relationship she learned that Wallace was an extraordinary man. Having earned a doctorate degree early in his professional career, he was a respected researcher and astute businessman. She found him to be a kind and compassionate person. And he was also a widower.

Eventually, he'd shared with her that he'd lost his entire family several years before meeting her. His beloved grandmother—who raised him in Charlotte—died after a lengthy battle with dementia and, tragically, his wife died shortly after from heart complications while giving birth to their daughter. Slowly, through tears at times, he'd told Janole the entire story.

Janole cried, too, as she listened and witnessed Wallace's pain. She learned that his wife's frail condition caused concern for doctors throughout her pregnancy. The doctors had warned the couple of the danger to her health when she became pregnant and their prognosis didn't change so it was no real surprise, according to Wallace, when his wife died. Sadly, the pregnancy was simply too much and took its toll on her already damaged heart. Wallace told of never leaving his wife's bedside and holding her hand as she took her last breaths. He spoke, with appreciation, of the medical staff's efforts. They did all that was humanly possible but, in spite of their best care, their infant daughter was too weak to sustain life and died hours after her mother.

Janole had not met a man quite like Wallace and, at first, he seemed almost too good to be true. Perhaps his painful losses accounted for his compassion and tenderness. Perhaps it was the loving example and expectations of his grandparents, Rudy and Thelma Jackson, who adopted him legally after his parents' untimely deaths. Or, perhaps it was a combination of all. Whatever the reasons, Janole found an amazing friend and love in Wallace at a time when she expected little.

She was consumed with shame and regret during that time of her life because of a stupid decision at a very vulnerable time that resulted in her being pregnant. Even now—almost thirty years later—feelings of guilt, shame and embarrassment are quick to surface. *What in the world was I thinking? How did I allow myself to get into such a compromising situation?* She had behaved in a way that was contrary to her values and beliefs.

Desperate, despondent, and afraid, she'd considered her options and decided that an abortion was the only answer. But, instead of being at peace with her decision, she was ill at ease. At a loss for what to do, she prayed, pouring out her heart and soul to God in confession, anguish and complete surrender. Incredibly, God spoke to her in a way that she had not experienced before and His message was clear and absolute, **"You are not alone."**

God didn't just speak to her, however. Miraculously, He infused Himself into her spirit such that peace replaced the desperation, a sense of calm replaced the anxiousness, and courage replaced fear. Janole was no longer confused about the direction for her life though there were many unanswered questions about her future. And, there were difficult times ahead.

Lying beside her husband, Janole continued to stare into the night, lost in the past, no longer focused on Wallace. Her mind was transported back to one of the most painful times of her life as she vividly recalled the ugly scene with her parents when she informed them of her pregnancy. Her father, an angry and controlling man, went into a frenzy referring to her as a slut and her unborn child as a bastard. For the first time, Janole stood up to her father unleashing all of her pent up feelings against this man who didn't seem to know the definition of love, constantly abused and berated his family, and put his needs and desires first.

Thank God for my brother, Janole thought. Marlo was with her that day as physical and moral support. It was a pivotal day of growth and insight for Janole and the beginning of drastic change for her entire family. Shortly after that fateful conversation, her parents—who had been married close to thirty years—separated and, sadly, Janole never spoke to her father again. Several months after her parents' separation, he died suddenly of a heart attack. It was a time of tragedy and triumph, pain and healing, reflection and growth.

Wallace abruptly turned over on his side pulling the bedcovers with him and, in spite of the chill, Janole was grateful for the distraction. She had not intended to reminisce about that painful time; enough of that. Slipping out of bed, she used the restroom and grabbed her robe before heading downstairs. The early morning was her treasured time. She relished in the quiet peace while enjoying a hot cup of hazelnut coffee.

Today was her birthday and Wallace was taking her out to dinner later for a special celebration. Neither event caused her to smile.

Later that night, Janole looked around the gathering of her family and friends at the Watercrest Hotel and knew that she was blessed. She was dressed in a flattering black cocktail dress complemented by diamond earrings. The two-inch black pumps and sheer hosiery accentuated shapely and well-toned legs. The short tapered hairstyle framed her attractive face, emphasizing big brown eyes. With smooth and flawless skin the color of caramel, Janole looked ten years younger than her actual age especially when she smiled. Tonight she was radiant.

The Watercrest Hotel was known for its ambiance, exquisite cuisine and impeccable service and was a popular option for various social and professional events. Wallace had surprised her with a party instead of an intimate dinner for two and the people whom she and Wallace loved most were with them to celebrate her fifty-first birthday. Yes, she knew they were blessed. Extremely blessed.

She also knew something was wrong. Very wrong. What was it? She couldn't yet identify it but the familiar tell-tale sign, her internal radar, was speaking to her loud and clear: a persistent, irritating knot in the center of her stomach. The recurring nightmare certainly didn't help to ease her mind. No time to focus on that now. Not tonight. Instead, she enjoyed the party, mingling and dancing, talking and laughing. Unexpectedly, she was grabbed from behind in a big bear hug and lifted off her feet. Immediately, she knew who it was.

"Put me down, boy. You'll ruin my dress," Janole said, pretending to be angry but unable to stifle her laughter.

Her oldest son, Marlon, laughed as he gently released her. "I'm just so happy to be home. I missed you, Mom."

"I'm happy to have you home, too, son." She turned to embrace this tall, handsome twenty-six year old man and her heart swelled with love and pride. "I had no idea you were coming but it's the best gift you could have possibly given me. How long have you known about this?"

"Not telling. We've got a few more surprises in store so get ready," Marlon said with mischief in his eyes.

"What are you talking about? As if this isn't enough. Don't know if I can take anymore," Janole said, smiling.

Just then Wallace approached Janole talking on the phone. "Hold on a sec," Wallace said to the caller. He then handed the phone to Janole.

"Hello?"

"Hi JJ! Happy birthday!" Jenn said, enthusiastically.

"Hi Jenn! Wallace threw me a surprise birthday party. Did you know about it? We're having such a good time. The only person missing is you," Janole said, not pausing between sentences.

"I can't believe you're partying without me. In fact, that is unacceptable," Jenn said.

"Jenn? Jenn? I can't hear you. There's a lot of background noise. I'll call you later," Janole said.

Jenn responded, "Is that better? Can you hear me now? By the way, I love your dress. You look gorgeous. Black was always your color. Talk to you later."

Janole disconnected the call and, simultaneously, realized that there was only one explanation for Jenn's ability to describe her dress. She slowly turned around and saw her friend of more than thirty years walking towards her, smiling and looking stunning, with her handsome husband, Paul, by her side. Janole couldn't contain her emotions.

Jenn embraced her friend, holding her close. "JJ, are you alright? What's wrong, honey?" she asked softly. Jenn knew her best friend well. These were not just tears of joy. "What is it?"

Because Janole was too emotional to answer, Jenn came to the rescue. "We're going to the ladies' room to freshen up," she said to Wallace and Paul. "Girl talk. Back in a few minutes."

Finally, after settling in the sitting area of the elegant restroom, Janole composed herself enough to glance at Jenn who wore a confused and worried expression.

"What's wrong, JJ? Are you okay? I wasn't expecting this reaction," Jenn said.

Janole looked at her best friend through red wet eyes. "And I wasn't expecting any of this. I'm so touched....and happy," Janole said in between sniffles. "Completely overwhelmed."

Jenn looked skeptical. "You sure you're telling me everything? I know you better than most. What's up?"

With sagging shoulders, Janole sighed. "I don't know, Jenn. I really don't know. Maybe it's the aftermath of all I've been through recently. I'm happy Wallace is home and safe. Really happy and relieved about that but—"

"But what?" Jenn asked.

They were interrupted by several loud giggling teenage girls dressed in gowns of differing styles and colors. They all wore high heels that looked extremely uncomfortable. Obviously, it was prom night for one of the local high schools. May is the season, Janole thought abstractedly, while blowing her nose and wiping her eyes. It seemed just yesterday when she was a high school student attending her prom. She was reminded of how quickly times passes.

"I need to get myself together," she said to Jenn. Dabbing at her eyes, she continued. "Let's get back to my party. I'm being rude. We'll talk later." Janole retouched her makeup and reapplied lipstick. Scrutinizing her face in the harsh light, she said, "Fifty-one years old. How in the world did that happen so quickly?"

"I don't know but we're still looking good, girl. Seriously JJ, you sure you're okay?" Jenn asked with concern.

"I'm fine....promise. Menopausal more than anything," Janole said.

"Lord have mercy. Don't mention that word." They both laughed. "Come on. Let's party like we're twenty-one," Jenn said.

Janole groaned. "Let's not. I'm trying to live to see another birthday."

She grabbed Jenn by the hand. "I want you to see everybody. Marlon, Nick, Mom and Marlo. Remember Reese, Sissy, Karen, Joy, Barbara? Everybody is here." Janole paused to hug her friend. "Most of all, I'm glad you're here."

Chapter Two

———————— ❋ ————————

$\mathcal{T}$he house was quiet and, as usual, Janole was the first up the next morning though much later than normal. She felt rested and actually found herself humming while making coffee and tidying the kitchen. As she slowly sipped her preferred decaf blend and munched on a bagel, it dawned on her that she'd slept through the night. For the first time in a long time, she hadn't dreamed. It was also the first time in a long while that she hadn't been alone in the house with Wallace. Her mom, Marlo, Jenn and Paul stayed overnight and it made her world feel complete having them there. She began reminiscing about the party. Aside from the uncharacteristic meltdown, she thoroughly enjoyed the evening.

Wallace had gone to a great deal of trouble and spared no expense, obviously wanting to do something special for her. The band was one of the area's best, the food delicious and abundant, and the room beautifully decorated in various shades of purple, her favorite color. The tiered cake offered three distinct choices: red velvet, chocolate, and vanilla. Tears came to her eyes when she remembered Wallace's toast. He said that God had blessed him with the most incredible woman on the face of the Earth and he couldn't imagine his life without her. And her precious sons, Marlon and Nick, surprised her with a special video tribute that caused many to wipe their eyes, including her.

"I could use a cup of whatever you're drinking," Marlo said as he joined his sister in the kitchen.

"You startled me. Didn't hear you coming," Janole said to her brother. "Let me get you a cup."

"You seemed deep in thought. You okay?" Marlo asked as he looked at Janole closely.

"I'm okay, just thinking about the party. I can't believe you kept the surprise from me. You know how I hate surprises."

Marlo smiled. "It was for a good cause." Continuing to watch Janole, he asked, "What got into you last night? I don't think I've ever seen you lose it like that in public. What's going on? I thought you'd be on Cloud Nine now that your life is perfect again."

Janole shrugged her shoulders. "I don't know. I haven't felt like myself lately. I guess I'm still trying to process it all. Plus, I'm menopausal. It's no wonder I haven't lost my mind."

Marlo smiled. Sister and brother sat in companionable silence for a few moments before Marlo spoke. "Jay, you scared me to death. When Nick called me sounding like a frightened little boy—"

"What are you talking about, Marlo?" Janole asked, staring at him.

"I'm talking about the day after Wallace disappeared. Nick found you upstairs in your bed. You asked him to call me."

Janole continued to stare at Marlo.

"Nick said he'd never seen you in such a state. Poor kid. He didn't know what to do. Don't you remember?" Marlo asked.

"No, I don't. I remember reading Wallace's letter but I don't remember much after that. The first clear memory I have is of Mom forcing me to get out of bed to shower and eat. After that, I vividly recall every detail," Janole said with bitterness. The anger caught her off guard. Refilling her cup, she stood with her back to Marlo willing her body to relax. *What is wrong with me?*

Finally, she turned to face her brother and said, "I never did thank you."

"Thank me for what?" he asked as he grabbed a plate from the cabinet and topped a bagel with several slices of ham. "You have nothing to thank me for."

"Yes, I do. You've always been there for me. They don't come any better than you as a brother and friend, Marlo. I'm so thankful for you." Janole was on the brink of losing her composure, just as she had yesterday with Jenn, so she stopped speaking.

Marlo was touched by Janole's sentiment and her sincerity. She, too, had a special place in his heart. Everyone who knew him knew how much he cared about his little sister and only sibling. "Awww, you're making me blush, Sis."

Janole smiled.

Satisfied that he'd gotten her to smile, he continued. "Since we're being sentimental, I will confess that you're my favorite sister and the ultimate unpaid assistant coach."

At that, Janole laughed outright. "I'm your one and only sister and speaking of coaching, how's the team looking this season? Good recruiting class?"

Marlo was a successful and highly regarded college basketball coach. After his record-breaking playing career ended at Old Dominion University, he was hired to coach at George Washington University and now coached at Michigan State.

"We'll see. We've got a tough non-conference schedule—both North Carolina and Virginia. They'll be huge tests for us. Tomorrow I'm heading to Vegas for an AAU tournament and our camp starts in a couple of weeks. Never a dull moment that's for sure."

"Everybody coming back next year?" Janole asked.

"Yeah, but there's one kid who worries me. Works his butt off but stays to himself a lot. Seems kinda sad. Distant. At times, angry. I've worked it out so that he can stay on campus this summer…hoping I can get him to open up a bit."

"Umm. I hope he's okay. No friends at all?"

"Don't think so."

"How about family?" Janole asked.

"Grew up in foster homes. Superb athlete, smart kid, too. Basketball is his ticket but he has trust issues. He's a good kid but could easily take the wrong path."

"What's his name?"

"Kenneth. Kenny Erving."

"I know he's in good hands with you. I'll send him a care package soon." Wistfully, Janole said, "This feels like old times. I really miss going to your games. Can't you find a job closer to us?"

Marlo noticed his sister's moist eyes. Until recent months, he had no cause to worry about Janole. He knew Wallace was a good man and never questioned Wallace's love for his sister. Granted, Wallace leaving her as he did and being away for months was a terrible ordeal for her. He knew firsthand that it was a living nightmare for her but found it surprising that, in spite of Wallace's return, Janole seemed different—less stable and sure of herself. Looking at his sister now, he realized that the recent crisis wasn't over for her. The situation seemed to have taken a bigger toll on her than, perhaps, any of them realized. Marlo was concerned but chose to say nothing at this time.

"I'm so disappointed that Amy and the kids didn't come with you," Janole said.

Marlo shrugged. "She said she wasn't feeling well...thought she was coming down with a cold but she sends her love. The kids, believe it or not, are gallivanting about Europe and won't be back for several weeks."

Janole detected a shift, albeit subtle, in Marlo's demeanor. "Everything okay with you and Amy?"

"I think so."

"What do you mean you think so? Don't you know?" Janole asked with raised eyebrows.

"Don't you know what?" Corie asked, as she breezed into the kitchen and kissed both of her children on the cheek. "I can't believe I slept so late. Where is the regular coffee, Janole? I don't want this flavored stuff. Don't you know what?" Corie repeated.

Janole and Marlo both smiled as they looked at their spry mother.

"Don't you know you're a beautiful woman, that's what," Marlo said, thankful for the diversion.

"Good morning, all," Jenn said as she joined them. "I was sleeping so good until my cell phone rang. Wrong number. Can you believe that?"

"Sounds like you need some coffee. Let me get it for you," Janole offered.

"That's exactly what I need. Paul didn't hear a thing. I swear he could sleep through a hurricane," Jenn said, shaking her head.

"Wallace too. Must be a man thing," Janole said.

"That's my cue," Marlo said, refilling his coffee cup. "I'll be in the den if anyone needs me. Don't want to interfere with girl talk."

Corie said, "I'll be on the deck reading the paper. Bernard is picking me up later. We're going to visit his sister in Maryland."

Making sure that Corie was out of hearing range, Jenn asked, "Why haven't they gotten married? Your mom and Bernard have been dating forever."

"They've been dating a long time, for sure. Mom always said that she'll not marry again. Said they're both happy with the way things are. If it ain't broke, don't fix it," Janole said.

"I guess you're right."

After a light breakfast, Jenn asked Janole about the plans for the day. "What do you want to do today? Whatever you wish, my friend. It's your birthday weekend."

Instead of answering the question, Janole said, "I've been thinking of Tam all morning. I really miss her, especially at special times like the party last night."

"It's funny you should mention Tam. She's been on my mind lately, too. After all these years, I still have a hard time believing she's gone. She was a good soul," Jenn said then chuckled. "You remember when she tried to set me up with a guy in her Anatomy class? She raved about how nice and cute he was and was adamant that we'd be the perfect couple."

Janole laughed as she recalled the situation. "I had forgotten about that. She was determined to connect the two of you," Janole said, shaking her head.

"And was devastated when she found out he was gay. She couldn't believe it...thought I was making it up. I wonder what he's doing now? What was his name?" Jenn asked more to herself than to Janole.

"Don't ask me. I have a hard time remembering what day it is," Janole said, smiling, as she checked her beeping phone. "Just got a text. You up for a little tennis? Doubles, not singles. One of our regulars had to bow out because she's not feeling well. They're all very nice. We have fun but play hard."

"Sure, I'll play. I'm a little rusty but it sounds like fun. What are the guys doing?" Jenn asked, referring to Wallace and Paul.

"I think they're going to play singles later. Either that or golf. We're scheduled to play at two so we need to get ready. You can use one of my rackets."

It was perfect tennis weather. Bright sunshine, low humidity, upper 70's with a slight breeze. Several members of the tennis club were engaged in friendly conversations as they waited for a free court. Janole and Jenn were having fun even though they lost the first set. At the beginning of the second set, Jenn received the serve and returned with a forehand down the line. Arlene hit the ball cross court to Janole who lobbed it. Kelly lobbed it back. Back and forth the ball was hit with all players focused on keeping it in play. It turned out to be the longest rally of the match. Janole and Jenn won the point and, excitedly, high-fived each other. As they walked back to the base line, it appeared as if they were discussing strategy for the next point but strategy was not uppermost on their minds.

Janole said, "Jenn, isn't this amazing? Look at how God has blessed us. It's a gorgeous day and we're spending it together. I'm fifty-one years old and in good health. A lot has happened since our college days but God has been so good to us."

Jenn responded, "Don't think I don't know it, my friend. There are no words. I thank Him every day—"

"Good playing, ladies." The voice came from the viewing deck behind them.

"Nate, what are you doing here?" Janole asked, surprise registering on her face.

"I'm a member of the club now. Played earlier. Finish your match. I'll talk to you later. By the way, happy birthday."

Jenn looked at Janole with an expression that said, "What in the world is going on?"

It was set and match point for Arlene and Kelly. The match was sealed with Kelly's backhand shot down the middle. Neither Janole nor Jenn moved to make a play on the ball and then looked at each other and burst into laughter.

"I thought you had it," said Jenn.

"And I thought you had it," said Janole.

After getting cold drinks and snacks, they settled on the viewing deck to watch Paul's and Wallace's match. The men were just beginning, tied at two. Neither had held serve. It was an exciting battle—both men skilled athletes—and several spectators had gathered to enjoy this competitive duel. As soon as the crowd dispersed allowing them enough privacy, Jenn leaned forward and hissed the question she'd been dying to ask.

"What's going on, JJ?"

"What do you mean?" Janole asked, confused.

"You know exactly what I mean. You crying like you did last night, Nate showing up at the courts. I saw the way he looked at you. And, was it a coincidence that he left shortly after Wallace and Paul arrived? What's going on?"

"Calm down, Jenn. Nothing's going on, I swear. Nate is just a friend. I'm just as shocked as you are that he joined the club. I had no idea."

Jenn stared at Janole. "JJ, I think Nate still has feelings for you and not just as a friend. You need to be careful."

"Thanks for the warning, Jenn, but I seriously doubt that after thirty years, Nate considers me anything other than a friend. That ship has sailed. Besides, Nate is the least of my concerns."

"What does that mean?" Jenn asked, still not convinced.

Janole looked around to make sure that no one was within ear shot. "I feel weird—out of sorts. I'm not sleeping well and—I don't know—I feel moody and anxious, at times. Initially, I attributed it to menopause but I'm also having the same awful nightmare every night."

"How long has this been going on?"

"A while. The nightmare started a couple of months ago…maybe before." Janole described the nightmare in detail. "What do you think it means?"

"I'm not sure," Jenn said, her brows wrinkled as she concentrated. "You're the psychologist, not me. Have you talked to Wallace about it?"

"No," Janole said softly, lifting her face to the warmth of the sun. Her eyes were closed as she continued. "I'm glad and thankful that

Wallace is home but things haven't been right for me for a while."
Janole exhaled loudly. "Jenn, I went through hell while Wallace was
gone. There were days when I wasn't sure...there were some very
tough days."

"I know it was tough, JJ, and I'm sure I don't know the half of
it." Jenn looked at her husband and Wallace, both drenched in sweat
but still going strong. "You think your dream is connected to what
you experienced?"

"I do but I can't make sense of it all," Janole confessed.

"How are things between you and Wallace?"

"Things are okay but...different. I just don't feel like the same
person. My world was shaken so badly that I'm constantly waiting
for the next terrible thing to happen. Instead of anticipating each
day with excitement as I've always done, I'm afraid...dreading what
might happen to ruin my life...waiting for the next bomb to drop."

"Honey, I think that's normal. It was a very tough time for you...
for both of you."

"Yeah, but Wallace doesn't seem to be experiencing any issues.
The 'hero' has no problems sleeping at night. He seems just fine."

"You sound angry. You know he did what he did to protect
you, right?"

Janole sighed. "Yeah, I know. But it still doesn't change the fact
that I went through hell."

Chapter Three

———————— ✳ ————————

(Three weeks after the birthday party)

"Seventy-three, seventy-four, seventy-five, done." Panting, Wallace lay on the bedroom floor after completing his morning workout routine. His body began to relax as he stared at the ceiling deep in thought about "the ordeal." That's how he and Janole referred to the situation that came to a head six months ago. He was home now—the ordeal over—and that meant more to him than he could express. "Thank You, Father, for this day—for life, health and strength. Thank You for bringing us through...for keeping my family safe...for taking care of me and guiding me. Thank You for making everything work out."

With tears in his eyes of which he was not ashamed, Wallace recalled the traumatic experience. He believed he was going to lose his life. Expected that at any moment he was going to be shot, attacked...somehow brutally murdered. His body discarded like trash never to be discovered. Or worse, the same fate would happen to Janole. Imagining all sorts of scenarios, he lived in constant fear for months and when he realized that he didn't know what to do or to whom to turn, he prayed. He had never experienced that level of fear.

Sure, he had worried about things before. There were situations over the years that gave him a few sleepless nights. But he had not experienced paralyzing, bone-chilling, gut-wrenching fear until he received the threats to his and Janole's lives. All because of the implications of his latest research findings, that if published, a

18

pharmaceutical company might stand to lose millions—perhaps billions—of dollars. When their bribes weren't successful, the company resorted to making threats.

His extensive research study was related to the etiology of schizophrenia. His findings suggested that birth order may have a more significant role than previously suspected in several disorders including personality disorders, dementia and schizophrenia. Further, his findings indicated that one of the most commonly prescribed medications for schizophrenia was harmful and ineffective in managing the disorder. This significant discovery had major implications for the pharmaceutical company, the major producer and distributor of the medication.

After weeks of receiving threatening messages, Wallace locked his office door and paced back and forth to the point of exhaustion. The more he paced the more anxious he became. The most recent threat—the one he'd received the previous evening—left no doubt that his life was expendable and time was running out. His greatest concern was for Janole. God forbid that something happen to her. He loved her so deeply that just the thought of losing her was unbearable. *God wouldn't be so cruel as to allow harm to come to her, would He? I've lost one wife. Surely, God would not take Janole from me.*

As Wallace contemplated his options, he found himself thinking about his grandfather wondering what he would do. His grandfather had been dead for many years yet Wallace yearned for his advice. He pictured the wise, unassuming man—who was so highly regarded by many—and was soothed by the image. He easily recalled Rudy Jackson's smile, kind eyes, and quiet strength. Wallace wondered whether his grandfather had ever experienced anything of this magnitude. Had he ever been faced with a life or death situation? Quite possibly, Wallace acknowledged. Rudy Jackson not only lived through the Great Depression, he also endured years of oppression, racial hatred and violence. After giving it more thought, Wallace was sure that his grandfather had likely looked death in the eye more than once. *I know what Grandpa would do. Before taking any action, he prayed.* He always told Wallace to seek God in all that he did. "Remember Son, wisdom comes from the Lord," his grandfather said to him on many occasions.

Though Wallace believed in God, he considered Janole the spiritual one. She was the one who prayed about everything and seemed never to waiver in her faith. She reminded him of his grandparents in that regard. Wallace believed God existed but didn't pray regularly. In fact, God was a last resort for him. Good to have around if really needed. God was for the big things; not for everyday life.

Janole believed differently. She saw God in every aspect of life, every expression of nature, and in each element of the universe, big or small. She referred to the world as His handiwork and admired the complexity and variety of all things, including mankind.

Wallace didn't have that kind of relationship with God but after acknowledging and accepting that the threats on his life and that of his family were too big for him, he finally prayed in earnest. He wasn't even sure who all was involved in this attack against him though he suspected he was being betrayed by one of his company's employees. "God, I don't know what to do. I don't even know what I'm dealing with, who I'm dealing with or who I can or can't trust. Please help me. Protect my family. Show me what to do. I need You, God. Please help me."

Wallace sat in his chair waiting for a revelation or a sign. He formulated several plans but there were major flaws with each idea. Flaws were unacceptable because the stakes were too high. Though time was his enemy, he sat in his office, immobilized…doing nothing as he waited for an answer. Eventually, he opened his desk drawer and reached for his grandfather's Bible. He kept the Bible close to him because it was a personal reminder of his beloved grandfather, the only father he knew. Touching its worn leather exterior comforted him but not enough to calm his racing heart or alleviate the telltale perspiration on his forehead and under his armpits. Usually looking at it or touching it was all he desired.

Today, he desperately needed more.

Opening the Bible, he turned to a page that was bent and began reading. Ironically, or perhaps not, he read about a person who was up against such a formidable adversary that most believed he stood no chance. It was the familiar story of David and Goliath. As Wallace read, he gained new insights. David used the weapon with which he was most comfortable to go into battle. He didn't attempt to fight using Goliath's tactics or armor. Rather, he used what was tried and true for him. Most importantly, he approached the fight confident in the power of God to deliver him.

Wallace read aloud. *"David said to the Philistine, 'You come against me with sword and spear and javelin, but I come against you in the name of the Lord Almighty, the God of the armies of Israel, whom you have defied. This day the Lord will deliver you into my hands....'"*

It's time to fight, Wallace thought, and began preparing himself for war. And, like David, he relied on his God-given assets which included finely honed research skills and the ability to think strategically and analytically. He began to develop a plan knowing that he needed to immediately identify the company spy while trusting no one. Each day Wallace prayed without fail. He read the Bible and committed certain verses to memory. One, in particular, was his mainstay. "Trust in the Lord with all your heart and lean not on your own understanding. In all your ways acknowledge Him and He shall direct thy path."

Wallace's plan worked though he'd had a nagging feeling that he was overlooking an important detail. It took months of painstaking and detailed planning while he compiled the incriminating evidence. There were times when he felt compelled to tell Janole what was going on but he did not. The days, exactly 152, separated from her were the worst. He missed her and worried incessantly but prayed that God would protect her. Wallace certainly was in no position to help as part of his plan was to discredit himself by posturing as a fraud on the brink of committing suicide. Extreme, perhaps, but he wanted to be certain that the pharmaceutical company no longer considered his research findings a threat to their profits.

Finally, 'the ordeal' was over and, in its aftermath, Wallace was viewed as a hero. Thanks to the wide coverage by news networks, he couldn't go anywhere without receiving attention. Complete strangers approached him to shake his hand in acknowledgement of his bravery and unselfish actions. He found it quite embarrassing. Everyone seemed to think he was a hero except the one who mattered most: Janole. They both were changed as a result of this ordeal. He knew that she was happy he was alive and well but something was different. This morning when he reached for her, she pulled away. She had never done that before in twenty-five years of marriage. Hurt and confused, Wallace didn't know what to do.

His thoughts were interrupted by the ringing of his cell phone. "Hello."

"Hi Dad. What are you up to?"

"Marlon? I'm good, man." Wallace immediately perked up. "What's going on with you? Got a game tonight?"

"Nah. Practice later on. Our next game is Tuesday." Marlon's usual chatter was absent and his voice lacked its normal enthusiasm.

Sensing that something was wrong, Wallace asked, "Son, you okay?"

"Yeah I'm fine, Dad, but I need to talk to you. I didn't call Mom 'cause I don't want to upset her."

"Okay. What's going on?" Wallace was alarmed and settled into a more comfortable position on the bed, unconsciously bracing himself for Marlon's news. This was atypical behavior for Marlon. He and his mom had a special bond. She was always the first person he sought when worried or in need of advice.

"I had my physical recently and the doctors told me that one of my test results was abnormal."

Wallace breathed a sigh of relief. Marlon was young, healthy as a horse, and extremely fit. "I'm sure there's nothing to worry about. Have you been feeling okay?"

"Yeah, I feel fine. Never felt better," Marlon said.

"Good. What exactly was abnormal?"

"It's called PSA. The doctor said it was elevated. It has to do with the prostate. I've—"

Wallace interrupted. "I'm familiar with that….an elevated PSA level could mean a number of things. It might even be a false positive. That happens a lot. Just last year, I had a false positive PSA reading."

"Well, the doctors here want me to be tested in the States just as a precaution….so I'll be coming home next week. I may need a biopsy."

Wallace detected fear and worry in Marlon's voice. "I'm glad they're being proactive. Don't worry, son. I'm sure there's nothing to worry about. It's not uncommon to have an elevated PSA level," Wallace said in an attempt to reassure Marlon though he had not heard of abnormal PSA levels in young men. "Umm—Is everything working okay? Sexually?"

Marlon laughed, slightly embarrassed. "Yeah, no problems there."

"How about urinating? Any changes or problems?" Wallace asked.

"Nope."

"Well, that's great. I know many guys whose PSA was elevated and turned out it was nothing. Everything will be fine. I don't want you worrying. That won't do you a bit of good. Understand?"

"I understand. Thanks Dad." He paused before continuing. "Dad, I don't want Mom to worry. She's been through a lot lately so can we just keep this between us?"

Wallace hesitated only briefly before answering. He'd do anything to spare Janole another trauma. "I'm sure it's nothing so I won't mention it to her. You're absolutely right. She has been through enough. Email or text me your flight plans."

Wallace continued to sit on the bed for quite some time after ending his phone conversation with Marlon. He was extremely proud of his sons and loved them equally though only one was his biological child. Janole was pregnant with Marlon when he met her and, shortly after they married, it was only fitting that he adopt Marlon as his own. It was a decision he didn't regret. In fact, he learned from Marlon what it really meant to be a father from the moment he held him in his arms. He vividly remembered the first time Marlon said da-da and took his first wobbly steps. He patiently taught Marlon how to play baseball, basketball and tennis. He taught him how to skate and ride a bicycle. He encouraged Marlon and coached him both on and off the field. He helped him with his homework and recalled the adoration and trust he saw in Marlon's eyes. He was the only father Marlon knew and Wallace considered Marlon his first-born son.

"God, please take care of my son. Give him safe travel and protect his health."

To himself he said, "Today has got to get better."

"Wallace, I'm going to the mall," Janole yelled from the kitchen. Not waiting for a response, she added, "See you later."

Janole knew Wallace was concerned about her but she had no answers for him. This melancholia and moodiness were foreign to her and she couldn't explain them. In fact, she was baffled by these feelings. God answered her prayers by keeping her husband safe and reuniting them but instead of feeling happy, she felt sad, discontent, and afraid…even anxious. For months she agonized about the situation in which she found herself, longing for Wallace, not knowing whether he was dead or alive.

She'll never forget the day she walked into their home to find his letter. It was an ordinary day with no foreboding of the personal catastrophe she would encounter. She'd read Wallace's letter so many times that she memorized it.

My Dearest Janole,

You are the best thing that has ever happened to me and I love you more than life itself which makes what I have to tell you so incredibly difficult. I have disappointed you, our children, myself and God. I just hope that, in time, you will be able to forgive me but I suspect that is asking too much. I'm a fraud and I've been found out. My name is not Wallace Jackson. It is an identity that I assumed for reasons that I can't explain. I've deceived a lot of people for a long time and I take no pride in that. I resigned from my position at the research center Thursday before I was terminated. It's just a matter of time before this information becomes public knowledge.

I allowed myself to believe that I could be Wallace and most days I was convinced that it would work. But I always lived in fear that I would be found out and my worst fear happened. My heart aches at the thought of you reading this letter. I'm sure you will question our entire relationship including my love for you. In spite of the lies and deceit, my love for you and our sons was and is real. Unfortunately, there is more. I have also been unfaithful to you. I allowed myself to get involved with a woman from my past. There is no justifiable excuse so I offer none. I am so very sorry. I know that I've hurt you deeply and you didn't deserve that. You have been an incredible wife and mother. You've

*shown me what true love is and I will be eternally grateful for that.
In you I have seen the love of God.*

*The last thing I wanted to do was hurt you. Please tell the boys that
I love them more than life and that they are to take good care of you
and each other. I can't continue to live with myself. You are the love
of my life and I hope in time you can find a way to forgive me.*

I will love you forever.
Your Husband

In the span of time that it took for Janole to read Wallace's letter
and fully comprehend its meaning, her wonderful, well-ordered life
was shattered. She went from being a happy, vivacious, secure, strong
woman to one who could barely function. The utter despair she felt
was unlike anything she had experienced before and she could not
have prepared for it. She had been completely caught off guard—
blindsided. And to make matters worse, her world had been publicly
exposed as a lie. For a period of time, thanks to Wallace's choices,
their lives were a media sensation. She shuddered as she remembered the gossip and unkind remarks, the questions and innuendoes,
the hushed conversations when she walked into a room, the stares of
accusation and sympathy. It had all been embarrassing and humili-
ating especially when her own integrity was questioned.

If there were such a thing as hell on Earth, she had lived it. It
was a time of utter confusion, devastation and desperation. She was
helpless to explain the circumstances, even to herself, because she
had no answers. Wallace was gone, leaving nothing but memories
and a letter describing himself as an unfaithful fraud. Oh, he had
professed his love for her but it was difficult for her to believe the
words of a self-proclaimed fraud. In an instant, she was thrust into
an unimaginable nightmare.

Recalling the anguish and despair she felt months ago during the
ordeal, she became exhausted and weary. Walking aimlessly in the
mall, she found herself near the Food Court and decided to sit at the
nearest table. So far, she had purchased nothing. Not surprising since
she wasn't in the mood for shopping. Her trip to the mall was a cover

for getting out of the house…and getting away from Wallace. She allowed herself to be entertained by the shoppers. Some, laden with packages, seemed excited with their purchases; some appeared frustrated or agitated perhaps concerned that what they had purchased cost more than they could comfortably afford. Others, mostly young couples and teenagers, seemed happy and content just to stroll the mall with no particular destination in mind.

"You look like you've lost your best friend. Mind if I join you?" Nate asked as he sat across from her, not waiting for an answer.

Surprised, Janole smiled. "What are you doing here and how are you?" As an afterthought, she asked, "Are you following me?"

Nate laughed. "No, I'm not following you. My daughter's birthday is next week so I'm shopping which I hate but I'm almost done." He sat back in the chair, crossed his legs and stared at Janole. He was dressed casually in tennis shoes, jeans and a black shirt. He also wore a black cap, containing the familiar Nike swoosh.

"I'd take you for an on-line shopper," Janole said.

"No way. I like to see in person what I'm purchasing." He looked at her more closely. "How are you? By yourself?"

"I'm okay and alone," replied Janole. "Just taking a break to people gaze since I haven't found any great bargains."

"Have you eaten?" Nate asked. "I'm starving."

"No, but I could eat. In fact, I'm actually hungry and I know exactly what I'd like. Bourbon chicken with lo mein, cabbage and a diet coke." She smiled. "I'll hold the table while you get the food."

"Okay. Watch my packages. Back in a minute," Nate said, winking.

Janole admired Nate as he walked away and was reminded of Jenn's warning. She was no longer in love with Nate but he was a very attractive man. She wondered how her life would have been different had they stayed together. College sweethearts, they had been very much in love at one time. Ironically, it was a change in circumstances—not a change in their feelings for each other—that ended their love affair. Immaturity played a big part, too. Young and idealistic, they were neither strong enough nor wise enough to weather the first big challenge to their relationship. They shared great times though. Janole smiled as she remembered those college days, the good times, the laughter, the ease of their companionship, the insatiable desire they had for each other, the football and basketball games, the long phone conversations. The many firsts that are made that much sweeter when experienced with one's first love. And she had deeply loved this man.

Everyone viewed them as the perfect couple and thought they were going to marry, even their parents. She continued to watch him as he stood in line and wondered why God sent him, of all people, to help her during 'the ordeal'. Over the years, she'd thought of Nate from time to time. Quite naturally, she couldn't reminisce about college without thinking about him, Jenn, Tam and her sorority sisters. They were such a big part of her life at that time but, as of late, she found Nate creeping into her thoughts quite frequently. Perhaps, too frequently.

While eating, they talked about mundane things keeping the conversation light. As he pushed aside a slice of green pepper, Nate was reminded of the first time Janole bit into a Jalapeño pepper. His smile turned into a grin and then into full-blown laughter as he told the story. "Your face turned beet red and you started perspiring. Then you began jumping. Jumping up and down, fanning your tongue. You actually cried."

"That was an awful experience and not funny," Janole said, laughing in spite of herself. "I kept ice on my tongue all night. I still hate those things. But before you get too cocky, I seem to remember a time you had just a tad too much to drink. You were sick all night long. Even threw up on my new shoes. I was so mad but you were hilarious. Slurring your words. You kept saying, 'Help me, Janole. Help me, shomebody. I'm dying.'" Janole laughed so hard that her stomach hurt.

Nate laughed, too, shaking his head. He said, "I thought I was going to die from drinking that cheap wine. Learned my lesson that day."

They continued talking about that special time, remembering events and people that were significant to them.

"Remember our special way of communicating?" Nate asked.

"Of course I do. We talked with our fingers." Janole smiled at the memory. It was a magical time.

Nate reached for her hand and held it while looking in her eyes and that was the scene that Wallace witnessed from the upper balcony.

As Nate began to tap on her palm with his fingers, he noticed her wedding ring and stopped abruptly. "This probably isn't a good idea," he said, releasing her hand.

"Probably not," Janole said.

Wallace was stunned. *What in the world is going on? Janole and Nate at the mall? Together? Holding hands?* He'd thought of Janole all day and decided to surprise her at the mall hoping they could catch an early dinner and perhaps talk about what was troubling her. Just as he was about to pull out his cell phone to call her, he spotted them in the Food Court below, holding hands. From his vantage point on the balcony, Wallace couldn't see Janole's face but he could clearly see Nate. *He's still in love with my wife. That much is certain. Is Janole in love with him?* Wallace refused to accept that as a possibility but he couldn't deny what he witnessed.

Chapter Four

---***---

*M*arlon watched the monitor as the nurse squeezed the blood pressure gauge. He willed his body to relax.

"Very good," the nurse said with a slight smile. "One twenty-one, over seventy-two."

Sitting in the sterile examination room, Marlon forced himself to breathe normally as he watched the nurse make annotations in his chart and on the computer. He was waiting to see the doctor and though his dad and Nick tried to reassure him, he was quite anxious. And jet lagged. His flight to Dulles was delayed by hours and didn't land until late two nights before. By the time he and Nick arrived at Nick's condo, it was early morning. He was able to snatch a couple of hours of sleep before his lab appointment to have his blood drawn.

"You're all set," the nurse said. "The doctor will be in shortly."

"Thank you," Marlon said.

Noticing the box of tissues, he grabbed one and wiped the perspiration from his forehead and clammy hands. Extremely uncomfortable in doctors' offices and hospitals, he avoided them if at all possible. Fortunately, except for his annual physical, he had not spent a great deal of time in either. He was meeting with Dr. Bowers, a highly recommended urologist, about his PSA level. Marlon knew there was a problem; otherwise, the doctor would have explained the results on the phone or simply mailed a letter. Still, Marlon wanted to believe that the problem wasn't extremely serious. After all, he felt fine.

Dr. Bowers, a middle-aged man of average height with premature gray hair that complemented his brown skin, walked in and introduced himself. He and Marlon hit it off immediately when Dr. Bowers shared with him that he played basketball in college. They talked sports for a few minutes and soon Marlon found himself more at ease if not totally relaxed.

"Let's talk about your lab results," Dr. Bowers said. "We have confirmed the previous findings. Your PSA level is definitely elevated. Now we need to find out why. We could put you on medication to see if that helps in lowering your level but, because of your age, I'm recommending that we do a biopsy first. That helps in ruling out certain things like a tumor. We can do the biopsy later this week. I also want to get a complete medical history from you."

"Okay. The sooner we get answers, the sooner I can get back to playing ball," Marlon responded.

"The biopsy involves me obtaining a tissue sample from the prostate entering through the rectum. You will need to give yourself an enema so that your bowels are as clear as possible. My nurse will explain the prep procedure in detail and provide what you need. The biopsy can be painful so you'll be given medication to deaden the pain. Once the medication has taken effect, I'll perform the biopsy. Questions?"

"How long will the biopsy take?" Marlon asked.

"The procedure, itself, takes less than thirty minutes. It really depends on the patient. I'll put a rush on the results and hope to have them back in a couple of days."

"Sounds good," said Marlon.

"I'm going to send my nurse in shortly. Are you allergic to anything?"

"No."

"No allergies to any medications or latex?"

"No."

"Taking any prescribed medications?"

"No, occasionally Aleve for pain."

"Great. You won't be able to drive immediately after the procedure. Is that a problem?"

"No, my father will be with me."

"Okay. Your blood pressure and all other vitals are normal so we should have you out of here in no time. My nurse will be in momentarily."

"Okay. Thank you."

Later, Marlon phoned his father to inform him of the biopsy date and time. Wallace assured Marlon that he would make himself available. Marlon also contacted his agent, Brian, who was slightly older than Marlon and more of a friend than a business associate. Brian could not hide his concern for his friend.

"Hey man, what's going on?" Brian said in greeting.

"Not much. Just saw the doctor," Marlon stated.

"Nothing serious, right? When are you leaving for Argentina?"

"I'm not going anywhere yet. The doctor said my PSA level is elevated and I need a biopsy which is scheduled for later this week."

"Okay. Forgive my ignorance. What is a biopsy? Is that like major surgery?"

"No. It's a minor procedure. The doctor said it's necessary to rule out certain things like tumors."

"Tumors as in cancer?" Brian asked.

"I don't think so. He didn't mention cancer," Marlon said.

"You okay?"

"Yeah, I'm good, man. Just ready to have this over and done with so I can get back to the team."

"I know that's right. You got dinner plans tomorrow?"

"None whatsoever. Are you in the area?" Marlon asked. Though Brian traveled frequently, his office was located in Arlington.

"Yep. We can meet in Crystal City. I'll hit you up later."

"Sounds like a plan," Marlon said before disconnecting the call.

Chapter Five

———————— ✳ ————————

At the appropriate time, Marlon followed all pre-biopsy instructions and was at the hospital an hour before he was to report. To his extreme relief, the biopsy was finally over. It was the most unpleasant and uncomfortable medical procedure he had experienced. At one point, the pain was so severe he wanted to punch Dr. Bowers in the face. Instead, he gritted his teeth and squeezed the table while tears leaked out of his eyes.

Dr. Bowers said during the procedure, "I didn't detect anything abnormal. That's a good sign."

Though Marlon was grateful to hear the news, he could only nod his head. After dressing, he met the doctor in his office and easily answered questions about his background but had very little to offer about his parents' health information.

"My dad is in the waiting room. He'll be able to answer more questions than I about my parents' and grandparents' history."

"Let's have him come in," said Dr. Bowers.

After introductions were made, Dr. Bowers explained to Wallace the importance of obtaining as much historical information as possible. "Not only is your history important as Marlon's father but also the history of your father and brothers. The same applies to Marlon's mother's family." Strange, Dr. Bowers thought as he looked at Wallace. He sensed reluctance in Wallace who had seemed eager to help before. Now he seemed somewhat uncomfortable.

Dr. Bowers continued. "I'm going to ask a few questions and then I'd like you to complete this medical questionnaire as thoroughly as possible."

Two days later Marlon and Wallace were back in the doctor's office. The news was not good.

Without preamble, Dr. Bowers said, "The biopsy revealed cancerous cells." He said nothing further giving Marlon and Wallace time to process the information.

"Cancerous cells? Wh—what does that mean?" Marlon asked, looking at Wallace and then at Dr. Bowers.

"It means we've detected cancer," said Dr. Bowers.

"I have cancer?" Marlon asked. "Are you sure? I mean…I'm only twenty-six years old…I don't understand."

Wallace looked as if he were sick. The color had drained from his face. Finally he spoke. "Dr. Bowers, are you absolutely sure? I think the tests should be run again. And, we should probably get a second opinion."

"I know this comes as a shock and, of course, you're welcome to get a second opinion. But I want you to listen carefully, okay?" Both men nodded though they were clearly in shock. "We did the tests multiple times. It's my practice to ensure that the findings are conclusive before I share them with my patients. So I have no doubt that the cancer diagnosis is accurate but we'll need to test further to determine the stage."

"Stage?" asked Marlon.

Dr. Bowers explained. "There are several stages of cancer. Stage one cancer is cancer that has been detected early and is confined in the place of origin. It is very treatable, usually. Stage four is the most advanced and means that the cancer has metastasized or spread to other parts of the body. The stage of cancer determines how we treat it and it is treatable. You with me so far?" Both men nodded their heads as if on autopilot.

"Prostate cancer is fairly common in men and especially black men. We usually see it in middle-aged or older men; less often in men your age, Marlon." He directed his next comment to Wallace. "Mr. Jackson, it's important that you review the medical history you provided. I'd like to be sure of just how much genetics is playing a role in Marlon's condition."

Again, Wallace nodded as he pulled out a handkerchief to wipe away tears that, in spite of his best intentions, were escaping his eyes.

"Do you have any questions for me?" Dr. Bowers asked, compassionately. He knew they were likely to have questions later after all of the information had soaked in and they had researched the Internet.

"How about basketball? When will I be able to play basketball?"

"I don't know because I don't yet know exactly what we're dealing with but I think you need to be prepared for the possibility of not being able to complete this basketball season. I think it best to address your cancer as quickly as possible. Can you come in next week?"

"Yeah," Marlon stated. "I'll be here. I guess I don't have a choice."

Dr. Bowers watched as the two men stood and walked out of his office. Though Dr. Bowers did not want to provide a premature prognosis, his gut told him that Marlon would soon be in a fight for his life. He hoped he was wrong.

Marlon and Wallace were each in his own way, trying to come to terms with the information they had received. Wallace drove to Nick's condo, making the appropriate turns while navigating traffic but with little awareness of what he was doing. It was as if the car were on automatic pilot. He was the first to break the silence. "You all right, son?"

"I-I just can't believe it. I never suspected cancer," Marlon said.

"I know but everything is going to be all right. We're going to fight this thing and beat it. You're a fighter. Always have been. Most importantly, son, you've got to put your trust in God."

Marlon nodded but when Wallace glanced at him he knew Marlon wasn't convinced.

Wallace continued. "Your mother has to be told. I'll tell her this evening. Do you want to tell your brother or would you prefer your mother and me to do it?"

When Marlon didn't answer, Wallace said, "Marlon?"

Marlon looked at his father as if he were dazed. "What?"

"I said do you want to tell Nick or would you prefer your mother and me to tell him?"

"I'll tell Nick when he gets home," Marlon said.

"Okay. We'll call Uncle Marlo and your grandma, too. Okay?"

Marlon nodded and noticed that the car was no longer moving. He looked around, recognizing his brother's familiar condo building. He saw his father unbuckling his seatbelt and, realizing his intentions, said, "Dad, I'm okay. I'd rather be alone for a while. We'll talk later. I just need some time. I promise, I'm fine. Just need time to think. Nick will be home soon."

Reluctantly, Wallace said, "Okay. I'll call you later tonight." Before pulling off, Wallace watched his son walk into his brother's house. Wallace had almost made it to the main street before stopping. He pulled the car over, put his head on the steering wheel and sobbed.

Finally alone, Marlon sank into the supple black leather couch in Nick's contemporary condo. He liked this space. It was stylish yet comfortable. Their mom had helped Nick decorate and though it was truly a man's space, he could see touches of her influence.

Marlon was sitting still yet his mind was racing. *Cancer. Unbelievable. I've never been sick a day in my life except for a cold. I've never even had the flu. Cancer? Of all things.* He felt betrayed by his body. Throughout his basketball career, he had been injury free, primarily because he took extra care of himself. Stretch exercises, deep tissue and muscle massages, weight training, cardio, and a healthy diet were all part of his regimen. He limited alcohol consumption and absolutely refused to smoke and engage in drug use.

He made money with his body, along with his basketball skills, and knew the importance of maintaining a well-oiled machine. If anything, he expected to get sidelined by a torn ACL or Achilles or just simple wear and tear. One of his teammates was forced to retire early due to continual back spasms after three surgeries. While unfortunate, it made sense. But cancer? *Not only might it end my career, it might end my life. I could die. A year from now, I could be dead. I don't want to die!* Marlon punched the sofa over and over and over.

Get a grip, man. The doctor didn't say anything about you dying. He said the cancer was treatable. Get a grip!

Nick walked in the front door as Marlon walked out of the restroom blowing his nose. Marlon's eyes were red. This can't be good, thought Nick. His stomach knotted but he willed himself to appear calm for his big brother. He couldn't remember the last time he had seen his brother cry but it was obvious that Marlon had cried today. Nick knew, intuitively, that it was important for him to be strong regardless of the news. The last thing Marlon needed was for him to lose it. Buying a few minutes, he grabbed two bottles of water from the refrigerator and threw one to Marlon who easily caught it with his left hand.

"What's up, bruh?" Nick asked. "What'd the doctor say?"

After taking a large gulp of water, Marlon responded. "Cancer."

Silence. Nick was rendered speechless, his arm suspended in midair with the water bottle in hand. He hadn't taken his eyes off of Marlon's face. "I'm sorry. What did you say?"

"You heard right. Cancer."

Nick had never seen his brother look so defeated...so scared. He walked from the kitchen into the living room and eased himself onto the recliner. *Stay strong.* "Well, wh—what else did he say?" Nick asked.

"I've got to go back next week for more testing to determine the stage. He thinks it's in the early stage. That's the good news."

"That is good news. In fact, that's great news. Stage one usually means the cancer is very easily treated." As a physical therapist, Nick was familiar with many illnesses, their effects on the body, and recommended treatments.

"Yeah, that's what the doctor said but I've been reading info on the Internet. Some of it is kinda scary—"

"Don't even go there," Nick interrupted. "The information on the Internet can be frightening. I always advise my patients to be very careful when researching the Internet about medical problems. Especially their own. Your best guidance will come from your doctor and Dr. Bowers is one of the best. Trust him and don't torture yourself, man." He paused for a few minutes. "You okay?"

"Yeah. I feel fine, physically. Just shocked. I was not expecting this," Marlon admitted. "I just didn't see this one coming." He took another sip of water. "Dad's telling Mom, Grandma and Unc tonight."

"Well, I'm sure they'll call us tomorrow. You and I have plans for tonight. We're going to play hoops. We are not going to sit here all night worrying. It's pointless. Won't change a thing." Nick talked as if he were trying to convince himself as well as Marlon. "Let's go to the gym and show them what time it is."

For the first time that day, Marlon smiled. "Yeah, let's do that."

Nick embraced his brother. "I'm with you all the way, bruh. You can count on that."

Marlon held his brother for a long time. "I know, man."

Chapter Six

———————— ✳ ————————

Wallace knew he'd find Janole in her favorite area of their home. Dressed in purple silk pajamas, she looked beautiful as she sat on the cream chaise lounge in the sitting room of their bedroom with an assortment of cards on either side of her. Her iPad, which contained the contact information for all of their friends, family and acquaintances, was laying on top of the chair arm. Though it was summer, the fireplace was lit giving the large room a warm and cozy feeling. The television was tuned to a movie. For a moment, the image of Janole and Nate entered Wallace's mind but he quickly dismissed it. He couldn't deal with that right now.

Taking a deep breath and summoning strength, he walked towards her. "Hi babe. How ya doing?"

Without looking up, Janole responded. "I'm good…sending out cards to friends and church members I haven't seen in a while. How was your day?"

"Not so good. Janole, we need to talk."

"I'm listening," she said as she began to address another card. "Something going on at the office?"

"I need you to put that away, please. This is important." Wallace sat on the oversized chaise lounge so that they could clearly see each other. He wanted to be as close to her as possible.

Janole stopped what she was doing and looked at her husband. *Has Wallace been crying? Why are his eyes red?* She felt a tightness in her chest. *What now?*

Wallace continued. "Marlon is home. He's been home for several days now." Reading the surprise and confusion on her face, he said, "Let me explain." He took a deep breath as if trying to fortify himself.

"Marlon had a routine physical a few weeks ago in Argentina and one test result came back abnormally high. The doctors there wanted Marlon to be checked out in the States to be sure. That's why he came home but he didn't want you to worry and I agreed. We were hoping the results would be negative and he could hop on a plane and return to Argentina." Wallace paused and grimaced. He appeared to be in physical pain. "We found out today that Marlon's PSA level is elevated and—" Wallace put his head in his heads, finding it difficult to utter the words.

"What is it, Wallace?" Janole asked, her voice no more than a whisper and her hands tightly clasped.

Wiping his eyes with his hands, Wallace said, "I'm sorry, babe. Marlon has cancer. Prostate cancer."

Janole inhaled deeply. *Dear God in heaven. Not my baby.* "That can't be true. He's-he's too young. There must be a mistake. We need to get a second opinion."

Wallace shook his head. "I thought the same thing. Dr. Bowers said that he had the test checked several times. Plus, he's one of the most experienced and respected urologists in this area. Marlon has cancer, honey. He'll be tested next week to determine the stage and how it should be treated. Depending on how things turn out, he may have to forego the remainder of this year's basketball season."

Janole tried to process this information. *My baby. Sick. Cancer.* She looked at Wallace hoping to see an indication that the news wasn't as bad as she thought. She didn't find reassurance in his expression. "Oh my God. He must be devastated. Where is he now?"

"At Nick's. He needed some time to himself," Wallace said, quickly glancing at this watch. "Nick is probably home now. He'll take good care of Marlon."

"Okay." After a few minutes, Janole asked a question. "Why didn't he call me?"

Wallace explained again. "He didn't want you to worry needlessly. He was trying to protect you."

Janole nodded, indicating that she understood. "I need to be alone," she said softly as if talking to herself.

Wallace was surprised. This was not the Janole he knew. "Baby, we'll get through this together."

"Please leave me alone," Janole pleaded, as she began rocking herself. "I just want to be alone. Please."

Wallace left the room with insult added to injury. He had not expected Janole to turn away from him at this painfully critical time. They had always rallied together and supported each other through tough circumstances, especially those pertaining to the boys. Together, they talked, made decisions and reassured each other. *Was it Nate she wanted?* Wallace dismissed that thought as he walked into Marlon's former room and lay on the bed. He was completely drained but the one thing he learned during his recent ordeal was to rely on God. His heart ached for his son but he knew he couldn't fix it. Not this.

"God, take care of Marlon. Please don't let this cancer kill him. Don't take him from us. I'm praying for his complete healing and recovery, Father. Take care of my wife and give us all we need as we confront this illness. Help us to keep our eyes stayed on You, Father." For the second time in one day, Wallace cried.

Janole was curled in a fetal position, partially covered by a throw, when Wallace checked on her an hour later. She wasn't asleep but it was apparent she had been crying. She looked exhausted and sad.

"Janole, we need to talk," Wallace said, softly.

"I don't want to talk right now," she said, hoarsely. Fresh tears ran down her face.

"I know this is a lot to take in but there is an important aspect of this situation we haven't discussed. And we need to do that today." Wallace sat beside her and gently caressed her shoulders and arms. He helped her sit up and held her hands.

"The doctor believes that genetics may be a significant factor in Marlon's cancer." Wallace paused as he looked in Janole's eyes. "Dr.

Bowers wants to know the complete history of both of Marlon's parents and their families."

It took a moment for understanding to dawn and when it did, Janole's eyes reflected pure terror. "Oh my God," was all she could say.

"We must tell Marlon about Eric and we need to contact Eric as soon as possible."

Janole nodded. *Will this nightmare of my life ever end?* "He'll hate us," she said, referring to Marlon.

Wallace attempted to reassure Janole. "Marlon adores you. He could never hate you. Plus, we don't have a choice. His life is at stake."

Chapter Seven

———————————— ✳ ————————————

ormented, neither Janole nor Wallace slept soundly during the night. Janole was not afraid of dreaming this time; instead, she was consumed with worry about her son. And, as afraid as she was to tell Marlon about his biological father—and how the news may impact their relationship—her biggest fear was his cancer diagnosis. Still, she couldn't wrap her mind around the devastating news. *My twenty-six year old son has prostate cancer. My baby could die as a young man. Would he need chemo and radiation? Just how sick would he get? And, after all that, would he still die?*

She lay in the bed unconscious of time…unaffected by the tears. She was in a familiar yet painful and lonely place where she felt she had no control over her life or destiny. **You are not alone.** She was reminded of God's promise once again in the stillness of the night and it comforted her but it didn't alleviate her fear that Marlon might die.

Sitting up, she wrapped her arms tightly around her body as if to hold herself together. Against her will, one sob escaped and then another. She couldn't contain her pain and anguish; the struggle was too great. She cried, uncontrollably, for her son as she prayed. "Please God, don't take him from me. Please don't. I know he's Your child and I know You are the giver and taker of life but I'm begging You, God, please spare Marlon's life. Please."

At the first sign of Janole's distress, Wallace jumped out of their king-sized bed and hurried to her side. Wrapping her in his arms, he held her as she released her despair and fear. He, too, cried as he held her tightly and slowly rocked her. Words were inadequate so he said nothing.

Later—neither of them aware of the time—Janole spoke with a raspy voice. "Would you get me a glass of water and some aspirin? I have a terrible headache."

"Sure," Wallace responded as he lightly kissed her forehead. "Why don't you lay back." He fluffed the pillows and helped Janole get situated before covering her with the comforter. "I'll be right back."

A few minutes later, Wallace was lying beside Janole. Reaching for her hand and holding it tightly, he began to pray. "Father, Janole and I are seeking Your help and strength. We thank You for how You have blessed us and we thank You for being a God of love, mercy and grace. Help us, God. Marlon has can—cancer." Wallace paused for a moment, unable to continue. Janole squeezed his hand in understanding, a gesture that gave him strength.

"Father, our son has cancer and we don't know what that means for his life. We don't know what it means for our lives. But this we know. You are a faithful God who loves us. Increase our faith, Father. Give us strength, wisdom, discernment, all that we'll need. Help us to look to You and rely on You. Protect Marlon, Father. We pray that this cancer is completely and permanently removed from his body. Help Marlon not to worry but trust in You. Bless my wife. Bless our love and our entire family. Keep us strong and united. We love You, Lord. Amen."

"Amen," Janole whispered. In spite of all that she was feeling, Wallace's prayer moved her. Not just the words but the fact that he prayed. Janole's body began to relax. The headache eased. She knew they were in for a battle and a major change because they had no choice but to tell Marlon the truth. But, while Wallace prayed, she felt God's presence and He reminded her of what He conveyed to her years ago when Marlon was a teenager. *You don't love Marlon as much as I do. He is My child and I love him more than you can comprehend. Thank You, God.*

"Thank you, Wallace. I love you for that," she said softly as they continued to hold hands.

"I love you, too, babe...more than anything in this world. Let's try to get some sleep."

The next day Wallace checked in with both Marlon and Nick and, after a brief chat, informed them that they needed to have an important family discussion. They agreed to meet at six o'clock. Meanwhile, Janole spent several hours on the computer trying to locate Eric, Marlon's biological father. She wracked her brain to remember his last name. *It begins with a C. Carson, Carter, Christian, Coleman. Pathetic that I can't remember the name of my son's father.* Again, she felt ashamed that she was intimate with a man who meant so little to her. And, as much as she wanted to forget that part of her life, it was now vital to her son's life that she recall as much as possible.

She was about to give up her search when it came to her. *Cutler. His last name is Cutler. Eric Cutler.* Quickly, she typed in the name only to discover that there were, literally, hundreds of men with the name of Eric Cutler. As a last resort she could contact her friend, Sarah Biltske. Sarah's husband, Will, was the advisor for students in her doctoral cohort at that time. Will was deceased but Janole was willing to bet that Sarah continued to maintain ties with the university and former students.

"Having any luck?" Wallace asked.

"No," Janole responded, rubbing the tension from her neck. "I just remembered Eric's last name a few minutes ago. It's Cutler. There are a lot of men with that name so I'm using UVA as a secondary search. That should narrow it down quite a bit."

"Okay," Wallace said, "but I think you should call your mom and Marlo first. The boys will be here soon."

"You're right. Better get it over with. Will you help me? They'll have so many questions."

"Of course I will," Wallace said. "We'll tell them together."

Chapter Eight

---------------❋---------------

*J*anole looked at her grown sons and her heart swelled with pride. Marlon—tall, muscular, and handsome with physical features similar to hers—was the outgoing one. Shy, he was not. He never met a stranger and had to be cautioned more than once as a child that not all people were good people. Perhaps because he believed the best about everyone, people gravitated to him. He was also quite the entertainer and impersonator. Marlon brought humor into their lives from an early age. He loved to laugh and took every opportunity to make others laugh.

Several inches shorter than Marlon, Nick—at 6'2"—was lean and wiry. His physique was deceptive. Most would assume that he didn't have brute strength because his muscles weren't as pronounced as Marlon's. They would be wrong. Nick was all muscle, lean and very athletic. Though he had many appealing attributes, women most appreciated his kindness and sensitivity. Men liked him because he didn't present himself as an alpha male, always competing to be the best, in spite of being a superb athlete. Nick never bragged or tried to outdo others as is typical of many males. More of an introvert, he loved intensely and nothing was more important to him than family. He had matured into a young man who was highly respected for his values, skills, work ethic and wise advice. He was considered one of the best physical therapists in the area and enjoyed his job because of the reward of helping others. It was not uncommon for him to be referred to as "an old soul." Janole often thought of him as a younger version of Wallace.

Not for the first time, Janole wondered about her sons and their relationship with God. She knew they believed in God and attended church regularly. But she wondered if they really had come to know Him. Was He a part of their daily lives? Did they seek His direction? Did they honor Him with their decisions? Did they desire to serve Him?

Understandably, both of her sons were subdued today. Marlon and Janole embraced for a long time when he arrived. She knew he would draw strength from her and she was determined to give him all the strength she could muster. She'd give her life if it would save his. Admittedly, she was afraid. Afraid that her son might die; afraid that he might live but hate her; afraid that what she was about to tell him would permanently wedge a divide in their relationship. Very shortly, Marlon would learn the truth. She hoped—no, prayed—that this news would not destroy their relationship. Or Marlon's relationship with Wallace, his father in every sense of the word. Realizing that she could no longer delay the inevitable, she indicated to Wallace that she was ready.

Wallace said, "Let's all sit in the family room."

Marlon and Nick sat on the couch. Janole and Wallace sat facing them on the love seat. The room smelled of vanilla spice and the view of the outdoors was spectacular, especially this time of year. The trees—dogwood, weeping cherry, elm, oak—were all in full bloom. Azaleas, hostas, and an array of perennials and annuals were artistically arranged on the deck and in the expansive yard. The lawn, neatly manicured, was a lush green. It was a beautiful display of nature and could easily be appreciated from any vantage point in the family room. The beauty, however, did nothing to lessen the somber mood of the Jackson family.

"Son, how are you doing?" Wallace directed the question to Marlon.

"I'm okay, Dad. I feel fine but, obviously, everything is not fine. But, I've decided I'm not going to dwell on that. I don't want everyone feeling sorry for me...looking at me with pity. I want everything to be normal. I know this has been a shock. Believe me. But, Nick helped me realize that it will serve no good purpose to sit around worrying and moping. In fact, we played ball last night and owned the gym."

Nick chimed in. "We sure did. They couldn't touch us. My jumper was hot, too."

Nick and Marlon high-fived each other though their usual exuberance was lacking.

Wallace said, "That's awesome. I think that's a healthy and wise approach." Janole nodded in agreement.

"It is what it is," Marlon stated matter-of-fact. "We'll deal with it and move on. You talk to Grandma and Unc?"

"Yes, earlier today," Janole stated. "Your dad and I both talked with them. It was tough. They were, of course, upset and shocked just as we expected. We told them we would give them regular updates and it's going to be important for us to do that. We can't leave them out. They both love you so much. You know that. They're hurting for you."

"They both said the same thing," Wallace added. "Tell him we'll be praying and that we love him very much." After a moment, Wallace continued. "Cancer is a scary word and people often panic when they learn that a loved one has been diagnosed with it. So you may find yourself trying to console others—even though you're the one who has cancer—when they first hear the news. You need to be prepared for that, son. We'll help as much as we can."

"I'll help, too," Nick offered.

Janole and Wallace looked at each other, communicating nonverbally. This did not go unnoticed by Marlon and Nick. All of their lives, they had witnessed their parents' interactions with each other, as if they were one...an extension of each other. The brothers, especially in recent years, often talked about how fortunate they were to have such great parents. It wasn't until they were teens that they gained a better appreciation for their parents and realized that all homes were not the same.

The parents of several of their friends and classmates were divorced. For those whose parents had remarried, they faced challenges with step parents and blended families that weren't blending too well. A few of their friends described situations where they all co-existed but the parents argued constantly or did their own thing separate from each other. They knew of one classmate, Jacob, whose father was never at home. Jacob lived in a beautiful luxurious home but, according to him, his father never had time for him because of work.

By contrast, Marlon and Nick had few complaints about their parents. As children, they were supported and given every opportunity to excel but they didn't get everything they wanted. Sometimes the answer was no and the only explanation given was "because we said so." The brothers hadn't always agreed with their parents' decisions, rules or expectations but they'd never questioned their parents' love for them or each other.

Wallace said, "Let's pray together."

"Okay," the boys said in unison though they were surprised. Their family prayed often but it was usually their mother who initiated it, not their father.

With joined hands, Wallace began. "Thank You, God, for Your blessings, provisions, bounty, and protection. We thank You for our family and how You've kept us and blessed us. Continue to hold us close. We pray especially for Marlon and his health. Remove the cancer completely, Father, and restore his health. We love You and thank You for being our Lord and Savior. In Jesus' name. Amen."

Janole, Marlon and Nick in unison said, "Amen."

Janole, strengthened by Wallace's prayer, began speaking.

"Marlon and Nick, I have something important to tell you and it's very, very difficult for me. It's probably one of the hardest things I've ever had to do." Janole paused to take a sip of water and Nick noticed that her hands were slightly shaking. When she put the bottle down, she began wringing her hands.

"Marlon, this will impact you more than Nick, understand?" She looked at Marlon and waited for him to acknowledge his under-standing. Satisfied with his nod, she continued.

"I'm going to ask that you both let me say what I need to say…that you hear me out without interrupting. I promise that I will answer all of your questions. Can you do that?"

Marlon and Nick both nodded despite their confusion. Never had they been called in for a family discussion like this. Nick, more adept at reading people than Marlon, looked at his father and mother. In their expressions, he saw pain and regret. Even fear. Something was very wrong.

"Are you getting a divorce?" Nick blurted out, his voice slightly higher than normal. "I'm sorry but is that what this meeting is all about?"

"No." Wallace was quick to respond. "Your mother and I love each other more than ever." He hoped that was true. "Just hear her out. Go ahead, honey."

Janole took a deep breath. "Years ago—before you were born—there was this guy, Eric, in my doctoral program at UVA who constantly pursued me. He was very persistent. I had no interest in him but one day, against my better judgment, I gave in to his advances. We had sex one time and I found out a few weeks later that I was pregnant. I never told Eric that I was pregnant for a couple of reasons. One, he was married and two, I didn't want anything from him. What we did was a mistake and shouldn't have happened." Janole took another sip of water before continuing.

"Because I was pregnant and had no means of supporting a baby, I couldn't stay in the doctoral program. I needed a job and with the help of a good friend, I was offered one in Fairfax. That's where I met your father and, eventually, we fell deeply in love. But I was already pregnant when I met your father."

She hesitated just briefly before saying, "Marlon, Wallace is not your biological father."

Marlon looked from one parent to the other in disbelief. Both of their faces communicated the same message…that what he had just heard was the truth. Unable to restrain himself, he stood abruptly and glared at his mother with rage. For a few moments, words failed him. He felt as if his entire world had just been blown apart by the people he most trusted.

"You can't be serious. You cannot be serious! What are you saying?" Breathing heavily with clinched fists, Marlon tried with all of his power to fight back tears. At that very moment he felt like a helpless child and despised feeling vulnerable and weak; but, he couldn't help himself. The very foundation of his existence was shattered. He looked from his mother to his father desperate for a different reality. "Dad, tell me this isn't true!"

Wallace looked at his oldest son whom he loved more than life.

"I am your father, Marlon, in every way that matters. Listen to me. I fell in love with your mother before you were born and held you in my arms when you were just hours old. Not only did I fall in love with your mother but I fell in love with you. One of the happiest days of my life was the day I legally adopted you as my son."

Reality hit forcefully when Marlon heard the words "legally adopted." As if pushed, he fell back on the sofa and stared at his parents with a stony expression.

Janole spoke. "Marlon, we should have probably told you before now—"

"Probably? You should have probably told me? You think?" Marlon retorted, sarcastically.

"I should have but I just couldn't bring myself to do it. I'm so sorry. I didn't want to relive those circumstances. I was so ashamed—and still am—about being intimate with a married man and, as your mother, I wanted to protect you from that stigma."

"So were you a whore or something?" The minute Marlon spoke the words, he was instantly regretful. He saw the pain in his mother's eyes…how those words impacted her but he offered no apology. Part of him was glad she was hurting just as he was hurting.

Nick, initially stunned, found his voice. "Marlon, ease up man. I know you're upset but that was not cool."

Meanwhile, Wallace walked over to Marlon and stood directly in front of him. He stared at Marlon with a steely expression and spoke slowly and deliberately. "Look at me, Marlon."

When Marlon looked into his father's piercing eyes, he saw a man who would go to any length to protect his wife.

"You were way out of line. Don't ever speak to your mother that way. Ever. That was ugly and beneath you. I will not tolerate disrespect from you or anyone else. She is your mother. Don't forget that. Have I made myself clear?"

Marlon said nothing as he stared at his father. He was angry enough to fight and considered punching Wallace. Though he was bigger and stronger, something held him back.

"Have I made myself clear?" Wallace repeated.

"Yeah." Marlon was ashamed that he made such a despicable statement. His need to strike out, to hurt someone—anyone—as much as he was hurting overpowered his better judgment. He knew at his very core that his mother was a good woman but right now anger consumed him.

Returning to sit beside Janole, Wallace asked, "What other questions do you have?" He tenderly rubbed Janole's hand.

Marlon looked at his brother. "Did you know about this?"

"No, man. I had no idea," Nick admitted. He, too, was angry with his parents. "So, you guys lied to us all of our lives?"

Janole looked at Nick then Marlon before responding. "I—we should have told you. I thought I was doing the right thing by not telling you or Eric. We made a mistake. I was trying to protect you—"

Marlon responded with anger, frustration and confusion. "Wow. This is too much. I found out yesterday that I have cancer and that I may not be able to play basketball for a long time, if ever. Today I find out that my father is not my father and that I'm a mistake. What's next?"

Janole had never seen Marlon so angry, disappointed or hurt. The stress of the situation was getting to her, too. Though she didn't realize it at the time, she was reacting to months of accumulated stress.

"Don't twist my words, Marlon. Do you feel like a mistake?" Janole asked, raising her voice slightly; her face contorted in anger and pain. Tears were falling freely but she ignored them. Her voice was thick with emotion. "At any point and time in your entire life did you feel like a mistake? Huh? I loved you from the minute I knew of your existence. So has Wallace. I know this is a lot to process. I get that but don't twist my words or this situation."

The tension in the room was palpable. No one spoke for several minutes. "I assume Uncle Marlo and Grandma know," Marlon said, dejectedly.

"Yes," Janole responded. "And your Aunt Jenn."

Marlon exploded again. "I can't believe this! Everybody knew about this except me! How could you do this to me? I trusted you. What other secrets are you keeping? You had no right..." Marlon put his face in his hands to hide the tears. This was a kind of agony that he had never experienced. It was the ultimate betrayal.

Janole, Wallace and Nick were each tortured as they witnessed Marlon's pain.

Finally, Nick spoke. "Mom, our entire lives you preached honesty and integrity. You both did. Your word is your bond you said.

Always tell the truth. We were punished when we lied. It all seems so hypocritical now. Surely you can understand that."

"I do." Janole sighed. "I hope in time you will understand how difficult it was for me. I hope in time you will forgive me and understand that I wanted to protect you. I've tried to live as honorably as I can but I'll be the first to admit that I'm not perfect."

Wallace spoke. "Marlon, the reason we chose today to tell you about Eric is because of your medical condition. Dr. Bowers made it clear that genetics could be a significant factor. Your mother has spent hours on the computer trying to locate Eric so that we can obtain his medical history. The most important priorities now are your health and your life."

Marlon stood and grabbed his jacket. "I guess it's a good thing that I have cancer; otherwise, my entire life would be a lie. I'm out. Come on, Nick. Let's get out of here. End of conversation."

Chapter Nine

———————※———————

*H*er family was broken. Janole hadn't spoken to Marlon since he learned that Wallace wasn't his biological father. He returned none of her calls. She hadn't heard from Nick either whose allegiance was, no doubt, torn. Nick knew that Marlon needed him right now. She and Wallace had each other. Janole understood that she was responsible for this situation but the pain of being shunned by her children was almost unbearable.

She aimlessly wandered around the spacious house feeling empty and restless. Custom built to their specifications, it was a beautifully designed house. Trey ceilings, crown moldings, architectural beams, built-in shelving, hardwood flooring, granite countertops, and numerous windows all added to the structure's appeal and character. The walls, painted a soft palette of buttery cream, displayed an array of tasteful art and framed photographs. Janole loved this house from the beginning and, over time, transformed it into a comfortable home for her family with an understated yet elegant sense of style and color. Visitors were often surprised, and impressed, that she was solely responsible for its décor without the aid of an interior designer. To her, this home represented the love of her family and their many wonderful memories.

Sighing, she continued to stroll from room to room. *The sins of my past have finally caught up with me. If only I'd listened to Tam and Jenn.* Years ago, her best friends tried to persuade her to tell Eric that she was pregnant with his child but she had adamantly refused. And, because she had never disclosed to Eric that he was the father of her son, she didn't feel pressured to tell Marlon the truth. Telling one would necessitate informing the other. She believed she was doing the right thing for everyone involved.

Now she was haunted by her decision. Perhaps if Wallace hadn't come into her life when he had she would have decided differently. The timing of their involvement, she'd felt, wasn't due to fate or coincidence. Rather, it was confirmation that she was being given divine permission to put the past behind her. Wallace was a Godsend; their relationship preordained. After all, how many women find their soul mate—their one true love—while carrying another man's child? In spite of her sin and complete lack of judgment, God blessed her with a kind and loving man. One who had his choice of beautiful women but chose her. She would have gladly accepted his friendship on a platonic basis but God had other plans. For that, she was deeply grateful.

She glanced at her reflection in the hall mirror and paused. "What have you done to your family, Janole?" she asked herself. "Your son hates you."

As she stared deeply into her own brown eyes—the windows to her soul—she saw sadness and pain. But there was more. There was strength, wisdom, conviction, integrity and love. She realized then that given the same circumstances she would, without a doubt, make the same decision. She knew with every ounce of a woman's—and a mother's—intuition that Eric would never have accepted or recognized Marlon as his son. And, if years ago, she had revealed to Marlon the true identity of his biological father, Marlon's life would have been very different and not for the better. All of their lives would have been different.

Option One: provide a secure and nurturing foundation for Marlon with two parents who love him and each other; provide every opportunity for his growth and development and proudly watch him mature into a successful and confident man. Option Two: tell Marlon about his biological father who has no desire to be his father or involved in his life; watch Marlon grow up questioning his worth, wondering why his own father would reject him.

The decision was easy. Option One, please. Janole decided then and there that she was going to release herself from guilt. It was never her intent to hurt Marlon—quite the contrary. She'd spent her entire life trying to protect her boys from the ugliness of life. Everything she did for them was out of a deep and abiding love.

She prayed that, in time, Marlon would come to understand her reasoning. "God, gently reveal the truth to Marlon. Help Marlon and Nick to understand my heart and give them the grace to forgive me in spite of my actions just as You did. Please heal Marlon's body and remove all of his pain. Reunite our family with Your love. I love You."

Janole decided to take a walk. No more brooding, no more worrying. One of her favorite scriptures came to mind. ***Be anxious for nothing...***

She continued her conversation with God as if He were standing in the room. "I'm releasing it all to You, Father. I can't fix it anyway. You have given me the gift of another day and I will not waste it worrying and sulking." As she dressed in walking gear, she decided to call Reese.

"Hi Janole," Reese said in her usual cheerful greeting.

"Hey Reese. I'm going for a walk. Want to join me?"

"Sure. Give me ten minutes to change."

"I'll meet you at your house," Janole said, excited to have Reese's company and leave her problems behind, if only temporarily. Janole had not met anyone more kind and generous than Reese. If she could help someone in need, she did. Friend or stranger, it didn't matter. If she had something that could be used by someone, she cheerfully gave it even if it was a sacrifice. Her home was always open.

Reese was also extremely intelligent and possessed a great deal of spunk. Not known to sugarcoat the facts, Reese's bluntness was difficult for some to receive. Janole appreciated Reese's honesty, finding it refreshing. Over the years, the two women had developed a friendship that Janole treasured. They watched their sons grow up, trusted each other with very personal information, helped each other through tough times, and celebrated life together. One of their favorite annual trips was to the CIAA basketball tournament where Reese cheered for her beloved Winston-Salem State University Rams.

Reese was on her front porch, stretching, when Janole arrived. "I'm so glad you called," Reese said. "I needed to get out of the house. Jack and I had a terrible argument and I mean terrible."

"About what?" Janole didn't particularly like Jack. He was selfish and critical of Reese at every opportunity. His comments about Reese angered Janole on more than one occasion. Jack was also argumentative with a skewed sense of reasoning; therefore, his points of view seldom made sense. When he was challenged during a conversation, he resorted to personal attacks and insults. Janole tolerated him because of Reese.

Reese responded to Janole's question as they began walking. "Because I have not changed my mind about retiring in a few months and he is adamant that I should work longer. I've told him over and over that the stress of the job is affecting my health but he seems more concerned about money than me. I've been working since I was fifteen years old and it angers me that he won't support my decision. I've carried our family, Janole, and I'm tired."

"You don't have to convince me. I get it. How much longer does he want you to work?"

"Three more years! I'll be dead by then," Reese said. "You know what really galls me? He retired early and I didn't say one word."

"So, what are you going to do?" Janole asked.

"I'm going to retire as I planned and trust God to work it out however He wants."

They walked in silence for a few moments before Reese continued. "Pastor Jones said something in bible study that helped me a great deal. He spoke about 'the enemy' and his cunning ways....how Satan takes such great delight in destroying happiness. Very subtly, he infuses himself in our lives—at every opportunity—causing doubt, insecurity, worry, sadness, discord, anger, even hate as the focus shifts more and more on our problems. Before long, to Satan's delight, everything is a mess and we're feeling overwhelmed, depressed and defeated. I refuse to let Satan claim my peace or my family. Well, now that I think about it, he can have Jack if he wants."

Both women burst into laughter at the same time.

"Girl, you are hilarious," Janole said, holding her stomach.

"Gotta laugh to keep from crying," Reese said. "Seriously though, I'm going to trust God and keep my focus on Him."

"Good for you," Janole said. "I'm proud of you. You've encouraged me to do the same thing," Janole said with a renewed commitment.

Janole inhaled deeply, pulling the refreshingly cool air into her lungs. She felt energized by the brisk walk and encouraged by Reese's comments. It was a beautiful day. The sun shone brightly and the sky overhead was a startling blue. She and Reese said good-bye and promised to talk in a few days.

As Janole neared her house, she noticed the flag was raised on their mailbox. Strange. For security reasons, they never used the mailbox for their outgoing mail. Perhaps the neighborhood kids were responsible. She lowered the flag and checked the box out of curiosity. Inside she found a plain white business-sized envelope. It was sealed but contained neither a mailing nor return address. This is strange, Janole thought.

After wiping her face and grabbing a bottle of water, she sat at the kitchen table and opened the envelope. She was glad to be sitting when she read the contents. The message was short.

"You'd better watch your back. It's not over." Dropping the letter as if it were hot, Janole stared at it not sure what to do next. This confirmed her biggest fear.

For months she had worried that the pharmaceutical company would seek revenge. Partly because of the information Wallace had compiled, the company had, reportedly, lost billions of dollars in revenue which resulted in people losing their jobs. Worse, some were facing long prison sentences. She'd even read of one person who had died by suicide as a result of his involvement with the company's illegal activities.

When she had shared her fear with Wallace, he dismissed it saying that there would be no point in the company harming them now. They had already given the evidence to the FBI and their situation was but one part of a much larger scheme implemented by the pharmaceutical company.

"What purpose would it serve for them to hurt us now?" Wallace asked when she'd first expressed her concern. She could think of a few reasons. How about payback? Retribution? Anger? Vindictiveness? Wallace, kiddingly, told her that she watched too many movies and she had, over time, accepted that perhaps she was worried for no good reason.

Until today.

She looked around her home feeling afraid and shaken yet she didn't phone Wallace. She remembered Nate saying that there were persons who could get into a locked home without anyone knowing they had been there. Still, she turned on the security system and checked that all doors were locked.

Janole began pacing. Anxiety and fear had returned. *I should call Nate. No, I should tell Wallace first. No, remember your help. Don't focus on the situation. Focus on your help. Okay.*

"Father, thank You for being the loving and faithful God that You are. You said to cast our cares on You and to be anxious for nothing. It is You alone, Father, who has all power, knowledge, wisdom and strength. Protect us. Keep us. Guide us. Help us to rely on You and not ourselves. I'm afraid and worried. And I'm angry. Please help me. Restore peace, joy and contentment. Keep us safe."

Later, Janole stared at the note as if it were a poisonous snake poised to strike — venomous, destructive, deadly. It was just a piece of paper but she didn't want to touch it, didn't want to be tainted by its implication. Someone meant them harm. Already, it was a source of contention between her and Wallace.

"No, Janole! We are not calling Nate," Wallace said, emphatically. "We don't need your old boyfriend involved in this." The old boyfriend who is still in love with you, he thought but didn't verbalize.

"I don't understand. Nate helped me find you and he's experienced in this sort of thing."

"I don't care," Wallace stated with anger in his voice. "The answer is no. We'll contact Agent Tyous but not Nate."

Unbelievable, thought Janole. Their lives were in danger and they were arguing. Janole was afraid, plain and simple. She wanted Wallace to contact the FBI and Nate. She trusted Nate and would be comforted knowing that he and the FBI were involved. Not one or the other; both. She explained that to Wallace.

"I don't completely trust that the FBI will consider this a top priority."

Wallace attempted to reassure her. "Babe, I know you're wor-ried. I am, too. Let's call the FBI now, hear them out and go from there. Agent Tyous said to call him any time and that's what I'm going to do."

Special Agent in Charge (SAC) Tyous and Agent Cochran arrived at their home several hours later. They looked the same. Professional, stoic, discerning…both muscular and fit, dressed in dark suits. Janole remembered them well from 'the ordeal.' After exchanging brief greetings, Wallace repeated what he had conveyed during the earlier phone conversation.

SAC Tyous took the lead in asking questions while Agent Cochran made notes in a small black leather notepad. "Mrs. Jackson, tell us how you discovered the note." Janole did.

"Did you see anything unusual or suspicious?"

"No."

"Cars that you haven't seen in the neighborhood before?"

"No."

"What time did you leave for your walk?"

"Around 11:30."

"And what time did you return?"

"12:45. I checked my watch."

"Was the flag in the raised position when you began your walk?"

"I don't think so but I can't be sure."

"Before you found the note when did you last check the mailbox? I'm assuming your mail is delivered and placed inside the box."

Wallace nodded. "You assume correctly. I remember getting the mail from the box yesterday evening after work. Probably around five-thirty or six."

"What time did you leave for work, Mr. Jackson?"

"My usual time, around seven." Wallace anticipated the next ques-tion. "I didn't pay any attention to the mailbox. I don't know if the flag was raised or not."

"Mrs. Jackson, are you usually at home during the day?"

"No, but I'm on vacation for a couple of weeks."

"Did you see anyone else at all?"

"I walked with a friend who lives in the neighborhood. Her name is Reese Vaughan. I saw our neighbor across the street mowing his lawn. His name is Peter Linton. Of course, there was car traffic but nothing that appeared out of the ordinary. Oh—I did see a woman pushing a stroller and walking her dog. I've seen her before but I don't know her name."

"Mr. Jackson, have you noticed anything unusual or suspicious?"

"No, not at all."

"How about at work?"

"Not really. I fired a secretary a week ago."

"Tell me about that," SAC Tyous said, his demeanor unchanged.

Wallace explained that the secretary was frequently absent and late to work and had been warned of the consequences. He provided her name as requested.

"Who else knows about the note?"

"No one," Janole answered. "We didn't tell anyone else."

"Keep it that way," SAC Tyous said. "We're going to run it through our lab and will let you know what we find."

Janole's fears had not been calmed. "Is that it? Is that all you can do? How about protection?" Janole was convinced that this was related to the pharmaceutical company's threat.

SAC Tyous did not succeed if his attempt was to provide reassurance. "We need to get answers first. Let us do that. Then we'll make a determination. Give us an opportunity to investigate. We'll be in touch soon. Meanwhile, if you think of anything or notice anything out of the norm, give one of us a call."

After the agents left, Janole looked at Wallace and said, "Feel better? Cause I sure don't. We did it your way and guess what? We have no answers, no protection, nothing." She angrily left the room not giving him an opportunity to respond.

Wallace sat down not knowing what to say or do. At times, Janole was so angry with him. He thought her fear was unwarranted but, he had to admit, the note had him worried. He just couldn't fathom what the pharmaceutical company would gain from threatening them now. It seemed foolish for them to do anything to make their situation worse. He recalled the words on the note. *You'd better watch your back. It's not over.* What's not over? It didn't make sense. And, it wasn't addressed to them specifically. It could be a harmless prank or intended for someone else. Maybe they should consult with Nate but Wallace's pride wouldn't permit it. Under other circumstances, he and Nate could probably be the best of friends but he knew the look of a man in love and Nate had that look. Wallace would be foolish to invite Nate into their lives knowing how Nate felt about Janole.

Chapter Ten

---❋---

*M*arlon and Nick were lounging around watching NBA basketball but neither was completely relaxed. After the meeting with their parents a few days ago, they'd had a huge argument almost coming to blows. Nick, livid with Marlon for suggesting that their mother was a whore, warned Marlon that he was never to say anything derogatory to their mother again. Marlon felt justified and refused to apologize. As a result, there was definite tension in the air.

Nick, too, had been stunned by the news regarding Marlon's biological father but Marlon had gone too far. The pain in their mother's eyes caused by the full impact of Marlon's verbal assault—plus what she had endured when their father was gone—was something Nick would not soon forget. He wouldn't be satisfied until Marlon apologized. Under the circumstances if Marlon had been speaking to anyone else, Nick would have given him a pass. But he was speaking to their mother and that was unacceptable.

Marlon was angry because his life was a mess. For the first time in his life things were spiraling out of his control and that infuriated him. Scared him, too. He knew his anger served no constructive purpose yet he felt entitled and dared anyone to tell him otherwise. He was anxiously waiting for the test results about the stage of his cancer and trying not to anticipate the worse. The unknown was proving to be quite terrifying as he considered each possible outcome. Meanwhile, the thing he loved most was on hold—basketball, his passion and livelihood.

He also felt betrayed and misunderstood by everyone he loved—his mom, father, grandmother and Uncle Marlo. They all knew the truth and not one of them ever hinted that Wallace wasn't his biological father...that there was another man responsible for his existence. He even felt at odds with Nick though he could provide no rational explanation. And, as if the anger, worry and betrayal weren't enough, Marlon was conflicted by feelings of guilt because he couldn't help but be curious about this man, Eric. *What kind of person is my biological father? Are there other children? What kind of work does he do? Where does he live? Does he love basketball like I do? Hate spinach like I do? Can he hoop? Will he want to have anything to do with me? Do I want to know him?*

Before, Marlon attributed his athletic prowess more to Wallace's genes though he knew his mom's side of the family was athletically inclined, too. He recalled proudly comparing himself to Wallace and beaming when others said about him, "You're just like your dad."

Now he questioned the sincerity of those comments. He questioned everything as he reviewed his life including the very beginning. He wasn't conceived out of love as he had thought. He was a mistake—unplanned, unwanted; the result of a brief, passionate but meaningless liaison between his mom and a married man.

Marlon had been quick to attack his mom but now he wondered about Eric. Just what kind of man was he? Is he? A playa going after everything in a skirt that looked good? He knew guys like that. They had beautiful, loving wives or girlfriends but never seemed satisfied. Their vows were completely disregarded as they pursued, deceived, manipulated and seduced their prey, often leaving behind a trail of pain. And, in some instances, leaving behind a new innocent life. *Like me.*

Nick interrupted his thoughts. "I think I'm going to stop by Mom's and Dad's. Wanna come? I'm sure it would make their day to see us."

Marlon, unshaven and dressed in sweats, was stretched out on the sofa staring at the television. He didn't bother to look at his brother. He knew Nick was trying to be supportive of him and restore family peace. "I don't think so, man. I'd just bring everybody down. You go ahead. I'll be fine."

Nick asked a questioned that gave Marlon pause. "What are you really angry about?"

Marlon did look at his brother then. "That's a stupid question. I'm-I'm angry about everything."

"But what makes you most angry? Is it the cancer? Is it—?"

"I'm pissed off because they lied to me," Marlon stated. "Nothing will ever be the same."

"Okay, I get that. It was messed up that they lied to us. But let me ask you this. What kind of life did you have?"

"That's not the point," Marlon said, angrily.

"But let's talk about it anyway. I repeat. What kind of life did you have, Marlon? Real talk."

Marlon hesitated before answering as he quickly reflected on his life. "I had a great life but that doesn't change the fact that they lied to me my entire life."

"No, it doesn't but who is responsible for this great life of yours?"

"But they lied to me, Nick. I feel betrayed. Get off my case. You don't know what it feels like. Don't minimize what they did. That pisses me off even more."

"I'm not trying to minimize it, Marlon, but it's done. You can't change it. Our parents aren't perfect and this news was a huge shock... but I've been thinking about this. A lot. I have a feeling they did what they did to protect you, not themselves. You need to get over this, man. Nothing changes the love they have for us. It's real and you know that." Nick paused for a few minutes to collect himself. "Let me ask you another question. When you needed someone, really needed someone, who did you call?"

Marlon said nothing, refusing to acknowledge Nick's question.

"You can ignore me if you want but you know the answer as well as I do. Mom and Dad have always been there for us," Nick stated. "And Uncle Marlo. Am I right?"

Marlon shrugged his shoulders.

Nick continued. "Man, we're talking real love. It doesn't matter how you were conceived. It really doesn't. Nothing can change the way I feel about you. Do you feel differently about me knowing that we're now just half-brothers?"

Marlon's expression conveyed the absurdity of Nick's question. "Of course not."

"Exactly. What matters is that we're family and we love each other. If anything, you should appreciate Dad more than ever. He has loved you as if you were his own blood because that's what you are to him. Who knows how your life would have been if Mom hadn't met Dad. It seems to me that you're angry at a gift. Maybe they were wrong for not telling you sooner. They made a mistake, man. You can question their judgment. You can disagree with their decision. But you certainly can't question their love."

Marlon laid his head back on the sofa and closed his eyes. "I just need time to work through this, man. I've got cancer, I can't play basketball, my future is up in the air and I've got a biological father somewhere that I've never met. And I don't even know if I want to meet him. Hell, he may not want to meet me either," Marlon vented. "I could have other brothers and sisters and I don't know if I care. My life—everything—is different now and I don't like it. I didn't want this...any of it."

"I know, Marlon, you've got a lot going on. But you have two choices. Accept it and move on or stay in a funk. It's your call." Nick grabbed his keys and phone. "You think you can put it all behind you for a few hours? Come on."

In spite of Nick's common sense urgings, Marlon decided to stay at home.

"I don't think so, man. I just want to chill here. You go ahead though."

Marlon admitted to himself that he wasn't ready to forgive, to submit to a release of his anger. Everything that Nick said was true. Marlon couldn't deny that; but, it was also true that he was changed by this news. He looked at them all differently now through somewhat murky lenses. He knew that they loved him yet they had a common thread that tied them all neatly together—blood.

He had no such common thread with Wallace, the man he thought to be his father. Marlon had always taken such pride in being his father's son. He was proud to be in the Jackson lineage...to know that the blood coursing through his veins was, in part, connected to his great-grandfather, Rudy, whom Wallace spoke of with great respect. Not only that, Marlon idolized Wallace; even questioned whether he could measure up to him as a man. The Jackson legacy of proud and noble men meant a great deal to Marlon.

All of that had been destroyed when he learned he was a Jackson in name only. And a more tangible and permanent reminder was his prostate cancer to which, it seemed, the Jackson men were not pre-disposed. Even if he wanted to forget and move beyond the news about his biological father, he really couldn't. His cancer and its possible genetic significance wouldn't allow him to do so.

His phone rang, interrupting his brooding thoughts. It was his Uncle Marlo again. This was not a conversation Marlon was looking forward to but recognized he was only delaying the inevitable. Reluctantly, he answered. "Hello."

"Finally you answer the phone. I've been calling you for a while. It's good to hear your voice," Marlo said.

Marlon could muster no excitement. "Yours too. Sorry I haven't returned your calls."

"No worries. So, how are you? Talk to me. You don't sound good," his uncle said.

Marlon wanted to talk to his uncle...to confide in him. Their relationship was special but Marlon considered him a betrayer, too. "What do you want me to say? Life stinks right now."

"You sound angry," Marlo said, with genuine empathy.

"I am angry. More than angry. I'm furious. You knew that Wallace wasn't my father and you said nothing." Marlon fought to restrain the emotion that was just below the surface.

"Marlon, listen to me. It wasn't my place to tell you. I know you're angry. You've got a lot going on now. I understand. But, as your uncle, it wasn't my place to tell you, man. I've always been straight up with you but I had to respect your mother's wishes."

"Well, it doesn't feel good to know that everyone was a part of this secret except me."

Marlo paused for a moment giving his nephew time to compose himself. "I think the question you should ask is why your mom didn't tell you."

"She said she wanted to protect me."

"But why? Protect you from what?" Marlo probed.

Uncertain, Marlon responded with questions. "The truth? The stigma?"

Marlo sighed. "It's deeper than that—much deeper. Let me tell you a story. True story. Your mother called me when she learned she was pregnant with you. She wanted—and needed—my support when she informed your grandparents. I'll come back to that.

"I knew Eric, your biological father. Now, he may have changed; I hope he has. But then he was a playa of the worst kind because he bragged about his conquests. I'd come visit your mom occasionally and hoop with the guys. When Eric's wife came to watch us play he was on his best behavior but when his wife wasn't there, he'd ogle over the women more than the single guys. And it wasn't just mindless flirting. He was sleeping with these women or, at least, trying his best to get in their panties. One day he said something about Janole who was watching us play and I told him she was off limits and then proceeded to kick his butt on the court. He didn't take too kindly to either. I think that's why he was so persistent in pursuing your mom."

"Reminds me of this guy on our team. He's a dog," Marlon said, with disgust, as he recalled his teammate's wife tearfully confiding in him one day.

"Well, like I said, Eric may have changed since then. I'm not trying to disparage him but I think it may help you to understand what your mom went through. So when your mom told me she was pregnant by Eric, I paid him a visit. This is something your mom doesn't know. And let's just say that I let him know he messed with the wrong woman. I've often wondered how he explained his black eye and bruises to his wife."

Marlon couldn't help himself. "You beat him up?"

"I did. I whipped his ass and threatened to tell his wife about him."

"Did he know Mom was pregnant?"

"No, and I didn't tell him. He used her, Marlon, partly for his own satisfaction and partly to get back at me and I wasn't having that."

"What happened next?" Marlon asked.

"Your mom had to tell your grandparents and it was ugly—real ugly. Times were different thirty years ago. Try to imagine a single woman like your mother having to inform her religious parents that she was pregnant from a one-time involvement with a married man. That was tough news. Your grandfather had issues—serious issues—and went ballistic. He said horrible things to Jay...called her names and told her she was no longer welcome in his home."

"He disowned her?" Marlon asked in disbelief. "Grandma too?"

"No, not your grandma but that's a story for another day. The point is your mom went through a lot. She didn't tell Eric about you because she knew the kind of man he was then. More importantly, she didn't tell you about him because she didn't want you longing for a father who would only disappoint you. Like our father. She didn't want that kind of life for you."

Marlon didn't say anything as he digested this information. He had convinced himself that there was no justification for his mother's actions. Now he wasn't so sure.

Marlo continued. "When our father disowned Jay, I vowed to be there for her and stand in as your father...to be the man in your life. Was proud to do it but there was no need because your mom met Wallace while she was pregnant with you and the rest is—as they say—history."

"Why didn't Mom tell me this?" Marlon asked.

"I don't know, man. Probably because it still hurts. It was a very painful time for her. Look, I'm sorry to cut this short but camp starts in a few so I've got to go but I want you to think about this. You don't get to choose family, Marlon. They're family whether you like them or not...regardless of how they treat you. Let me say it this way. If I had to choose a father and the three options were my father, Eric, or Wallace, without a doubt or a moment's hesitation, I'd choose Wallace. Take it from me. Blood doesn't always make it better."

Nick rang the doorbell before opening the door and announcing his presence. "Anybody home?" he yelled from the foyer.

Janole was in the kitchen finishing the final preparations for vegetable lasagna and a salad. "I'm in the kitchen," she called out as she wiped her hands on her apron and headed towards Nick. "You're just in time for dinner."

She held him tightly knowing the significance of his presence. It represented more than a routine visit. It meant that he understood her decision, at least, in part. Enough for him to embrace her and, more importantly, forgive her. He said as much. He also explained that Marlon was in the process of coming to terms with his new reality.

"He'll come around. Give time time," Nick advised his mom. "That's what Grandma always says. Give time time."

Late that night as Janole was preparing for bed, the phone rang. Hoping it was Marlon, she quickly answered. Wallace was already asleep.

"Hi JJ. Did I wake you?"

"Hi Jenn! No, I'm wide awake."

"How are you? Feeling better? Still having nightmares?" Jenn asked.

"I'm hanging in there and I haven't had nightmares for the past few nights." Janole chose not to share the news about Marlon...that her nightmares had been replaced with worry about her son's life. Exhausted, she didn't want to rehash the situation. Not tonight.

"Good." After a brief hesitation, Jenn said, "JJ, I've got exciting news. You get three guesses." Jenn's excitement was contagious.

Janole walked down the hall to the guest room so as not to disturb Wallace. She sat in the chair and tucked her feet under her. "Okay. You're pregnant," Janole said, smiling.

Jenn laughed loudly. "Girl, shut up. No! Guess again."

Laughing, Janole said, "Okay. You won the lottery. Oh—that's right. You're already rich so that would be no big deal to you. Hmmm, let's see. You won the lottery and you're giving all the money to me?"

Jenn laughed. "No, you're way off base." Unable to contain her excitement any longer, Jenn exclaimed, "We're moving!"

"Moving? Into a new house?" Janole asked, confused. The house they lived in was beautiful and perfect, in Janole's opinion. She couldn't imagine why they would want another home.

"No. Moving as in relocating. Leaving Seattle."

Janole was surprised by Jenn's news. She had no idea that Jenn and Paul were even contemplating a change of this magnitude. They loved Seattle where they met years ago. "Moving? Why? Where?" Janole asked.

Jenn explained that an opportunity presented itself for Paul that he found quite appealing and had given a great deal of thought. "The proposal grew on me over time. The more I thought about it, the more excited I became. The twins were initially disappointed but as long as they have each other, they can adapt to any location."

"Don't keep me in suspense, Jenn. Where are you moving?" Janole asked.

"Let me tell you about the job first," Jenn said, relishing in prolonging the suspense. "Paul and one of his law school buddies are opening a practice specializing in criminal law. It's going to be a small firm which ideally suits Paul because he'll be able to teach at the university and still do missions work at church."

"That sounds exciting. Congratulations! I'm so happy for you both," Janole exclaimed.

"Now for the best part," Jenn said with intrigue.

"Well, tell me for heaven's sake," Janole said.

"Are you sitting down?" Not waiting for an answer, Jenn continued. "We're moving to DC! Can you believe it? We'll be less than an hour from you."

Janole sat up. So many thoughts went through her mind. "Jenn, are you telling me the truth? You're not kidding, are you?"

"No way. I wanted to tell you when we were there for your birthday but Paul made me wait until it was definite."

"Oh my God. Oh. My. God." Janole was at a loss for words. This was the best news in the world. She began to cry.

"Janole, I hope those are happy tears."

"Very happy. Jenn, your timing…couldn't be better. I'm so happy."

"I'm happy, too. Are you sure everything is okay?" Jenn asked, her excitement replaced with concern.

"We'll talk later, not now. It's no big deal, anyway," Janole lied not wanting to spoil the joy of Jenn's news. "I promise. When are you moving? Have you found a house?"

Reassured, Jenn asked, "Are you still sitting down? We'll be there by summer's end. For good. Permanently."

"What?" Janole asked, incredulously. "I can't believe it."

"Yep. We'll be moving, if all goes according to plan, by the end of August or early September. We'll rent a home in DC until we find exactly what we want. You and I can go house hunting together. We can do a lot together."

"Jenn, this is the best news ever. You have made my day. Wallace will be so excited."

Chapter Eleven

———————✳———————

*J*anole approached her computer with excitement and trepidation. It had been a week since she'd fired off emails to several men with the name of Eric Cutler. One of them had to be the right one but, so far, there had been no responses. She'd included just enough information to convey her identity and desire to reconnect with former classmates.

She'd considered writing a more urgent appeal but thought better of it. *Please contact me. It's a matter of life or death.* No, that would raise too many suspicions before she had an opportunity to explain. She wanted to be in control of this situation and the information shared.

It occurred to her that Eric may not remember her. After all, almost three decades had passed since their brief but fateful liaison. Or perhaps he remembered but didn't want to connect with her. That was a possibility, too. She meant nothing to him; no delusions in that regard. For a brief moment in time, she fed his ego and satisfied his body. She wondered how many other women had served the same purposes.

Janole looked out of the window, mesmerized by the unrelenting rain. It had been falling steadily all day and was predicted to continue for the next two days. The local news reported flash flood warnings were in effect for the entire viewing area. The dreary weather matched her mood.

After turning the computer on, she warmed her coffee and made a decision. If she didn't hear from Eric today, she would contact Sarah

Biltske. And if Sarah had no information, she'd hire a private detective. She was going to find Eric, come hell or high water.

Today was pay day. There was an email from an Eric who lived in North Dakota and had never been to the state of Virginia. He wished her good luck. The next email caused her heart beat to accelerate as she read it.

Hi Janole,

I am one of your former classmates. We were in the doctoral program at UVA in the 80's. As I recall, you left the program rather suddenly. Hope you're well. I heard that Dr. Biltske died a few years ago. Do you go back to UVA often? I've only been once or twice. I live in Phoenix now. Let me know who else you connect with. I'd be interested in attending a reunion….

Regards,
Eric

He was the one! Marlon's father. Calm down, Janole. Picking up her laptop, she walked down the hall into Wallace's home office. Until the mysterious note writer was identified, Wallace was committed to staying close to home and even closer to Janole.

"Wallace, take a look at this," Janole said, trying to downplay her excitement.

Wallace read the email, looked at Janole and asked, "Now what?" He was unsure of how to handle himself with Janole because of her unpredictable moods.

"I'm going to Phoenix. I can't deliver this kind of news over the phone. Plus, I've got to convey to him how badly we need his medical history."

"I'll go with you," Wallace offered.

"No, you stay here. Marlon may need you before I return. Plus, I need to do this alone."

Wallace watched as Janole typed a response to Eric.

What a coincidence. I'll be in Phoenix later this week for a conference. My schedule is flexible Friday and Saturday. Want to have lunch or dinner?

While Janole was contemplating the remainder of the message, she noticed an incoming message from Nate. Wallace saw it, too, and immediately, his jealousy flared.

"Aren't you going to open your message from Nate?" Wallace asked more as a challenge than a question.

Oblivious to Wallace's annoyance, Janole said, "Yeah, in a minute. I want to finish this first." Janole included her cell phone number in the email to Eric and, when satisfied with the message, hit the send button.

Nate's message read: *Hi Janole. Need your help with a situation. Could really use your advice. Can we meet for lunch one day soon? Let me know what day is good for you.*

Wallace was incensed. "How often do you email each other?" He didn't wait for an answer. "I can't believe this. I know you don't plan to meet with him. That ain't happening."

For some reason, Wallace never mentioned to Janole that he saw them together in the mall holding hands. Interestingly, Janole hadn't mentioned it either. And, Janole hadn't mentioned that Nate had joined their tennis club. She could only imagine Wallace's reaction when he found out. He was being extremely unreasonable where Nate was concerned and she was tired of it. She slowly closed her email, stood and faced Wallace, and stared at him with an expression Wallace had not seen. He was taken aback.

"Wallace, I don't know what your problem is but I don't appreciate you giving me orders as if I'm a child. What exactly is your issue with Nate?" Janole's stance and entire demeanor communicated hostility.

"Janole, he's in love with you," Wallace said though it sounded more like jealous pettiness than a factual statement.

"That is so ridiculous. He was in love with me. Past tense. Until recently, we hadn't seen or talked to each other in almost thirty years. You expect me to believe that he's been in love with me all these years? That's absurd!"

"Well, I don't like it and I don't want you to see him."

She continued to stare at Wallace. "Too bad. Nate was there for me when nobody else was, including you. I was able to depend on him when I was going through hell and that's more than I can say for you."

And then Janole's truths poured out of her as if a dam had broken. The feelings she had suppressed, the anger she didn't want to acknowledge, all came gushing out—pure unfiltered anger.

"I'm your wife—your partner—yet you didn't even trust me enough to tell me that the pharmaceutical company was threatening us. When we were facing the biggest crisis ever, you left me out. Months before you disappeared I anguished over what was wrong." She said the word 'disappeared' as if it were a dirty word.

"I know you, Wallace, and it was obvious to me that something was very wrong. I thought it was me. I thought you didn't find me attractive anymore. You didn't talk to me...you were never at home... when you were at home you were on the computer all night...when we did talk you seemed distracted. You didn't want to play tennis or go out. I thought our marriage was in serious trouble and I didn't know what to do about it."

"I was trying to protect you, Janole," Wallace said, angrily. "I thought I explained that."

"Really? Really? Protect me from what? Pain? Devastation? Heartache? That's a joke," Janole said, sarcastically.

"You did what you usually do when faced with a problem. You clam up and shut me out." Janole wasn't concerned about the tears on her face as she continued to unleash her anger. Wallace could only stare at this woman he barely recognized.

"Do you have any idea what you put me through? Do you?" Janole asked, her voice raised, eyes ablaze, hands emphasizing her frustration.

"I went through hell for months. You had a plan but guess who had no clue about your plan? Me! When I read your letter, I was utterly devastated. For the first time in my entire life, I understood a person feeling such despair that they think life isn't worth living. You weren't here to deal with the fallout, Wallace. I was. You were spared from facing the public. Not me! You didn't have to go to work and pretend that everything was okay. I did! You weren't exposed to the ridicule and questions. That was ME.

"Ev-er-ry night you went to sleep with complete knowledge of the situation. Me? I'm wondering if you're alive or dead...trying to figure out how I can make another life for myself without you... praying that God will give me enough strength to get through the next day." Janole hesitated for a moment to take a breath. She had more to say.

"Do you know what I did at night? I kept telling myself over and over to hold on to God's hand. I kept reminding myself about God's unchanging hand. I would literally lift my arm in the air and say, 'Hold my hand, God. Please hold my hand.' I did this for months!"

Wallace was stunned and speechless. He had no idea that Janole harbored such resentment and anger. He offered no defense as she continued.

"You left a note for me in your tennis bag that I may or may not find."

Wallace said, "I knew you would find—"

Janole held up her hand to silence him.

"You knew nothing," she spat. "You chanced it. And you know what's ironic? You came back a hero. Imagine that." She laughed harshly. "You're the hero in everyone's eyes for your unselfish actions when I was the one who went through hell. The person who suffered the most as a result of your brilliant plan—that excluded me—was me. Not you. And you think you can now tell me what to do? You don't approve of me having an innocent conversation with Nate? Nate was a Godsend when I had no one else. Without him, I would not have found you. Don't forget that."

Throughout her unleashing, Janole's expression never changed. It was filled with disgust, anger, hurt, disappointment, and hostility. Equally as telling as her words was her uncompromising body language and posture. Wallace was actually relieved when she stalked out of the room. The way she regarded him was hurtful. He walked to the window and stared out at the falling rain. Now it was clear to him why Janole appeared different since his return; at times, sullen and unapproachable.

He recalled the numerous occasions when others congratulated and commended him for protecting innocent people and exposing the pharmaceutical company that threatened their lives. He clearly saw now what wasn't apparent to him then because he was too busy soaking up the attention. Janole stood beside him, time after time, drawing no attention to herself, forcing a smile. Not once did anyone praise Janole for her bravery, patience, strength and endurance. Sadly, that included him.

"Aren't you proud of him?" they would ask Janole.

"You've got a good man."

"What a courageous thing to do."

He sank into his chair and put his head in his hands as he replayed Janole's words and relived her anger and pain. *God, help me. What have I done to my wife?*

As he reflected he was forced to be honest with himself. Truthfully, he hadn't considered the full impact of his plan on Janole when he devised and implemented it. He knew she would be hurt and confused by his letter but those emotions merely skimmed the surface of what she actually experienced and endured for months. In retrospect, he realized that he should have confided in her. He should have, in some way, prepared her for what was going to take place. She was right and had the situation been reversed he would feel the same.

Wallace's plan, though successful in many ways, was flawed. At the time, he thought it was the best way to accomplish his goal of deceiving the pharmaceutical company and convincing them that he and his research findings were no longer credible threats. In that regard, the plan was brilliant. But as he looked at the situation from Janole's perspective, he clearly saw what he was ashamed to admit. His "brilliant" plan included an escape for him but only for him. Janole, on the other hand, was forced to deal with devastation, humiliation, confusion, shock, loss, innuendo, public disgrace and a world torn apart. She lived a tortured existence because of a plan—his plan—she knew nothing about.

How could you be so stupid, Wallace? What were you thinking? You should have talked to her. Or Marlo. Somebody. Another perspective would have been helpful but, as usual, you wanted to handle things alone. Yes, you prayed but you know that God would not sanction you keeping a secret from your wife; certainly not one of this magnitude.

It was all so clear to him now. He couldn't disagree with Janole. When faced with problems, he retreated. Shut down, to use Janole's words, until he resolved the problem his own way in his own time. This time he prayed for direction but he ignored part of it. He was supposed to tell Janole and he hadn't. *Good job, Wallace.*

Janole escaped to her bedroom, closed and locked the door, and released all of her frustration. Sobs wracked her body as she slid to the floor. She had been in denial about her pain; conflicted between gratitude and anger. That was no longer the case. Her anger had exploded like an erupting volcano and continued to ooze. Analogous to the volcano's lava, her anger was heated, festering and destructive, a force to be reckoned with because it had been building ever so slowly and restrained for much too long.

Initially, Wallace's safety overshadowed all else and she was overcome with relief when they were reunited. She wanted her life back and kept trying to convince herself that his safety was all that mattered. That, now with 'the ordeal' being over, it would be foolish to focus on any type of negativity. Forget all that she endured in the months prior to his disappearance. Never mind the suffering she experienced while he was gone. It was worth it, right? After all, she reasoned, she made it through thanks to her loving God.

But a seed had been planted even while Wallace was away. She realized the turning point for her was when she found the note in his tennis bag. The clue he left for her. So many times she had been at a breaking point and all the while there was a clue within her own home waiting to be discovered. And that was the source of her anger. Wallace left a clue for her which meant he knew what was happening.

He wasn't a victim of foul play or some other unfortunate circumstance over which he had no control. There had been a plan or, at the very least, knowledge of impending danger. Otherwise, he would not have written the words, *"It's not what it seems."* Wallace knew exactly what was going on. Even though his note gave her hope it also revealed to her that Wallace was a part of this scheme or whatever it was. Something changed for her that day and, unbeknownst to her, it had been festering ever since.

The tears were purging, a welcome release but they did nothing to lessen her anger. It was unforgivable that Wallace didn't come to her...that he didn't trust her with this situation...that he caused her to suffer as he did. She would not have done that...could not have done that to him. She even questioned her love for him and that scared her. This was all too much. Her marriage was in trouble, Marlon was sick and not speaking to her and she had to fly across the country to tell Eric he was the father of her son and beg for his help. And, as if that weren't enough, someone was continuing to threaten them.

Chapter Twelve

✳

*S*everal days later, Janole was on a flight to Phoenix. She was actually meeting Eric later for dinner as he suggested. She would have preferred lunch but felt she was in no position to make demands. They were meeting. That was most important. As the plane climbed into the air, she allowed herself to relax for the first time in days. It felt good to escape the tension between Wallace and her...to get away if only for a short while. She leaned back, closed her eyes and permitted her mind to wander. She thought of Nate, Eric and Wallace. Men whose lives were intertwined with hers, differently, significantly, permanently.

Wallace thought Nate was still in love with her. Preposterous. She and Nate were friends with a shared past. That's it. Nate had done or said nothing to suggest otherwise. Wallace was jealous and he had no one to blame but himself. In spite of Jenn's warning and Wallace's feelings, Janole had every intention of maintaining a friendship with Nate. Before leaving, she had responded to his email letting him know she'd be out of town for a few days and suggested that they connect one day the following week.

She was meeting Eric at six o'clock at Valencia's in downtown Phoenix. According to Eric, the eclectic food options were all delicious and the restaurant was within walking distance from his office.

Threatening rain clouds loomed overhead which kept the temperature in the mid seventies. After checking in the hotel, she texted Wallace to let him know she had arrived safely. Usually, she phoned

80

him but, today, she was grateful for the distance afforded by text messaging.

Standing at the window admiring the view, she began rehearsing what she would say to Eric. The more she rehearsed, the more tense she became so she stopped. Instead, she prayed.

"Give me the words, Father. This information is important to Marlon's health. Please touch Eric's heart to help my son."

Nothing could have prepared her for the evening with Eric. First of all, she didn't recognize him. Sure, almost thirty years had passed but there was little resemblance to the charismatic, handsome man she remembered. No longer thin, he was carrying an extra forty pounds, at least. His face was round, he wore glasses and was bald. The only adornment on his face, other than eyeglasses, was a neatly trimmed gray beard. He used a cane to assist in standing when he embraced her. The charming smile and beautiful white teeth were still apparent as well as the deep baritone voice. Janole also noticed his attire and was reminded of his impeccable sense of style. Today he was dressed in a navy suit and light blue dress shirt that fit him nicely in spite of his girth. She suspected they both were custom made.

Eric was pleasant and kind, quickly putting Janole at ease. He immediately explained his appearance as if he felt the need to apologize. He shared that due to an automobile accident several years ago, he sustained a serious leg injury and experienced severe back pain from time to time.

"I'm so sorry," Janole said, meaning every word.

"Thanks. Tragically, my wife, Joan, was killed in the accident." When Eric spoke of his wife, his eyes misted. "I loved her deeply. My life hasn't been the same without her."

Janole expressed her condolences and decided that she would tell Eric the reason for her trip, no holds barred. And she did. Eric listened attentively while she explained that she became pregnant as a result of their sexual encounter. "That's why I abruptly left the doctoral program."

Eric's face registered surprise and shock, but neither anger nor denial. "What are you saying? I have a child?"

Janole nodded.

"Are you sure?" he asked.

"Of course I'm sure," Janole said, indignantly.

"I'm sorry. I didn't mean it that way. I just can't believe it. I'm not questioning whether it's true. This is quite a surprise. I just can't believe it." There was an awkward pause as Eric processed the news. Janole couldn't read his expression. The server's arrival with their food choices afforded them a convenient distraction. Satisfied that they were pleased with their order, the server left but neither of them touched their food.

Finally, Eric looked at Janole. "Boy or girl?" he asked.

"Boy," Janole answered.

"I have a son," Eric said, as if the news was miraculous. "Why didn't you tell me before now?" he asked though he suspected he already knew the answer.

"What we did was a mistake, Eric, and I regretted it immediately," Janole said. "I was so very angry and ashamed of myself. Plus, I didn't think it would matter to you. I liked Joan and didn't want to cause a problem in your marriage. Honestly, I didn't want anything from you."

"But didn't you think I had a right to know that I had fathered a child?"

"Would it have made a difference had you known? Really?"

Eric stared at Janole before finally admitting the truth. "Probably not. I was such a jerk back then and have many regrets. Joan deserved better than me. I hurt a lot of people, including my wife...and you. I'm sorry," Eric said, sincerely.

The server checked on them again. Janole waited until they were alone before resuming their conversation. Prior to their meeting, she had decided not to engage in a lengthy discussion with Eric about the past but she had always been curious about his relationship with his wife. "Did Joan know about your affairs? You had quite a reputation on campus."

Eric sighed heavily. "She knew I was unfaithful if that's what you're asking. To my knowledge, she didn't know names."

"I often wondered why she stayed with you knowing you were cheating on her. She was very pretty and nice," Janole said.

"I've asked myself that so many times. I think she loved me in spite of me."

Surprisingly, Janole felt compassion for the man she was facing. He appeared to be in a great deal of pain, physically and emotionally. "Eric, I'm sure she knew how much you loved her."

"I hope so," he said, wistfully. "Now, tell me about this son of mine and why you're really here."

Janole felt uncomfortable with Eric possessively describing Marlon as "his" son but she chose not to address her concern at this time. As she talked about Marlon, the love and pride she felt for him were apparent. She told Eric he was an exceptional person — intelligent, kind, funny, and loving — who was also an extremely talented basketball player.

Eric noticed the sparkle in her eyes when she spoke about her son. "What's his name?"

"Marlon. Marlon David Jackson."

Eric stared at Janole for a moment before speaking. "Are you telling me that Marlon Jackson who played at UVA is my son?" Eric asked. "I watched almost all of his games. He was a great player. I'm one of his biggest fans."

Janole smiled at the irony before continuing. "He needs your help, Eric. Marlon has prostate cancer and he's so young. The doctor wants to know as much about his genetic history as possible. That's why I'm here. I need to know your medical history, anything that can help the doctors help Marlon."

Without hesitation Eric said, "I'll help in any way I can. Just name it. I can tell you that my father died of prostate cancer at the age of fifty-five. My brother was diagnosed with it when he was in his late forties so it definitely runs in our family. I'm tested regularly and, so far, my results have been good."

Then Eric made an offer that, without him knowing, was an answer to Janole's prayer. "I'll come to Northern Virginia next week to speak with the doctor, personally. I just need to make arrangements at work and I have no issue with having a copy of my medical records sent to Marlon's doctor. I can talk to my brother, too, if you think that would help. Can you give me the name of Marlon's doctor and his fax number?"

"Yes, of course. Thank you, Eric. I can't thank you enough," she said, extremely relieved. She looked at her food with desire now that she had an appetite.

"Can I see him, Janole? Do you mind if I meet Marlon?" Eric asked, somewhat tentatively. He saw the shock and fear in her eyes and quickly reassured her. "Joan and I didn't have children. It would mean a lot to me if you and your husband are okay with it. I'm not trying to replace your husband or insert myself where I'm not wanted. I'd just like to be his friend if you and he will accept that."

Janole hesitated before answering. "It's really Marlon's decision, not ours. Unfortunately, he's not speaking to us right now. Feels as though we deceived him. We just told him about you, Eric. He didn't know anything about you...thought Wallace, my husband, was his biological father until a few days ago. He's quite angry with us right now."

Eric wasn't sure what to say. It was apparent to him that this entire situation was causing a great deal of pain for Janole. "If he is the kind of young man that you just described to me, he'll come around. And if I can help in any way, I will."

Janole was grateful for Eric's support. Their meeting was nothing like she had nervously anticipated. She whispered a silent prayer of gratitude before saying, "Thank you. Let me know your travel plans when you've made them. Meanwhile, I'll talk to Marlon when he's ready."

Janole's return flight was smooth and uneventful. She excitedly replayed the conversation with Eric and was surprised to discover that the plane was beginning its descent to land at Dulles Airport.

Chapter Thirteen

The call wasn't unexpected; it was just...unsettling. Marlon walked into the kitchen after speaking with the nurse from Dr. Bowers' office. Grabbing a bottle of water from the refrigerator, he twisted the top with hands that slightly trembled. He gulped the water hoping it would help to settle his nervous stomach.

His first inclination was to phone his parents. It continued to anger him that they kept Eric's identity from him but he'd had plenty of time to think. No doubt the news changed his world and with that change he was forced to redefine himself somewhat.

"I look like my dad. I have my dad's nose. I inherited that—whatever that was—from my dad." Those statements he could no longer make in reference to Wallace.

But there were many statements that were definite and true. *"My dad taught me everything I know. He taught me how to compete. He demonstrated the importance of honesty and integrity. He showed me what it is to be a man. He has been there for me whenever I needed him. He is a man I can love and respect. He loves me, unconditionally."* Those were powerful statements.

The conversations he'd had with Nick and his uncle helped put things in perspective, too. He thought about how devastated his mom would be if he were to die. Then, for an inexplicable reason, he thought about how devastated he would be if something were to happen to her. He couldn't imagine his life without her because, more than any one he knew, she was the essence of love. He realized, as he reflected, that he'd not bothered to think about her life before his existence.

He had no idea that her father disowned her because of him. It was difficult to imagine a parent doing that. Any parent. Certainly, he could not imagine his parents disowning him or Nick for any reason. And, he knew that his mother would do nothing intentionally to hurt him. As he continued to assess his entire life from his earliest memories, he concluded that he was extremely fortunate and blessed. Who knows how things would have been if he'd known about Eric? He had to admit that knowing the truth may not have made his life better.

Marlon's life had been quite easy until now. While things weren't handed to him on a silver platter, he had experienced few challenges. But he was no longer a little boy. He was a man now and needed to respond to situations as a man. Perhaps these situations were tests for him. Tests of his character, strength, spirit and, yes, his maturity and manhood.

Life wasn't fair and people weren't perfect. He looked at his phone and made a decision. Rather than phone his parents, he'd pay them a visit. He had a few things to say.

As Marlon suspected, his parents were elated to see him though he noticed they both looked somewhat tired. He embraced his mom and then his dad for a long time.

"It's the prodigal son. I've returned," Marlon said. "Better late than never."

They all laughed, each relieved that Marlon was no longer angry. As was his usual habit, Marlon looked in the refrigerator and was happy to find pasta salad and grilled chicken, two of his favorites.

"Dr. Bowers' office called. I have an appointment Thursday at one," he stated matter-of-factly.

"Did they say anything else?" Janole asked, unable to hide the anxiousness she felt.

"No, nothing else."

"Well, we can go together. How about we pick you up at noon?" Wallace offered.

"Sure, works for me."

Though Marlon didn't express it, he was relieved that his parents would be with him on Thursday. No matter the news, he would be able to receive it better with them by his side.

After serving himself a generous bowl of pasta salad topped with chicken, he sat at the kitchen table and asked his parents to join him. "I want you both to know that I've done a lot of thinking since learning that—since learning about Eric. It was a blow and I would be lying if I said it didn't hurt. Still hurts. It shook my world. What I thought was true wasn't true and I had no inkling. It was truly a shock. And, the more I thought about it, I realized that the shock of it was really a good thing."

He looked at his father. "I never questioned whether I was your son…was never made to feel that I was anything less than someone you loved very much. You never treated me differently from Nick. What I'm trying to say is that I'm very thankful…for both of you."

Wallace looked at his son and nodded. He didn't trust himself to speak but he knew Marlon understood.

Janole reached for a napkin to wipe her eyes. "We love you so much, Marlon, and never meant to hurt you."

"I know that, Mom. Now stop crying. This pasta salad is good," he said, sheepishly. "So good that I need another bowl." Marlon was an expert at redirecting conversation, usually with humor.

"We have some news for you," Janole said.

"What is it? Don't tell me you're not my mother," Marlon said, jokingly.

"Shut up, boy," Janole said, laughing in spite of her tears. This was the Marlon they both knew and loved. "It's about Eric. I talked with him."

Janole proceeded to tell Marlon the entire story of her trip, her meeting with Eric and the outcome including the fact that Dr. Bowers should already have Eric's medical records.

"Wow," Marlon said. "I don't know what to say."

"He wants to meet you. He actually kinda knows you because he followed your games at UVA. Said he's a fan of yours. He'll be in town Thursday night and has offered to speak personally with Dr. Bowers if that would help. He'd like to see you while he's here."

Marlon was definitely curious. He looked at his parents with a questioning expression. "You guys okay with this?"

Wallace and Janole had already discussed the situation at length and were in agreement that it was Marlon's decision. "It's your call, Marlon," Wallace said. "We're okay with whatever you decide."

The news could have been better; it could have been worse. Marlon, Wallace and Janole sat in Dr. Bowers' office, waiting, tension reflected on each face and in each posture. Marlon was positioned between his parents. His mother held his hand while his father discreetly rested his hand on Marlon's other forearm. When they heard the words "stage one", their relief was obvious. Marlon exhaled deeply. Wallace smiled. Janole said, "Thank You, God."

Dr. Bowers went on to explain that though the cancer was stage one and confined solely to the prostate, there were three concerns that made Marlon's situation somewhat unique. One, the early onset; two, his genetic predisposition; and three, it was an aggressive type cancer. As Dr. Bowers predicted, their relief was short-lived. This was the part of the job he most hated. He delivered bad news frequently; in fact, much worse than this. It never got easier.

Dr. Bowers spoke. "Marlon, listen to me. Your cancer is contained in the prostate. That's very good news." And it was. Dr. Bowers had expected the cancer to be more advanced simply because in young patients, this type of cancer tended to spread quickly.

"You understand? But we have important decisions to make. You have several options. One, we can watch it for a while to see what happens. Two, we can treat it with chemo and radiation. Three, we can surgically remove your prostate."

Marlon found his voice. "What would you recommend?"

Dr. Bowers thoroughly explained the pros and cons of each option and answered their questions. "Think about it over the weekend and let me know what you decide. Just call my office next week and ask for my nurse. I'm giving you information about the options including several good websites. Take a few days to review this, discuss it with your parents and let me know your decision."

"Dr. Bowers, you didn't answer my son's question. What would you recommend?" Wallace spoke directly.

"Usually, with an aggressive type cancer, I recommend surgery to remove the prostate," Dr. Bowers stated without hesitation. "Because of Marlon's age and the fact that it is stage one, we may want to consider chemo and radiation."

Janole asked a question that he wasn't expecting. "Do you believe in God, Dr. Bowers?"

Dr. Bowers smiled. "I do, Mrs. Jackson, without a doubt. He orders my steps."

"Good." Janole was reassured by Dr. Bowers' answer. She knew Marlon was in capable hands.

Chapter Fourteen

———————— ✳ ————————

arlon ordered his favorite appetizer, Calamari, but could only eat a couple. It was as tasty as usual but his nervous stomach simply couldn't tolerate it. He had suggested this restaurant because the food was good and the atmosphere conducive to conversation. Not too formal yet not a place to bring small children. He dined here frequently and often recommended it to friends. As he scanned the room casually checking out the diners, he thought he saw someone who looked familiar.

"Is that Brandy?" he asked himself. *"And who is that dude she's with? Yep, it's definitely Brandy. She is so fine! Should I speak or not?"*

He had no right to be jealous but he was. He cared deeply for her but the long distance relationship just didn't work. They had been good together while it lasted. Really good. *This dude is all over her. What is he doing?* Without thinking twice, Marlon approached Brandy's table.

"Marlon! Hi! This is a surprise." Brandy stood to embrace him. It was obvious by her radiant smile that she was happy to see him. She felt good and was wearing the most enticing fragrance. He didn't want to let her go.

"Hi yourself. How are you?" Marlon asked as he appraised her with his eyes, very much enjoying the view.

"I'm fine. What are you doing home? Is the season over already?" Brandy asked.

"No. Long story—"

Marlon was interrupted by Brandy's date. "Baby, aren't you going to introduce us?"

Marlon looked at Dude and saved Brandy the trouble, "I'm Marlon. Marlon Jackson," he said abruptly but extended his hand in an attempt to be cordial.

"Nice to meet you. I'm Cameron. Cameron Rivers. I remember you. You played ball at UVA."

"I did," Marlon answered, curtly. "Look, I didn't mean to interrupt. I'm actually meeting a friend but I wanted to come over to say hello. It was great seeing you, Brandy. You look good."

She was dressed in all black and oozed sexiness in an understated way. Nothing too tight or revealing but her curvaceous figure could not be hidden.

"You too. How long are you going to be home?" Brandy asked, ignoring Cameron.

"For a while. Taking care of some business."

"Call me. I'd like to catch up with you. Let me give you my new cell number."

So it wasn't that serious, Marlon thought. Brandy would not have offered her number if she were seriously involved. While he waited, he noticed Cameron's irritated expression. *Too bad, Dude*. Marlon meant no disrespect but he definitely planned to call Brandy. No doubt about it. Maybe tonight.

Marlon had returned to his table but Brandy continued to be distracted. The last person she expected to see was Marlon. All of her feelings for him came rushing back with an overpowering force. Flushed and dizzy with excitement, she was grateful to be sitting. No man affected her like Marlon. They ended their relationship over a year ago but she'd never let him go. Not in her heart.

Her dinner companion noticed the change in her.

"I take it that this guy is special to you. You're blushing," Cameron said.

Brandy sipped her tea and patted her face with a napkin before answering. "We were very close at one time. I didn't expect to see him."

"Uh huh," Cameron stated. "Sounds like there's more to that story."

Brandy offered no additional information. Instead, she redirected the conversation to next week's church activities while trying to slow her heart rate and cool her body temperature. Cameron reluctantly took the bait but the evening was ruined for him. Brandy never looked at him the way she looked at Marlon. The joy was so pure that her face glowed; the energy between them so charged he felt the current from where he stood. Awkwardly, he had stood there like a third wheel feeling as though he was intruding on an intimate moment and should, at the very least, look away. But he couldn't. He was enthralled—and envious—by whatever it was that existed between the two of them. Though they talked for only a few minutes it seemed to him that time stood still.

Usually, he dominated the conversation but tonight Cameron ate his dinner in virtual silence letting Brandy do the talking. There was no future for Brandy and him, he realized. She had been nothing but honest with him, sometimes painfully so, but he hoped she would eventually fall in love with him. Prayed that she could love him one day as deeply as he loved her. Tonight, he acknowledged defeat as he accepted the truth.

Brandy noticed Cameron's despondency but was still reeling from Marlon's embrace. As she replayed the feel of his body next to hers, she felt tingling. He was as fine as ever and he was home! There had to be a good reason for him to be away from basketball during the crux of the season. What could it be, she wondered.

Shortly after Marlon returned to his table, a tall portly man slowly walked towards him with the assistance of a cane. "Marlon? I'm Eric."

Marlon's father looked nothing like he expected. *Was this the debonair man who seduced my mom? Hard to believe.* But as the evening wore on, Marlon gained a deeper understanding and appreciation of the man. Eric was what Marlon would describe as an intellectual because of his knowledge about many things. It was basketball that dominated their conversation, however. To Marlon's delight, Eric was a basketball junkie and had an impressive memory of games, players and their stats.

Eventually, the conversation turned more personal.

"Any news from the doctor? I hope you don't mind me asking," Eric said.

"No, I don't mind. The cancer is stage one which is good but it's aggressive so the doctor recommended chemo and radiation or having my prostate removed. I really don't want to go into details tonight…it's all I've thought about since meeting with the doctor. By the way, thanks for your medical records. I really appreciate it."

"No problem. Happy to do it." Eric had also gone to the doctor's office today to complete a medical history questionnaire.

Changing the subject, Eric said, "I noticed you talking to the young lady over there. She's a real beauty."

"Yes, she is. We're old friends." Marlon noticed that Brandy and the Cameron dude were leaving. She waved and smiled as they walked out.

"She reminds me of your mother. She was a beautiful woman, too. Still is. Back in the day all the guys described her as a ten."

Marlon did not particularly like Eric talking about his mother this way. Eric seemed to get the unspoken message and changed the subject. "She told me you were quite angry with her when you found out about me."

Marlon nodded. "I was. It was a real shock to say the least. I was hurt by their deception but I'm over it now for the most part."

"I'm glad to hear that, Marlon. I'm not condoning dishonesty but I think she did the right thing by not telling you. She really did."

Marlon looked at Eric. "Are you saying that had you known about me it wouldn't have made a difference to you?"

"I can't say that for sure. But I probably would have made life very difficult for your mom and very painful for you. I only thought of myself then. I guess you could say I was a real jerk. An unscrupulous jerk. I take no pride in that but it's the truth."

"No disrespect but I know guys like you. They're disgusting. I just don't get it."

"Marlon, my behavior was disgusting. I'm the first to admit it. I have many regrets," he said, sadly.

Marlon stared at Eric trying to gauge the character of the man sitting across from him. "My uncle told me about you. Said he paid you a visit."

"He did indeed." Eric took a sip of his drink. "I couldn't understand then why he was so furious but now I understand. He'd just found out your mom was pregnant, right?"

Marlon nodded, affirmatively.

"And you're named after your uncle?"

"Yep," Marlon stated proudly. "He and I are very close. Our families are close. Do you have kids?"

"Unfortunately, no. Nieces and nephews but no children. We wanted kids but it never happened. My wife and I had a good life together until her death. She was killed several years ago in an automobile accident. My leg and back were seriously injured." Eric wanted Marlon to understand and accept him so he continued talking. He reasoned he had nothing to lose at this point.

"I picked up all of this weight after the accident. Used to work out regularly but the accident changed things...changed everything. When I lost my wife there was such a huge void. I used food as comfort but found out sixty pounds later that nothing could fill it. I was also consumed with guilt. It was an accident but I was driving the car. Joan was such a kind and compassionate person. I've often wondered why I lived and she didn't."

Marlon didn't know what to say so he said nothing. He was sorry Eric's wife died and they had no children but if he expected Marlon to be his family, to be the son he never had, he would be disappointed. Too late for that.

As if reading Marlon's mind, Eric made his intentions clear.

"Marlon, I'm not trying to be your father. You have wonderful parents. And, I'm comfortable with no one knowing I'm your biological father if that's what you want. What I'd like is for us to get to know each other. I'd like to be included in your life from time to time but on your terms. Perhaps we can be friends. I'd like that but let me be clear. You owe me nothing."

Eric paused briefly. "When I found out about you, I thought maybe it was God's way of showing me that He had forgiven me. And maybe it is because, believe it or not, I'm happy that you exist. And I'm happy that I am, in part, responsible for your existence." He looked towards the ceiling as if searching for the right words.

"It's been a long time since I've been happy. I guess I feel as though my life has been given meaning in a special way. From my seed, a life was created. That makes me very happy. But the last thing I want to do is cause a problem for you or your family. Understand?" Marlon nodded. "I'm going to be praying for you and I'd love for you to keep me posted on how things are going. Okay?"

"Okay," Marlon said, thinking there was much about this man that he'd like to know.

Chapter Fifteen

*J*anole forgot about meeting with Nate. It was his phone call that jogged her memory as she was driving to the indoor tennis club. She had a date to play doubles with friends, something she had been looking forward to for days.

"Nate, I'm so sorry. We've got a lot going on and I simply forgot. Today is probably my best day. How about we grab a quick bite after my tennis match? Two thirty?"

"Works for me. You name the place," Nate said.

After deciding on a convenient location, Janole wondered about the purpose of their meeting. Nate seemed eager to talk to her. I guess I'll find out soon enough, Janole thought, as she pulled into the club parking lot.

For two hours, Janole was carefree. Excited about doing the thing she most enjoyed with women she genuinely liked. They played hard and had fun. During changeovers, they talked and laughed, even gossiped. They all had one thing in common: a passion for tennis. If it were possible, Janole would play tennis every day. She loved the game just that much.

Janole saw Nate before he saw her. He was talking on the phone, seemingly deeply engrossed in the conversation, when she arrived at the restaurant. An irritating thought of Wallace entered her mind which she quickly dismissed. She was doing nothing wrong and would not be made to feel guilty about an innocent friendship.

After exchanging greetings, they ordered. Janole, famished, decided to forego her normal diet and ordered a burger and fries. Nate ordered the same.

"What's up, Nate? You said you needed my advice."

"I'll get to it in a minute. I can't believe you forgot about us getting together. What is going on in your world that is more important than me?" Nate asked in a joking manner.

"You wouldn't believe," Janole said, sighing deeply. "My life is a nightmare right now."

No matter how often she told the story, it continued to be very difficult.

"We found out that Marlon has prostate cancer."

"What! He's so young. Are you sure?" Nate asked.

"We had the same reaction. Yes, we're sure. Fortunately, it was detected early but still cancer is cancer. And, because the doctor wanted to know the medical history of both parents, I searched for Marlon's father and flew to Phoenix to meet with him." Janole noticed the confusion on Nate's face and realized that he had no knowledge of the specific circumstances about Marlon's father. She sipped her drink while debating how much to reveal to Nate.

"I made a mess of things, Nate. Neither of them knew the other existed until a few days ago. Marlon was livid with me."

"Wow, Janole. You have been going through a lot. I'm sorry. How is Marlon? Is he going to be okay?"

"We hope so but only time will tell. We're trusting God...that's all we can do."

Nate watched Janole closely before speaking. "Is there something else troubling you, Janole?"

Janole looked at him and saw the concern in his eyes. Even though she and Wallace were advised not to mention the note, she knew she could trust Nate. "Um— we received a threatening note. I found it in our mailbox."

"A threatening note? What did it say? Why didn't you call me?" Nate asked, alarmed.

"We contacted your friend from the FBI, Agent Tyous. He's handling it and directed us not to talk about it," Janole said, evasively. "I shouldn't have mentioned it to you."

Nate continued to stare at Janole in an attempt to gauge her level of worry and fear. His thoughts led to more questions but he chose to say nothing more for the time being. He was hoping that Janole would elaborate and was disappointed when she offered no additional information.

Their order arrived and they ate in silence for a few moments.

"This is delicious. I don't remember the last time I've had a burger. All we've talked about is me. What's going on with you? I really don't have a lot of time...need to get home and you know how traffic is," Janole said in between bites.

Nate looked at her with concern. "My situation pales in comparison to what you're dealing with. I wanted advice from you about this woman I've been seeing but it's no big deal. I'm actually embarrassed now. You're dealing with major problems. My situation is nothing. Really. What can I do to help you?"

"Just pray for us, Nate. We need all the prayers we can get."

She had no idea whether Nate was a believer. She assumed he was but they had not discussed his religious beliefs recently.

"Will you keep me posted on Marlon's status?" he asked.

"Of course."

"And, you'll let me know if you get more notes?"

Janole hesitated and avoided looking at him. "Um-Wallace would prefer that the FBI handle it. I really shouldn't have mentioned it to you. He would be furious to find out that I told you. But I know how to reach you if I need you. You understand, don't you?"

"I understand. Just know that I'm available to help."

Janole smiled, her relief obvious. "I'm sorry to cut this short but if I don't leave soon, I'll be sitting on 95. Thanks for lunch."

After Janole left, Nate ordered another drink and pondered all that Janole shared with him. He also thought about the unspoken messages including the implication that Wallace did not want him involved in their lives. He couldn't blame Wallace considering the love affair he and Janole shared years ago but he was going to be available for her if she needed him. Fate brought them together and it would take more than Wallace's insecurities to get rid of him.

Wallace was waiting for her when she walked in the house. In spite of the tension between them lately, they both shared a common concern—and pain—about Marlon. She looked at him anxiously. It seemed that, as of late, she was always on alert bracing herself for bad news.

"Is Marlon okay?" Janole asked.

"Yes, he's fine. I talked with him earlier. Don't worry so much. He's fine." Wallace said, hoping to reassure her.

"Good. Did you hear from Agent Tyous or Cochran?"

"Yes, but there's really no news. Agent Cochran called about an hour ago to say that they were continuing their investigation. There were no discernible fingerprints and the neighbors didn't see anything helpful. He asked whether we'd received another note and said to keep them posted of any new developments."

Noticing her attire and wanting to change the subject, Wallace inquired about tennis.

"It was wonderful. Played with Jeannine, Noriko, and Candace. We had the best time. Just what I needed." She didn't dare mention her lunch date with Nate.

She seems to be in a receptive mood, Wallace thought.

"Janole, can we talk? With all that's going on, we haven't had a chance to focus on us. We can't continue avoiding each other."

Janole sighed. Suddenly she was tired and wanted to take a nap.

"We can talk," she said, her voice flat. "I'm listening."

Wallace mistook her fatigue for indifference.

"Janole, don't do me any favors. If you don't want to talk we don't have to." Though he considered himself a patient man, her moods were becoming intolerable.

"Wallace, I'm tired. I didn't sleep well last night. Haven't slept well the last few nights. I'm sorry but I just don't have a lot of extra right now. I haven't had a lot of extra for a while," Janole stated, making reference to all that she had endured the past months.

"I hear you, Janole. Loud and clear. You don't have to talk...just let me say a few things. You don't have to say a word. Are you willing to listen?"

Janole sat down and waited. She really was tired. It was an overwhelming mental exhaustion that spread to every bone and muscle in her body.

"I love you more than anything in this world," Wallace began. "I had no idea that my plan would hurt you as it did. You were absolutely right when you said I should have confided in you or somehow warned you. My only defense is fear. I've never felt such fear in my life and my biggest fear was losing you. I prayed like I never have before and God helped me. I know He did. In hindsight, I realize I should have included you. Something was nagging at me and now I know what that was. I could and should have handled things differently. But you must know that I didn't do what I did to hurt you. I did it to protect you because I can't imagine my life without you. I hope you will forgive me. I'm so very sorry. Hurting you is the last thing I'd ever want to do. I would never hurt you, intentionally."

Looking at her husband, Janole had no doubt that Wallace was sincere. She knew he was sorry and yes, she knew that he wouldn't hurt her intentionally; but, it irritated her that he felt he could make important decisions about her life without including her. It continued to gall her that during this major crisis he felt justified in not informing her that her life was in danger.

Not only that, he devised a plan that impacted her more than anyone, leaving her helpless and devastated. The agony and suffering she endured could have been avoided or, at least, minimized if he had confided in her. She considered all of these things before speaking. He needed to know the truth. After all, that's what this conversation was all about. Being open and honest—no secrets.

"Wallace," she said wearily, "thanks for your apology. I'm sure you meant it; but, sometimes saying I'm sorry just isn't enough. It's because of your fear that you should have told me. You left me completely in the dark and I'm having a hard time with that."

Wallace opened his mouth to respond and closed it. It was as if his wife was a stranger. There was no getting past this it seemed. Throughout their marriage, an apology was enough but, then again, they had not dealt with anything of this magnitude. He didn't know what else to do. He would do anything to rectify the situation and that's what he said to Janole.

"Baby, tell me what I can do to make this right," he pleaded.

"I don't know if there is anything you can do," Janole said before walking slowly out of the room.

Overcome with exhaustion, Janole stretched out on the bed and almost immediately fell into a deep sleep. She laughed as she watched young Marlon and Nick play in the front yard. Marlon was around five years old; Nick was three. The boys were dressed alike in denim shorts, blue short sleeved tee-shirts, white socks and tennis shoes.

It was a beautifully warm day. Flowers were in bloom and a soft breeze was blowing. Her heart was full of pride and joy as the boys played and skipped around without a care. Butterflies were flitting here and there and the boys began to excitedly chase them. Marlon decided to follow a beautiful black and yellow butterfly that appeared to fly in slow motion, enticing him. His chubby arms were outstretched as he tried to reach it but always the butterfly was just beyond his fingertips.

Janole's heart began beating faster as she watched Marlon follow the butterfly. He was running towards the street. Her joy turned to fear and then terror as she watched the speeding car approach. Marlon was oblivious to the car, so intent was his focus on the beautiful butterfly. She watched in horror, first Marlon then the car. *It's going too fast! It's going to hit him! Oh no!* She tried to run but her legs seemed to weigh a ton. She couldn't lift them high enough or make them move fast enough.

"No! No! No! Marlon!" She yelled to him but he didn't respond. Nick was standing close to her, watching and still, as if he sensed the danger. The car was getting closer and wasn't slowing down. Marlon still hadn't seen it.

My baby. God, please save my baby. Her terror intensified as she watched helplessly. The car was just a few yards from Marlon's tiny body. He was smiling at the butterfly, arms still outstretched.

"No!" she screamed, just as the car made impact with Marlon's body.

Janole awakened with a start. Tears stained her face, her heart pounded loudly, and she was drenched in perspiration. It took her a few minutes to collect herself and realize that she had been dreaming. *Thank God. It was only a dream.* She sighed deeply as she wiped her wet face. The dream seemed convincingly real though she knew her sons were no longer little boys. Was this a premonition? A fore-warning of Marlon's destiny? Would he die as she helplessly watched unable to change the course of events?

"Janole, are you okay? I heard you scream." Wallace's concern was apparent.

"I had a horrible dream," she said hardly able to utter the words. The image of Marlon being hit by the car would not leave her mind.

"You want to talk about it?"

"No. I'll be fine," she said, refusing any consolation from Wallace. "Please close the door on your way out."

"I'm here if you need me, Janole," Wallace replied softly.

He stared at the door separating him from his wife. More than a physical barrier, the closed door was a symbolic representation of their relationship. He didn't envision there ever being a barrier in their marriage. He and Janole were as one, so in tuned with each other that it was comical at times. They completed each other's sentences, ordered for each other when dining out, and anticipated each other's desires. When playing tennis, other couples marveled over how well they communicated and complemented each other. At times, they were in sync with each other to the degree that words weren't neces-sary. They were comfortable and confident in each other's abilities. But this was not tennis. They were not playing a game. This was life and, at the moment, their relationship could best be described as adversarial rather than loving and harmonious.

Once again, Wallace was in despair as he walked to his office. Truthfully, part of him had a tough time accepting Janole's feelings. After all, his intentions had been good. Noble even. He could under-stand Janole's anger better if he had an affair or spent an astronomical amount of money without discussing it with her. Or suddenly quit his job leaving them in a lurch. Or, heaven forbid, became involved in criminal activity or was a heavy and irresponsible drinker.

He had done none of those things. Ever. He'd just…he'd just… what had he done? The answers were not reassuring. Scared her half to death...destroyed her security...deceived her...severely compromised her mental and emotional well-being.

A husband is supposed to protect his wife and, at the time, he thought that was what he was doing. But he hadn't protected her in very important ways. For the first time, Wallace was very concerned about their marriage and questioned whether it could survive. Janole was showing no signs of forgiving him. He sank in his chair, completely disillusioned. If he were a drinker, he'd fix himself a double shot of whiskey. He longed for his best, most trusted friend. But, in spite of the pain and emptiness, he was not going to give up on Janole or their marriage. He remembered to pray.

The weekend was strained. They were cordial, talking only when necessary. For the most part, they remained in separate parts of the house. Janole wanted to be alone and Wallace, reluctantly, honored her need for space. The joy and fun were missing. Both were suffering; neither happy with the current state of affairs. Janole didn't want to be angry and miserable but those emotions consumed her, fueled by recent memories.

They followed their usual Sunday routine but it felt as if they were miles apart. Janole sat stiffly in church making sure there were inches between them so that he understood, literally and figuratively, her desire for distance. Wallace understood and made no effort to close the gap.

Pastor Jones' message was a continuation in a series addressing the family. Today he focused on the realities and challenges of marriage. The subject of his message was *Grace*. He spoke about divorce statistics and a prevailing mindset of many couples when they enter into marriage.

"If you don't like it, you can leave, right? Isn't that the mindset nowadays?" Rev. Jones asked. "Marriage is no longer a permanent commitment. In the back of our minds, we know we have an out when things don't go our way, am I right? Divorce is no longer taboo as it was in my day. It happens all the time so it's no big deal. We'll just get a divorce if things get too messy because we are not going to tolerate being hurt or disappointed. Let me ask you three questions that I really want you to consider. Are your expectations realistic? In other words, do you expect your spouse to never make a mistake in action or judgment? Second question: Are YOU perfect? Third: Since when isn't an apology enough?"

Did Wallace talk to Pastor Jones, Janole wondered.

Pastor Jones elaborated. "There are certain behaviors that no one should be subjected to. Abuse of any kind, adultery, habitual lying, criminal involvement, and behaviors that repeatedly compromise trust, health and safety. Those behaviors do not make for a healthy relationship and often have at their core deep-rooted issues that can't be remedied without help. Usually, professional help. An apology alone shouldn't suffice in these types of circumstances.

"I'm not referring to those behaviors. I'm referring to disagreements, misunderstandings, miscommunications, irritations, differences of opinion and personality differences. There will be times in your marriage when you are hurt or misunderstood by your spouse. At times, you may feel betrayed by your spouse whom you deeply love and consider your best friend. You may expect that your spouse should see things as you do and always act in a way that you understand and approve of. And when that doesn't happen, then what?

"How do we handle pain and anger? How do we handle disappointment? How do we handle betrayal?

"There are times we become so focused on our pain and disappointment that we forget all of the good. Instead, we dwell on the negative. And, sometimes, we know we're wrong but pride prevents us from admitting it.

"I want to pose another question and this may be the most important question of all. When things are going wrong in your marriage, who is the real enemy? Is it your wife or husband? I think there's something else — or someone else — at work.

"Recognize who has the most to benefit from your marriage falling apart. Don't fall for the enemy's tricks. Satan is real, my friends, and he knows how important marriage is in the life God has ordained for His people. If Satan can attack and destroy a marriage, he's happy. And, the impact is far reaching and not just limited to two individuals. Am I right? What did Jesus say in John 10:10? *The thief comes*

only to steal and kill and destroy. I came that they may have life and have it abundantly. Who is the thief? None other than Satan."

He could be talking to me, thought Janole. *He IS talking to me.* There was more.

"What makes us not accept an apology when we know the other person is remorseful and trying to do better? Did God accept your apology?" Pastor Jones paused for effect.

"Perhaps a better question is how many times has God accepted your apology or have you apologized for your sinful behavior? He, The Perfect One, can forgive us over and over and over but we can't forgive each other? What's wrong with that picture? My friends, it's so easy to hold on to anger, pain, and disappointment. Holding on to those things gives us power and control, doesn't it? We've been hurt so we want to hurt back.

"I'm here to tell you that anger and payback are very destructive to a marriage but Grace is divine. Nothing is as powerful or liberating as bestowing grace. That's what God does for each of us daily..."

Grace is divine. Janole tuned out the remainder of Pastor Jones' message. She had gotten what she needed. And, if she hadn't, it was made crystal clear as she listened to Sissy—her voice clear and soulful—sing a familiar hymn. Janole didn't join in though she knew the words from memory. Instead, she allowed Sissy to minister to her.

Amazing grace how sweet the sound
that saved a wretch like me.
I once was lost but now I'm found
Was blind but now I see.

Twas grace that taught my heart to fear
and grace my fears relieved.
How precious did that grace appear,
the hour I first believed.

Through many dangers, tolls and snares,
I have already come.
'Tis grace that brought me safe thus far,
and grace will lead us home.

When we've been there ten thousand years,
bright shining as the sun.
We've no less days to sing God's praise,
than when we first begun.

Janole walked into church wrapped in a cloak of self-righteous anger. She walked out feeling two feet tall, exposed and diminished in her own eyes. Usually one to analyze situations and behaviors, she had not been inclined to look at herself closely. Had she taken the time to reflect, she would have perhaps realized sooner that the root cause of her pain and disappointment was much deeper and more complex than Wallace's recent actions.

Wallace was paying the price for the behaviors of other significant men in her life beginning with her father. As a young girl, she was subjected to her father's unfair rules and self-centered decisions. She was made to feel insignificant and of no consequence. Her opinions, feelings and desires were not important.

Then there was Nate. Deeply in love, they had discussed plans and dreams for their future which included marriage and beginning a life together after graduation from college. Their happiness seemed to have no limits until Nate made a decision without her knowledge or input. He, alone, decided their future according to his plans and time-line. Again, her feelings weren't considered by the man who supposedly loved her. It was a devastating and difficult time for her years ago.

Then, a few months ago, Wallace made a decision about their lives that, in spite of his intentions, put her through hell. Perhaps if Wallace was the first to disappoint her in this way, she could have rebounded more quickly, given him a pass and resumed life but the scars were too deep. Understandable but inexcusable, Janole thought much later.

God showed her an abundance of grace when he sent Wallace to her and her to him. They shared a wonderful life together but, instead of demonstrating the grace that God extended to her, she was acting as Satan's accomplice by focusing on her anger and disappointment. She intended to rectify this situation immediately and plead God's forgiveness.

After the service, Janole briefly chatted with Reese, Sissy and other friends and acquaintances before walking to the car to wait for Wallace.

She, distractedly, removed the folded flier under the windshield wiper wondering why the advertisement was placed on the car and not left on the information table inside the sanctuary. She soon had her answer. It wasn't a flier. It was another note. It read, "I'm watching."

Chapter Sixteen

———————— ✳ ————————

*M*arlon faced a big decision; one that would affect him for the rest of his life. One that could potentially determine the length of his life. He'd read all the literature and information provided by Dr. Bowers but was unsure of which option was best. It was mind boggling how drastically his life had changed in just a few weeks' time. Cancer, newfound knowledge about his biological father and a career interrupted. Though he didn't want to accept it just yet, he had an inkling that his days of playing professional basketball were over.

If the cancer were not aggressive, his decision would have been easier. He'd opt for chemo and radiation though he was anxious to have the invasive disease out of his body as quickly as possible. He had no idea what cancer looked like but imagined a tiny gray blob growing bigger and wider by the day, threatening to overtake his prostate and invade his other organs. A miniature octopus with tentacles able to reach through and around blood vessels, tendons, nerves, glands and bones; feeding itself on his body, leaving him depleted.

Surgery would take care of removing it quickly and, from all he'd read, it was a relatively quick and easy procedure. He wasn't concerned about the surgery itself. What concerned him was living without a prostate. The literature consistently referred to several possible occurrences which were disturbing—no, frightening—to Marlon: impotence, erectile dysfunction and incontinence. He didn't know what the word incontinence meant until he checked the dictionary. Oh no! He might wet himself occasionally at least in the first few months after surgery. Okay. Not pleasant but he could live with that temporarily if necessary. But impotence? Erectile dysfunction? He understood the meaning of those words...didn't need a dictionary. And they scared the living day lights out of him.

Dr. Bowers had explained that with the removal of the prostate he would become sterile but could father children with his own sperm using artificial means. Not desirable. To make matters worse, there were no guarantees that erectile dysfunction would be temporary. Terms were used like "improvement over time" and "residual problems" and "improved functioning."

What did that mean? He was a young virile man in the prime of his life dealing with the possibility of his manhood being compromised. Either procedure involved risks. Removal of the prostate was frightening because of sterility and possible impotence but chemo and radiation might not completely remove the cancer. Marlon was emotionally drained. He'd thought about his options for several days and still hadn't made a decision. I'm choosing between my life and my manhood, Marlon thought. *This sucks.*

His cell phone vibrated indicating an incoming call. Not in a talkative mood, he let it go to voicemail. Probably his parents who were just getting home from church, he thought. But it wasn't his parents he discovered later. Surprisingly, it was Brandy. At any other time, he would have eagerly returned her call. Now, he hesitated.

What's the point, he asked himself. I have nothing to offer her anymore. Perhaps that was a bit dramatic, he admitted, but he questioned whether he wanted her to know about his diagnosis. He was in a quandary. His simple life had become quite complicated and, because of that, he realized that what he needed most right now was a friend and there was no better choice than Brandy. Nothing more; just a friend. He had nothing to lose. Brandy was the only bright spot in his life right now, he thought, as he dialed her number. He was relieved when she answered. They chitchatted briefly before making plans to meet later for dinner.

"Hi," Marlon said in greeting, kissing Brandy on the cheek. "You look beautiful as always." Her hair was pulled into a ponytail exposing her prominent cheekbones and full lips. "I like your necklace," he said. He had given it to her as a gift while they were dating.

"Thank you," she said, smiling. "It's one of my favorites. You look nice, too."

"So, what have you been up to? How's life?" Marlon asked.

Brandy filled him in on the latest news. She continued to love her job as an interpreter. Fluent in three languages, in addition to English, Brandy was a highly sought interpreter at the Pentagon. She had earned a master's degree in International Relations and routinely traveled with high ranking government officials as an advisor. Most often, her work was classified which prevented her from sharing specific details. It was obvious from her enthusiasm that she found her work exciting and fulfilling. She also told him about her involvement in church especially with the young adult ministry and, yes, she was still a fitness buff. Recently, she'd even begun golf lessons.

"Wow. You have been busy. When do you sleep?" he asked, jokingly. "You still live in Arlington?"

"Yep. It's expensive but the commute is easy and with my hours that's important. I've been looking at houses but haven't found anything yet. Taking my time."

"Good for you. How are your parents? Alyson?" Marlon asked.

"Everybody is good. My parents just returned from a month of traveling abroad." Brandy's parents owned several successful businesses. She explained that Alyson, her younger sister, was being groomed in the businesses and had already made significant changes that were proving to be very lucrative. "She has an incredible business sense. I'm really proud of her," Brandy said. "She's planning to begin law school in the fall."

"And I'm proud of you, Bran. I'm happy that things are going well." As an afterthought, he inquired about her recent date. "So who was the dude with you Friday?"

Brandy smiled at Marlon's question. "A guy I met at church. Nothing serious. I enjoy his company from time to time."

"Does he know it's nothing serious? He seemed pretty intense the other night."

"He should know. I've told him over and over that I consider him a friend only. Obviously, he wants more but I'm just not into him like that."

Marlon was relieved. As he listened to Brandy, he realized how much he missed her. He always enjoyed talking to her and valued her opinion. She didn't accept the status quo but gave careful thought to issues before forming an opinion.

In spite of their commitment to each other, their relationship was complicated by the distance that separated them. Often they missed each other's phone calls and became frustrated when the other wasn't available. When they did see each other, their joy was stifled by the fact that their time together was short-lived. Calling it quits was difficult but, they agreed, the best decision at the time. Her life was here. His was in Argentina and they both were at such pivotal places in their careers.

After placing their drink and appetizer orders, Brandy said, "Your turn. What's going on with you?"

Marlon forced a smile. "Everything is good. I'm—" He sighed, leaned back in his chair and stared down at his hands. Finally, he looked at her.

"What is it, Marlon?"

"I don't know where to begin."

"Begin at the beginning," Brandy said in an encouraging tone.

"I have prostate cancer," Marlon blurted out.

Surprisingly, Brandy said nothing but waited for him to continue. He told her everything that had occurred from the time he learned of his elevated PSA level to now. No detail was omitted.

She covered his hand with hers and lightly squeezed it transferring strength, compassion and support. She had not stopped loving him. Faced with the reality of this life threatening situation, it became clear to her how deeply she cared for this man. She spoke compassionately but with conviction.

"Marlon, I'm sorry that you have cancer. Really sorry. But, as I see it you don't have a tough decision. With your prostate removed, the cancer will be gone and the chance of it returning is nil. It's that simple. You'll still be able to father children and the other side effects you're concerned about are possible, not probable. There's one thing

I know about you. You're a fighter and if there's anyone who can beat this thing, it's you."

He listened and was almost convinced. Surgery might be the best option for him in light of his genetic predisposition. But, not if it meant he'd be impotent.

"I don't know, Bran. Suppose I become impotent after surgery. What kind of life is that? For me? My girlfriend or wife? I'm twenty-six, not seventy-six."

"Do you believe in God?" Brandy asked.

"Of course I do. You know that."

"Well, have you prayed about it? Have you really taken this issue to God in prayer and asked for His direction?"

Marlon hesitated. "No, I haven't."

"Why not? If you believe in God and in who He is, then why not?"

"I don't know. You make it sound almost magical. Pray and magically the answer will be revealed or, better yet, I'll be cured and everyone will live happily ever after."

"No, faith is far from magic. Marlon, I'm the same Brandy you've always known with one difference. I've committed my life to God. And I pray about all of my concerns, desires and decisions. Brandy doesn't know it all, can't do it all or see it all but God can. He has a plan for my life and I trust that. He has a plan for your life, too." She sipped her tea wondering whether to share with Marlon one of the issues about which she'd specifically prayed. She didn't want to scare him away but decided to take her chances.

"What?" he coaxed. "What are you thinking?"

"Do you think we reconnected by chance?" It was a rhetorical question. "Because I don't. I specifically prayed for you and about you. About us. When I saw you the other night I couldn't believe it but then I realized God was at work." She looked deeply into his eyes and felt encouraged to continue.

"I love you. I am in love with you," Brandy said. "I never stopped loving you, Marlon. You being here is an answer to my prayer," she stated with certainty.

Something special was happening but Marlon had to be sure.

"And you still think that I'm an answer to your prayer even though I have cancer? Even though I could be impotent? Or worse?"

"Of course. Maybe you didn't hear me before. I love you," Brandy said.

Marlon smiled as he locked his fingers with hers. He didn't trust himself to speak. As cliché as it may sound, the padlock on his heart was unlocked by its rightful owner. Brandy alone had the key. He felt himself exhale as if he had been holding his breath for months. Sweet Brandy.

After their appetizers and drinks were placed in front of them, Brandy said, "I'd like to bless the food. You okay with that?"

Marlon nodded.

Brandy continued to hold his hand. "Father, thank You for Your love and faithfulness. Thank You for answering prayer. Take care of Marlon, please, and guide him. I ask that You give him peace, heal his body and show him the plans You have for his life. I ask that through this experience, he comes to know You better and understands the purpose for his life. Thank You for this food and all of Your blessings. In Jesus' name. Amen."

Marlon smiled and squeezed Brandy's hand.

"Thanks Brandy. I'm sorta at a loss for words and that rarely happens."

Later that night as he lay in bed, he thought about Brandy and his future. He marveled at Brandy's strength and composure when he mentioned the dreaded word, cancer. Seemingly, it didn't faze her though she said nothing to minimize its significance. Unknowingly, she conveyed to him that his cancer diagnosis was a situation—a circumstance of life. One to be faced and dealt with; not one to which he should succumb. And, he wouldn't allow it to define him. He so appreciated Brandy's support and he admired her faith.

Life had thrown him a curve ball. Or had it? He wondered for the first time about God's plan for his life and it was with anticipation that he did so, not dread. Perhaps, a degree of good fortune had come out of this situation already. After all, he thought, his cancer diagnosis was indirectly responsible for reuniting him with the only woman he loved. He considered that an encouraging sign.

After much soul searching and more conversations with those closest to him, Marlon was finally at peace with his decision. So were his parents and Nick. He'd opted for chemo and radiation. Brandy wasn't completely sure but respected that it was his decision.

With a newfound contentment and excitement—due, primarily, to Brandy Janae Nichols—Marlon was seeing the world in a different light. He no longer felt defeated or consumed with worry and was excited to get on with living. He was now eager to begin treatments, deal with the consequences, and trust God as he moved on with life. A life he planned to share with Brandy as his wife.

Up to now, he had avoided contact with his teammates including his best friend, Zo. Calling them was long overdue. Marlon knew he also needed to talk with Brian and his coach to inform them of his status. He would make those calls today. But there was someone else he wanted to call first whose number was on speed dial.

His uncle picked up on the second ring. "What's up, nephew? How's it going, man?"

Marlon could tell his uncle was happy to hear from him.

"I'm good. My first treatment is scheduled for next week so I'm just waiting but all is good."

"You sound great. You want me there? I'll rearrange a few things—"

"No, don't do that. I—uh—need your help in a different way."

"Name it," Marlo said.

"I need help getting a coaching job here in the States. I'm not going back to Argentina. My days in the league are done."

"Are you sure you're not making a hasty decision? I'm happy to help...but are you sure?"

"Positive," Marlon assured his uncle. "My family is here...everything I love is here. Don't get me wrong. I enjoyed playing but I want to build a life here. Coaching. It's what I've always wanted to do. You know that," Marlon said. "I want to be just like you," he added with humor.

Marlo smiled. Marlon sounded more like himself than he had in quite some time. Happy, funny, positive and upbeat.

"Okay nephew. Let me make some calls. When would you be able to begin?"

"Let me check with Dr. Bowers to be sure. I'll get back to you soon."

"Sounds good. Meanwhile, you take care of you. I'll call you next week. Oh—before I go. How are things between you and your mom?"

"Everything is good, Unc." Marlon told his uncle about his meeting with Eric and their conversation. "I'm still working through some things but I know Mom and Dad love me. That I know. No worries."

Chapter Seventeen

———————— ✳ ————————

*J*anole would not be sidetracked from what she considered to be of paramount importance. Above all else, she needed to make amends with God and her husband. After retrieving the note from the windshield, she was momentarily stunned. But, she had on her spiritual armor and, in spite of all she was experiencing, she was ready for battle. Spiritual warfare.

She anxiously waited for Wallace and began talking before he put the key in the ignition.

Touching his arm, she said, "Wallace, I've got to get this out. I'm so sorry...so sorry. I know you didn't hurt me intentionally. God must be quite disappointed in me right now. He brought us through this ordeal. I prayed. You prayed. We both prayed and God answered our prayers. He protected us.

"This situation could have had a very different outcome but God didn't allow that to happen. I think of all He's done for me, for us; how He's blessed us and, as Pastor Jones said, demonstrated divine grace. Yet, I can't find it in my heart to forgive you. That's terrible. It's sinful." She forced herself to pause. "I do wish you had figured out a way to warn me before you disappeared. I think of all that I endured that could have been avoided or extremely minimized. I—"

Wallace interrupted. "Janole, I understand. You have every right to be angry. I wasn't thinking clearly. I can't express to you how sorry I am for what I put you through."

"I know. I forgive you, Wallace. Life is too short...much too short for us to be angry with each other but no more secrets. We've got to work as partners. Agreed?"

"Agreed," Wallace said.

Janole looked at her handsome husband through clear eyes that were no longer shrouded in anger and resentment; her desire for him, once subdued, was now intense.

"How quickly can you get us home?" she asked leaving no doubt as to her intention.

Wallace smiled before passionately kissing his wife.

When they parted, a soft moan escaped her lips. "I've missed you so much."

"Not more than I've missed you. We'll be home in record time."

After an exhilarating and passionate reunion, Wallace and Janole decided to eat dinner at one of their favorite restaurants. They were both famished but giddy about their newly restored relationship. It was during dinner when Janole told Wallace about the note.

"What? Another one? On the car? At church?" In disbelief, Wallace echoed the information shared by Janole. "I don't know what to make of this. I'm really baffled."

"I am, too, but we need to trust God through this, Wallace. We've got to. If we're in danger, God will protect us just as He's always done."

Wallace nodded. "But no going anywhere alone for the time being, Janole. No walking, nothing. We'll call Agent Tyous tomorrow morning first thing. Whoever it is is becoming quite bold. They want us to know that they're watching. That's what I don't understand. Watching what? It just doesn't make sense to me," Wallace admitted.

"Somebody could be watching us right now," Janole said, trying not to show her fear.

"Listen to me, Janole," Wallace said as he gripped Janole's hand. "We can't live in fear. And, think about it. If someone wanted to hurt us, they could have without sending a warning. Right? Whoever this is doesn't want to hurt us. They're trying to send a message about something. We need to figure out what the something is." Wallace paused for a moment before continuing. "Now no more talk about the notes. There's something else I need to discuss with you and it's a pretty big deal. A lawyer contacted me last week."

Janole looked at Wallace with surprise. "A lawyer? About what?"

"Representing us in a civil suit against the pharmaceutical company. He thinks we should pursue it. Not only that, he thinks we have a very good chance of winning," Wallace explained.

"I'm confused. Is he referring to your research company filing suit or us as a couple?" Janole asked.

"Us. The amount of money he mentioned is staggering. He thinks we could be awarded millions of dollars based on similar cases," Wallace said in a hushed voice.

"What? What?! Did I hear you correctly?" Janole lowered her voice. "Did you say millions? Why are you just now telling me this? Is he a crook?" Janole voiced each question as it popped into her head.

Wallace replied calmly. "Yes, millions. I didn't tell you because we had a lot going on and you were angry with me. I was waiting for the right time. And, no, the attorney is not a crook. He's very reputable and has won a number of cases. I researched him and made a few calls. He's one of the best."

Janole said nothing but her mind was in overdrive. "What do you think? Are there risks?"

"I've given it a lot of thought," Wallace said. "I think we should do it. The only risk that I can see is reliving the ordeal during the trial. There are no financial risks. The question is what do you think?"

"I don't know, Wallace. My goodness. I don't know what to think," Janole admitted. "This is overwhelming."

"Tell you what we'll do. First, we'll pray and seek God's guidance. Then, we'll meet with the attorney so that we can get all questions answered. I'll call him tomorrow and, hopefully, he can fit us in later this week. Sound like a plan?"

Janole nodded. They ate in silence for several minutes.

"Wallace, we could become rich. Filthy rich, right?"

"Yep, according to the attorney, that's a good possibility."

"Our lives could be so different," Janole mused.

Wallace smiled. "We'd just have more money, babe. Our lives don't have to change. At least not in a negative way. I like our lives."

"But there are so many things we could do. Travel extensively, give more to charities and to the church, pay off the house and our other debt. With the money you mentioned, we'd be able to do just about anything."

"I guess we could but let's not get ahead of ourselves," Wallace cautioned.

"You're right." Suddenly Janole grinned as an idea occurred to her. It felt good to be carefree if only for a brief time. "We could buy a house with a tennis court on the property and have tennis parties. How cool would that be?"

Her next thought remained unspoken. *None of it would matter if Marlon died.*

When they arrived home, Janole made a cup of coffee and checked the home phone for messages. She smiled as she heard Jenn's familiar voice and decided to FaceTime her best friend. At times, such as these, she missed her so much.

Jenn immediately began telling Janole about the twins and their latest activities. Exceptional soccer players, they were approaching their sixteenth birthdays. "I'm worried, though," Jenn confided.

"Worried about what?" Janole asked.

"Everything. Sex, drugs, boys. Girl, I don't know how you survived raising teenagers. These girls don't tell me anything."

Janole laughed. "That's normal teenage behavior. I'm just glad I had boys. Boys are easier, I think, at that age. Do the girls have steady boyfriends?"

"No. I don't think so. No one that we've met," Jenn admitted.

"Do you think they're having sex?" Janole asked.

"Honestly? I'm not sure. They're good girls but during the past year, they've become so secretive. Whenever I try to talk with them, they act as if I'm invading their privacy."

"Privacy? They're sixteen, Jenn, and living in your house. You are responsible for them. They ain't got no privacy."

"Well—"

"You don't need to be the Mom Police but you need to know what they're doing. And, you've got to talk to them. They might act like they're not listening but they are. They need you. One of the current trends is for teenagers to engage in oral sex so they can maintain their virginity. They don't realize that they can still contract venereal diseases. And today's drugs are scary. Access is too easy. You need to monitor their computers, too."

"They'll be so angry with me," Jenn said.

"Who cares, Jenn? These are your daughters, not your best friends. Their anger comes with the territory if you're doing your job as a parent. They're not always going to like your decisions or actions. They're clueless about many things but think they know everything at that age."

"I guess you're right," Jenn said. "I'll talk to Paul." She went on to share her concerns and felt better after confiding in Janole. "I've been doing all the talking. What's going on in your world?"

Janole sighed before answering her friend. "Too much."

"Too much like what?"

"You're not going to believe this. Marlon has prostate cancer and will be undergoing treatments soon."

Janole watched Jenn's face transform from horror to shock to disbelief and back to shock.

"Oh my God, JJ. I'm stunned. I—I don't know what to say. I'm so sorry," she said as she wiped her eyes. "I'm so sorry. You need my strength and I'm the one crying."

Janole understood only too well. She explained the entire situation to Jenn who continued to wipe her eyes throughout. She also told Jenn about searching for Eric and meeting him. "My life has been crazy, Jenn."

"Is that why you were so emotional at your birthday party? You just didn't seem yourself."

"No, I didn't even know about Marlon's cancer then." Janole sighed. "My problem then was Wallace. I was so angry with him."

"Because he went away?"

"Because he left and didn't tell me anything. I went through hell as a result of the ordeal with the pharmaceutical company. I thought I had dealt with it but apparently not. I couldn't sleep at night and began having nightmares and severe headaches. Remember? I told you about the nightmares."

"I remember. Why didn't you call me?" Jenn asked.

"I don't have a good answer, Jenn. But it's all in the past now. Thank God." She sipped her coffee.

"Did you see a counselor?" Jenn asked.

"No. Well, yes. The ultimate Counselor. Pastor Jones talked about marriage in his sermon and said a few things that I couldn't ignore. He talked about the importance of forgiveness in spite of disappointments, pain and mistakes…that your spouse isn't going to be perfect or make decisions that you always agree with. Bottom line, I finally accepted that Wallace did not intend to hurt me though I was hurt deeply. I was so bitter, Jenn. God answered our prayers; yet, I had the audacity to be angry."

"Well, I think you were entitled to some anger. What did Wallace have to say?"

"He acknowledged that he could have handled things differently. But, we both have grown from this experience. I think we're better… stronger…as a result. After I opened up and told Wallace how I really felt and asked God's forgiveness, the symptoms went away. No more dreams or headaches. No more anger." Janole paused for a moment.

"Wallace is definitely changed. The relationship he has with God is different. I used to take the lead in praying but now he does. He made a spiritual connection with God that is evident. One of the most intimate things we've ever done is to kneel beside our bed, side by side, and pray. And, it was his suggestion."

"Amazing. So everything's good now?"

"Yep, everything's good." Though she could trust Jenn, Janole decided not to tell her about the notes.

"Just worried about Marlon. Will you pray with me for him? Will you be my daily prayer partner?"

"You know it—"

"Excuse me, Jenn. My cell phone is beeping. It's Nate. Let me send him a quick text message."

Jenn asked, "Why is Nate calling you?"

"He's probably just checking on me. He does that from time to time."

"Janole, is that a good idea? What does Wallace have to say about your relationship with Nate?"

"It's not a relationship," Janole said, defensively. "We just talk from time to time and occasionally have lunch. It's no big deal."

"No? You didn't answer my question. How does Wallace feel about it?"

"He doesn't like it but Nate and I are just friends, Jenn."

"Friends who were once very much in love. Listen to me, Janole. You'd better be careful."

"Jenn, we're just friends," Janole emphasized.

"Yeah, I hear you but I wonder how you would feel if one of Wallace's old flames called him regularly. Or if they got together for lunch? How would you like that?"

Janole shrugged. "Depends on who it was."

She knew she wasn't being truthful. With her jealous tendency, she would have a major problem if the circumstances were reversed.

"You mean like someone he was once madly in love with?" Jenn asked.

"Jenn, while Wallace was away I prayed that God would send someone to help me. The very next day I heard from Nate. Why would God send him to help me if we weren't meant to be friends?"

"I don't know, JJ. Maybe it was meant so that you could bring complete closure to that part of your life. Maybe it's some other purpose. I have no clue but we both know that there ain't nothing good or Godly about your involvement with Nate if it makes Wallace uncomfortable."

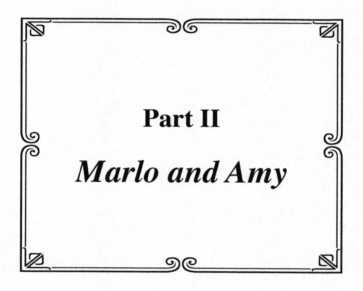

Part II

Marlo and Amy

Chapter Eighteen

———————— ✳ ————————

After Janole's birthday party, Marlo flew to Vegas for an AAU tournament that featured some of the best high school basketball talent from across the country. As head coach of a top college program, he was selective about the tournaments he attended but felt obligated to make an appearance at the major ones.

He hardly remembered the car ride to the airport; the scenery from Fairfax to Dulles was a blur of residential and commercial buildings, trees and steady traffic. He had hoped to speak to Amy en route just to hear her voice and tell her about Jay's party.

Who was he kidding? More than anything, he wanted assurance that Amy was okay...with him...and their marriage. His wife was different somehow. Happier, carefree, more light-hearted but, at the same time, distant and emotionally disconnected. Because of Amy's close friendship with Janole, it had surprised him when she decided not to attend Janole's party.

Usually, his sister and wife looked forward to spending time together. The more he thought about Amy's changed behavior the more he wondered about the cause. He was worried and Janole, who could read him like a book, had sensed that something was troubling him. Thankfully, he was able to avoid an in depth conversation with his sister. He hated being evasive with her but his worry about the status of his marriage was the last thing he wanted to acknowledge or discuss.

He tried calling Amy again while waiting to board the flight to Vegas. This time he left a message. "Amy, it's me. I'm at the airport headed for Vegas. I should be home Tuesday or Wednesday. I-uh-just wanted to hear your voice. I'll call you later."

Awakened by the ringing of her cell phone, Amy was disoriented not immediately recognizing her surroundings. Her naked body was moist and contained residue from sexual activity. Grabbing the phone from the nightstand, she saw the familiar number of her husband and quickly sent the call to voicemail.

She glanced at Doug lying beside her. He continued to snore lightly, undisturbed by the phone. Must not be a light sleeper, Amy thought. She couldn't believe they had both fallen asleep. Truthfully, there was a lot she couldn't believe beginning with the fact that she was in bed with a man other than her husband.

Amy turned her phone off but it was too late. Sleep and relaxation were no longer options for her; Marlo's phone call was a wake-up call in more ways than one. I am officially an adulterer, Amy admitted to herself as she stared at the ceiling. Today she had crossed a point of no return and, heaven help her, it felt good.

The sex itself was amazing but what she and Doug shared was more than sex. He made her feel alive and vibrant…sexy and desired… important. Her days, once routine and unfulfilling, were now exciting as she looked forward to her 'meetings' with Doug. When they weren't together, she enjoyed their text and email exchanges and lengthy phone conversations.

Where was this leading? She had no answer and did not want to speculate. One thing she knew for sure. She couldn't tell anyone about this liaison not even Abbie, her very best friend and confidante. Abbie would not approve. No, this was her and Doug's secret which made it all the more special and exciting.

And sinful.

A heated debate was occurring inside Amy's head with two distinct voices. One was the voice of reason, the one with a moral conscious.

"Amy, what are you doing? This is wrong and you know it. Your mom and dad would be so disappointed. What would MJ and Brianna think of you if they found out? Marlo? Janole?"

Tears were threatening but Amy angrily blinked them away.

The other voice—the one justifying and defending Amy's cause—spoke for her. "To hell with Marlo. All he cares about is his basketball program. Why should I be concerned about his feelings?"

"Because he's your husband," Moral Voice answered.

"Well, somebody needs to tell Marlo that he's my husband. Tell him that he's married to me, not basketball. I'm tired of being lonely and neglected," spoke Defensive Voice.

Moral Voice didn't respond right away. Amy thought Defensive Voice had made a convincing argument until she heard Moral Voice's warning, "You're going to regret this."

At times, the guilt Amy experienced was overwhelming and at those times she was tempted to do the right thing. But, strangely, she also felt vindicated by her secretive and adulterous actions. Liberated even. Later—much later—she would remember how Satan can twist one's mind to justify any action, no matter how horrible, but that was not a consideration for her now.

Amy was tired of hurting, so sick and tired of being a basketball widow though her husband was very much alive. She was beyond tired; she was weary. And angry. Most of all, she was miserable. She just wanted something—or someone—to take away her unhappiness if just for a short while. In her wildest dreams she could not imagine—or anticipate—the regrettable consequences that were on the horizon.

For years, she sacrificed her desires and needs for those of her family. It was easier to keep herself distracted from her loneliness and emptiness when the kids were living at home as she busied herself with their activities and the things she enjoyed doing for them. They were her pride and joy, after all, and she had no regrets where they were concerned. Marlo Jr. (MJ) would soon be graduating from Michigan State and Brianna had just completed her freshman year at the University of Michigan-Lansing.

Children aside, the more Amy thought about her life, the angrier she became.

This mess of a marriage was all Marlo's doing and if he were to honestly place blame where it belonged for the current state of their marriage he needed to begin with himself. It was all his fault. He was responsible for her pain, loneliness, and a union that was beyond pathetic.

Yes, she had been warned more than once about the challenges of being a coach's wife. The unending road trips, demanding schedule, emotional ups and downs, practices and meetings, late night phone calls, interruptions during family activities, the ever present reminder of the university's expectations, even the women who were aggressive in their pursuits.

She'd wondered more than once whether Marlo had been unfaithful to her and suspected that he had though she had no proof. Just a feeling. Maybe it was her own guilty conscience. She could forgive his infidelity, perhaps. After all, people who lived in glass houses shouldn't throw stones.

What she couldn't forgive was how he took her for granted time after time as if she were a comfortable fixture in his life. At times, he made her feel invisible. He acted as if basketball were more important than anything. And, he never shut it off. Never.

Of course, she couldn't complain about the lifestyle they enjoyed because of Marlo's hefty salary and the other perks he received. Their home was her dream home and was paid for, the kids had attended the best private schools, her wardrobe was enviable and they had travelled extensively. She wanted for no material possession yet her marriage was empty and she was filled with resentment.

Because of that resentment, she took every opportunity to disassociate herself from Marlo and basketball. In her mind, the two were one. Games, she no longer attended. She didn't offer to host coaches meetings. She did only what she considered necessary to maintain appearances. Social gatherings were the worse and she had come to loathe them because the conversation, inevitably, was dominated by basketball whether it was the most recent game or the next opponent, the latest high school prospect, the unexpected performance of an unranked college team, the firing of a coach, alleged NCAA violations or 'The League.'

In the beginning of their marriage, Amy was hopeful that Marlo would recognize that there was more to life than basketball. That he would be so in tuned to her—and so eager to please her—he would understand and share in her need for a multi-dimensional life. When that didn't happen, she tried talking to him…then begging and pleading. Over time, conversations turned into arguments. Arguments turned into angered silence.

She doesn't recall when she stopped trying. When she no longer attempted to engage him in conversations, no longer cared who won or lost, when functions became obligations, when it was no longer a big deal to her whether Marlo was home or not, when she began viewing her life as one she didn't want.

Maybe I'm the problem, Amy thought. In their coaching circle, she knew of many wives who seemed quite happy…marriages that were balanced…husbands who were attentive and seemed genuinely interested and engaged in family activities…children who thrived. If not perfect, their marriages seemed solid. She envied these couples who were true partners and friends, whose love and commitment to each other were apparent. What was the X factor, she wondered.

Perhaps she could have dealt with it all if Marlo had been more affectionate and passionate. More present. Expressions of affection and romance didn't come easy for him. There were times she craved a compliment, a spontaneous and passionate hug or kiss, or just cuddling while watching a movie. She would settle for him showing a sincere interest in her desires or plans for the day. Perhaps, if he'd call her during the day to tell her how much he loved her or if he really listened to her and actively engaged in the conversation when she tried to talk to him. Or took a walk with her where she was made to feel there was no place on Earth he'd rather be. She craved these things from her husband.

"Hello Beautiful. A penny for your thoughts," Doug said as he pulled her naked body close to his. He began caressing her. "You are so incredibly beautiful. Your eyes, your skin, your sexy body. I just can't get enough of you."

She was so deeply in thought that she didn't realize Doug was awake until she heard his voice. Looking into his eyes, she saw passion and desire.

"Hmmmm. That feels good but I'm famished. Why don't we order room service or go down to the restaurant," Amy suggested. The truth? Marlo's phone call was as effective as being doused by a bucket of icy water.

Doug had come to know Amy well and didn't persist.

"I'm hungry, too. The restaurant is fine. What time do you need to leave?" Doug asked as he brought her hand to his mouth and kissed it gently.

"Not for a while," she said. *What was there to go home to?* "Why don't you shower first?"

Doug tenderly touched her face as he looked at her. "Are you okay with this? With us? Like this?"

Amy hesitated before responding. She decided against sharing her most recent thoughts.

"I so enjoy being with you. Your friendship—you—mean so much to me. You make me feel things I haven't felt in a long time. And when I'm not with you, I think of you constantly. But—I've not done anything like this and never thought I would. Never in my wildest dreams."

Doug responded, "I understand. My life hasn't turned out as I thought or hoped, either. We're not bad people, Amy. And I want you to know this. You are incredibly special to me. You've made me very happy so let's enjoy our precious time together. Okay?"

"Okay," Amy said before kissing Doug gently on the lips.

While Doug showered, Amy slipped on the robe provided by the hotel and looked out of the window. They had agreed to meet in the city and Amy was intrigued by the car and bus riders, pedestrians, and bikers as they travelled in various directions, anxious to leave work behind. *I wonder if they have family at home eagerly waiting for them.*

It had all started so innocently. For an entire year, she and Doug worked on a fundraising campaign together to benefit the area YMCAs. Frequent face-to-face meetings, telephone conferences and email exchanges were required to adequately plan for this huge endeavor. The committee hoped to top last year's amount of $750,000. Doug and Amy also volunteered to co-chair the publicity subcommittee and discovered that they worked well together as a team.

Doug was a highly successful graphic artist by profession and Amy was an athletic trainer who became a stay at home mother when she became pregnant with MJ. She was also a talented painter though she considered it a hobby. Over time, their business meetings became a convenient cover for spending time together that had nothing to do with the fundraiser. They found that they had a great deal in common including being lonely and unhappily married.

They enjoyed each other's company, talked about many things, commiserated about their marriages, and shared a passion for Art. They frequented art galleries, something she'd longed to do with Marlo, and listened with interest to each other's interpretations of the artistic work they viewed. One day, Doug slipped his hand through hers as they strolled through the gallery and it felt perfectly natural and wonderful.

Amy remembered the electric shock of Doug's touch. No other man, except Marlo, had touched her in a way that gave her chills. He caressed her cheek and looked into her eyes with longing, desire and appreciation. For Amy, it was the most sensuous experience. He awakened feelings and responses in her that had been dormant much too long. A month later he kissed her on the lips. A soft chaste kiss that left her longing for more.

For months, they continued like this with discreet touches and soft kisses. The crescendo continued to build while the thrill of it all intensified. By the time Doug suggested a more private setting she was more than willing and felt quite justified in her behavior. She had done all she could to appeal to Marlo including sacrificing her pride; yet, nothing changed. Granted, things were good in the beginning but only because she allowed herself to be consumed by Marlo's world. When she gradually tried to introduce other activities and events for them to share as a couple, he always had an excuse and it was, without fail, related to basketball.

If Amy had reservations about Marlo's priorities, she was pushed over the edge when her parents died. Marlo was seldom there for her emotionally and that was never so apparent as when she received news about her parents' unexpected deaths over a year ago.

Her parents were on their way home from an evening church service. From what the police were able to determine, her father—who was driving—saw the deer too late. Swerving to avoid them, he collided with a truck in oncoming traffic. Her parents died instantly, the police said. The other driver sustained serious injuries but was expected to fully recover.

Amy knew she would never forget that day. She listened to her youngest brother, Gary, in disbelief as he conveyed the details.

"Mom and Dad? They're both gone? Oh God. No!" Amy said in utter distress. After receiving the news, she immediately phoned Marlo only to get his voice mail.

In between fits of grief and disbelief, she called him several times leaving frantic messages. She remembered being distraught... at times on the verge of hysteria. She had difficulty standing and thinking clearly but knew she needed to pack, make flight reservations to her parents' home in upstate New York, and tell the kids.

Overcome with the pain of losing both of her beloved parents, she gave in to her grief and sobbed for what seemed like hours. After a while, she had the presence of mind to phone Abbie, who rushed over and sent her husband, Ahmad, to the gym to inform Marlo.

When Marlo walked into the house over an hour later, he wore a pained expression and rushed to her side. He embraced her holding her tightly but never offered an apology for being unavailable. To his credit, he was very attentive to her that night. He made the flight arrangements for them and said all of the right things.

At her parents' home, he helped by running errands and doing whatever was asked of him but, to Amy's disappointment, was frequently on the phone with his coaching staff. Amy wanted—no, needed—him to be completely attentive to her during this time of crisis. For once, she didn't want to compete for his time and attention.

Angrily, she said, "Can you forget basketball for a few days? Just give me a week. My parents are dead, Marlo, and you spend more time talking to your coaches than you do to my family."

"Don't you think you're exaggerating a bit? I have to make sure everything is in order, Amy. I'm sorry but there are things I have to take care of because we left suddenly."

"That's why you have a coaching staff," Amy retorted. "They can do it. Cordell has been on your staff for years. Surely he can handle things. I need you."

Amy sat on the bed and cried; the impact of her loss, at times, was sudden and overwhelming. "I need you."

Marlo felt helpless in his ability to console Amy who was constantly in tears. And, just the mention of Cordell's name irritated him.

According to the rumor mill and a very reliable source, Cordell was trying to undermine Marlo's actions and ruin his relationship with the players. It was no secret that Cordell wanted a head coach position but it was surprising to Marlo that he was trying to make it happen by discrediting him.

Out of frustration, Marlo said to Amy, "I'm here. What more do you want?"

Amy said nothing while looking at him in disbelief, hurt that he could be so insensitive at this time.

Marlo walked across the room and sat beside her on the bed.

"I'm sorry," he said, taking her hand and rubbing it. "That didn't come out right. You know how sorry I am about your parents. They meant a great deal to me, too."

They sat in silence for a few moments. "It's just that there's a lot going on right now at work. I left quite a few things up in the air." Marlo took a deep breath before continuing. "Have you all decided on the funeral date?"

Amy wiped her bloodshot eyes and blew her nose. "We're thinking Sunday." Warning bells were ringing. "Why do you ask?"

"We have a scrimmage Wednesday. I thought I would fly out on Tuesday and fly back Wednesday night or Thursday morning."

Though he shared none of this with Amy, Marlo was concerned about the damage Cordell could do during his absence.

Amy looked at Marlo and realized she'd been fighting a lost cause. *My parents are dead and he's thinking about a scrimmage. A freaking scrimmage.* And as quickly as flipping a light switch, her internal capacity to fight for her marriage was turned off. Who was she kidding? She couldn't compete with Marlo's love for basketball. Obviously, it gave him something that she couldn't.

"I want you here but if you feel you need to go, go."

"I'll be back on Thursday morning at the latest."

During the period of Amy's greatest need for her husband, he left. To hell with you, Marlo, she screamed but only in her mind.

Again, Doug interrupted her thoughts bringing her back to the present.

"The bathroom is yours. I'll call the restaurant to see if reservations are necessary."

Freshly showered and dressed, Amy and Doug enjoyed dinner and the ambiance offered by the upscale restaurant. A jazz quartet played a variety of hits. The restaurant's bar was crowded with professionals of all ages taking advantage of the camaraderie and Happy Hour deals. Amy and Doug talked and laughed and actually celebrated their milestone with a toast.

Today they were no longer just friends, they were lovers. In spite of their new status, they didn't stand out to casual observers as they did nothing extreme to bring attention to themselves. Unbeknownst to them, however, there was one observer who had more than a casual interest in them.

Chapter Nineteen

———————— ✳ ————————

*A*fter pulling into the spacious garage of his 5,000 square foot home, Doug remained in the car for a few moments. He was exhilarated from his time with Amy and needed to regroup so as not to arouse his wife's suspicion. He expected to receive the usual stony reception—void of warmth and kindness—and wasn't disappointed. Grace—the irony of her name never escaped him—was sitting at the kitchen counter paying bills and drinking a cup of coffee.

"Hi Grace."

"You finally made it home," she said, never looking up.

Ignoring her statement, Doug asked, "How was your day?"

"Same as usual. Dealing with those incompetent people at work. They're all a bunch of airheads. Sylvia had the nerve to ask me for a week off because her mother is ill. She knows we have a big deadline coming. I looked at her as if she were crazy. She probably is crazy."

"Sylvia works hard and has always been there for you, Grace. Show some compassion. It's her mother."

"I'll show compassion after the deadline. I think I know what I'm doing...don't need advice from you. When I need your advice, I'll ask for it. I got this."

Grabbing a beer, Doug said, "I'm sure you do. I'm gonna watch the game." *Why am I still married to this evil woman?*

"Don't forget the dinner party tomorrow," she said to his retreating back.

Doug relaxed in his oversized recliner and nursed his beer, deep in thought. The NFL game promised to be a thriller but he was distracted. The question he asked himself earlier continued to plague him. He was miserable, finding his current state more and more intolerable. His and Grace's relationship was a marriage only in the legal sense.

Why, then, had he not left? Why did he remain in this union that offered not one shred of love or happiness? He knew the answer in part. His marriage to Grace was his second marriage and he didn't want to be considered a failure...again. He'd made a mistake in marrying his first wife which, in hindsight, could only be attributed to a youthful error in judgment.

Against the advice of family and friends, he married Debbie because she was beautiful and he was in love. It mattered little at that time that she lacked aspiration and refused to work, preferring to watch soap operas all day. To make matters worse, she drank excessively and gradually became an alcoholic. Though suspicious, Doug didn't realize the magnitude of her problem until he came home one day and found her soiled and drunk on the floor. It was a rude awakening especially when he became aware of how her alcohol consumption had drained their limited savings.

Needless to say, he was forced to admit that his family and friends clearly saw what he could not. It wasn't long before he understood that what he considered love was actually a short-lived lust affair. He regretted making Debbie his wife. They divorced two years after they exchanged vows.

Months after his divorce, he and Grace met at a social for business professionals. She impressed him as a go-getter and hard worker. Because of his experience with Debbie, he appreciated those attributes. Though there were no fireworks, Grace was nice enough and they dated off and on for several years.

Scarred from his relationship with Debbie, Doug made it clear to any woman he dated, including Grace, that he was not interested in a permanent commitment. The one woman, Deidra, who had the potential to change Doug's mind suddenly stopped communicating with him, changing her phone numbers and refusing to take his calls at work, with no explanation. Doug was baffled—and hurt—by her actions because he believed their affection for each other was mutual. With Deidra out of the picture, Doug wasn't considering marriage — certainly not to Grace — until she became pregnant despite taking the pill. Because of the nature of their relationship, he initially questioned whether he was the father but didn't go so far as to request a paternity test. Eventually he accepted the baby as his child; however, he did not rush into marriage which angered Grace and her family. He finally proposed shortly after DJ's first birthday. Did he love Grace even then? Probably not, but he grew to deeply care for her. He adored DJ and enjoyed life as a family. They were financially comfortable and took time to travel and vacation. Outside of work, their lives centered around DJ, shuttling him to and fro, and they looked forward to attending his various activities.

There were problems, however. Significant problems. Grace's mother, for one. Grace permitted Irene to have too much of a voice and presence in their marriage. Irene offered her opinion whether or not it was solicited. She felt entitled to insert herself at any time which caused a major problem for Doug because he regarded her as the crudest, most obnoxious woman he had met. Grace didn't know the identity of her father and was fiercely loyal to her mother. When together, the two women often criticized and ridiculed Doug. As a result, he stopped participating in their family functions and made a point of making himself scarce whenever Irene visited them.

The other problem was Grace's jealousy. At times, she was insanely jealous and possessive. She had accused him of having an affair with his assistant who was happily married with four children. He remembered the incident well.

In order to meet the deadline for a major client, he was working in his office with the door closed when he heard loud voices. He was surprised and embarrassed to discover Grace confronting — attacking — his assistant, Cassie, reducing her to tears. Doug thought highly of Cassie, professionally and personally. Smart and efficient, he had come to rely on her and included her in business meetings.

Grace accused them of having an affair because she had seen them together at a nearby restaurant the day before. Doug and Cassie both tried to explain, to no avail, that they were meeting a client to discuss business. Finally, Doug sent Cassie home after apologizing profusely and begging her not to quit. Grace eventually calmed down but never apologized for the scene she caused. Not to mention, her unwarranted accusations.

There were several embarrassing instances of her jealousy flaring throughout their marriage. One such rampage resulted in him losing the lucrative business of a potential client. The deal was almost final until Grace made her presence known. The client, Shannon Smith, was an attractive woman who appeared to be in her early thirties.

Apparently, Grace was set off when she called the office to speak with him and was told that he was in a private meeting with Ms. Smith. Earlier in the week, Doug had shared his excitement with Grace about the deal and showed her the business proposal which included a photo of Shannon. After Grace learned about the meeting, she showed up not bothering to have her presence announced. Barging into his office, she immediately began making accusations. This time, Doug was unable to undo the damage. Shannon stormed out of the office taking her business with her.

Doug's attention was drawn to the television. Though he had missed most of the game, he was happy about the outcome. His favorite team—the Carolina Panthers— won, impressively. The question he asked himself at the onset of the game continued to plague him, however. *Why am I still married to this evil woman?* Something needs to change and soon, he concluded.

The last place Doug wanted to be was at a dinner party with Grace, full of pretense. But he had dutifully gone and was trying to make the best of it. He knew most of the people seated at their table, all of whom worked with Grace. He looked at his wife and couldn't resist comparing her to Amy. They were polar opposites. Grace grew up in the projects and was raised by a mother who had a reputation of being tough as nails and mean as a pit bull. Most men would think twice before confronting Irene. Grace was very much like her mom except she was college educated and had learned to use more tact and diplomacy when handling conflicts. More, not much more. Doug wouldn't describe Grace as a pretty woman—her eyes were set too close and her nose was too big but she took care of herself. Hair and nails were always perfect—though he disliked the weave—and her clothes were expensive and stylish. Grace had an edge about her, a 'don't mess with me' attitude. If you did get on her bad side, which he had on numerous occasions, she could be very vindictive. No doubt, a trait she had learned from Irene. She was definitely a take charge type which appealed to him at one time. Now he detested her over-bearing personality and no longer found her attractive.

Amy, on the other hand, was pretty and feminine yet gracefully athletic. She was also kind, considerate and respectful of individual differences. He admired her creativity and intelligence and how she made him feel. She listened to him and valued his opinion. Amy's short natural haircut framed her face and complemented her facial features. Her skin was a creamy cocoa complexion and, to him, her big hazel eyes were extremely sexy. She, too, wore expensive and tasteful clothing but was less flashy than Grace. People were forced to notice Grace's flashiness whereas people were drawn to Amy's elegance.

Though he had not met her parents, Amy described them as loving, kind churchgoing people who were highly regarded in their community. A far cry from Irene who had affiliations with a number of unsavory characters including several reputed to be hardened criminals.

Tonight, as usual, Grace monopolized the conversation talking about herself and making snide remarks about other coworkers or their family members. Lillian—seated to Doug's right—drew him in to the conversation.

"I hear you are involved with the YMCA fundraiser. How's it going?"

Doug excitedly shared that it was going well though they were still short of their goal.

"We have several months so we're quite optimistic that we may even exceed our projection."

Everyone talked about what a worthwhile cause it was and complemented Doug's efforts.

Grace said, "They probably won't reach their goal. Doug can be so passive. They need me on that committee. I'd have people giving their rent money."

Grace laughed loudly while others chuckled or discreetly glanced at each other. Doug thought her statement was demeaning.

"Call me at the office tomorrow, Doug. I'd like to contribute and I have a few other contacts who I'm sure would be interested," Mitchell said to Doug. Mitchell was one of the senior vice presidents.

"I will. Thanks Mitchell."

"How's business going? Still thinking of expanding?" Mitchell asked.

"Well, I'm considering—" Doug began but was interrupted.

Grace snickered loudly. "He's hardly keeping this one in the black and only with my help. Doug doesn't know how to run a business. I'm the brains behind his success and I can tell you he won't be expanding any time soon."

Doug was embarrassed and livid. "Well, there you have it. Just ask Grace. She knows everything about everything."

Silence. No one said a word including Grace who was stunned by Doug's comment. He never challenged her publicly. She was stunned even more by his next statements.

"Please excuse me, everyone. It has been good seeing you all but I need to leave. Mitchell, I'll call you tomorrow. Grace, I'm sure you can find a way home. Good night."

Grace was humiliated knowing she would be the topic of office gossip and jokes. She failed to recognize her fault in the situation; only that Doug had gone too far. As if his insulting comment wasn't enough, he left her at the party, stranded. Surprisingly, none of her coworkers offered to give her a ride so she'd been forced to call a cab. *Jerks.* Fuming, she was determined that Doug would pay.

She stormed in the house, ready to explode but found no signs of Doug after yelling his name and searching the entire house.

"He's afraid to face me. Coward. Probably at a bar. That's okay. I can wait. I'm gonna cuss his ass out," she muttered to herself. "I don't know who he thinks he is. He has lost his freaking mind. When I'm done with him—" She stopped in mid sentence when she saw the note on the kitchen counter. In Doug's familiar handwriting were the words, "I'm moving out. Will get the rest of my things later. I want a divorce."

Payback would have to wait.

Chapter Twenty

---——*——---

$\mathcal{M}$arlo's concerns about Amy and the status of their marriage grew. When he had finally spoken to her from Vegas, she was polite but withdrawn. Evasive even. Her explanation for not answering the phone earlier was that it was turned off while she was out. Out where, he wondered. She seemed interested in the details of Janole's party but when he told her he missed her, she responded by asking him when he planned to come home. He got the weirdest feeling that she wasn't asking the question because she missed him.

He began noticing things. New perfume and lingerie. Or were they new? She seemed to spend more time on her appearance, he thought, though he couldn't be sure. She always looked good but seemed to have a glow these days. At times, he'd hear her humming or starring off into space with a dreamy look on her face. One morning he asked her about the fundraiser and could have sworn that her face registered guilt for just a moment.

"It's going really well," she answered. "I think we'll surpass our goal. Keep your fingers crossed."

"You really enjoy your involvement, don't you?"

Defensively, she responded, "Of course. It's a worthwhile cause. What kind of question is that?"

"It's just that you seem happier than you have for a while. I'm glad you found something you really enjoy."

"Me too."

Marlo's comment angered Amy. *Because I have an inattentive husband, I've been forced to find happiness outside of my marriage...*

reduced to sneaking around like a lowlife. If only you knew, Marlo, how much I enjoy "my" involvement.

Amy and Doug had been seeing each other for several months and were beginning to have serious conversations about their future together. Unlike any other time, the flaws of their marriages were blatantly exposed and difficult to ignore. Though the flaws were different in each marriage, the outcome was the same. Doug and Amy were unhappy and dissatisfied, yet guilt-ridden. The question they each faced was what to do about their marriages.

Doug had taken a big step by moving out; one he didn't regret. But, there were unpleasant consequences. His lifestyle had definitely changed and he was worried about their son, DJ. If true to character, Grace would distort the truth and make Doug out to be the villain to DJ and anyone else who listened. Though it pained Doug to admit it, DJ was very much like his mother. Spoiled, selfish and mean-spirited. Truthfully, he was a bully who showed no remorse for his hurtful actions. Of course, Grace undermined everything that Doug tried to do to instill a moral compass in their son. And now that Doug was no longer in the home, DJ would have free rein.

For Amy, there was always the fear of Marlo finding out the truth. She couldn't keep up with her own lies and Marlo was becoming more suspicious. She hated being in this position but not enough to end her relationship with Doug.

As a culminating activity, the entire fundraising committee met to celebrate their success and determine immediate steps for next year's fundraiser. The goal of $750,000 had been exceeded as they raised in excess of one million dollars in donations and pledges. Prior to the meeting, Amy and Doug met at Doug's hotel for their own private 'meeting.' The two lingered over coffee after the committee meeting, not wanting to end their too brief time together. They always found things to talk about and sometimes conversation was not necessary. Being together was enjoyment enough.

Reluctantly, they decided it was time to leave not knowing their worlds were about to drastically change. As they exited the restaurant through the revolving doors they found the sidewalk crowded with moviegoers who were arriving and leaving the theatre next door. Amy and Doug pushed their way through the crowd only to be confronted by a loud voice. In slow motion it seemed, their attention was drawn to a woman standing directly in front of them, pointing a gun at Doug's chest. Amy had time for only one thought before Doug violently pushed her away from him, causing her to fall.

She looks deranged, Amy thought as she scampered away.

By now, the crowd was aware of danger and began running in different directions. There was loud chaos. Someone yelled, "Gun! Gun! She's got a gun!"

Crawling on all fours, Amy made it to a nearby alley where she thought she'd be safe. Her knees were scraped and bleeding, her left elbow and hip ached and she felt blood seep through the torn sleeve of her shirt. She, unconsciously, tried to soothe the pain on her elbow by covering it with her hand as she focused on the woman with the gun.

Consumed with fear and worry about Doug, she watched the horrifying scene and heard Doug say, "Put the gun down, Grace. You're going to hurt somebody."

Had Amy heard correctly? *Grace? The crazy woman with the gun is Grace? It can't be!* Amy had seen a photo of Grace. This woman looked nothing like the put together woman in the photo.

Doug looked into Grace's crazed eyes. He'd seen her angry but never like this. It was as if she were possessed by a demon.

"Grace, put the gun down before someone gets hurt," Doug gently implored.

"Damn straight somebody's going to get hurt," Grace yelled. "And it's going to be you. Where is your whore? You think you're going to leave me for that tramp? You must be crazy! I'll kill you first."

"Grace don't. Please. Put the gun down." Doug tried to project a calmness he didn't feel. His heart was pounding at an astonishing rate and his knees were trembling.

"Where is she?" Grace yelled. "The slut! You thought I didn't know?"

She laughed but there was no humor. "I've known from the beginning. Paid a private detective to follow your sorry ass."

"Grace, you don't need to do this. We can talk about it—"

"Shut up!" she yelled stepping closer to him. "Time for talk is over."

The events that occurred next would haunt many for a long time. A family of four, oblivious to the danger, exited the restaurant through the revolving doors. At the same time, Grace began shooting. The bullet intended for Doug grazed his forearm before entering the chest of an innocent bystander. The little boy collapsed immediately. His mother's scream could be heard over the chaos.

Police had finally arrived and ordered Grace to drop the gun. "Police! Put down your gun! Put down your gun now!"

Grace, who seemed to be overtaken with anger and revenge, paused but it was as if the words didn't register. Ignoring the numerous warnings from the police, she raised the gun again and aimed it at Doug. A policeman fired at Grace numerous times but it was the first shot that was fatal. The gun dropped from her hands as she fell heavily to the ground.

From the alley, Amy watched in horror as the entire scene unfolded. Tears streamed down her face and her body trembled uncontrollably. *What just happened? This can't be real.* She tried to stand but couldn't. She felt faint.

Where are those screams coming from? Willing herself to focus, she saw three bodies on the ground. *Oh my God! Doug is hurt! Please God don't let him die.* Police and paramedics had arrived and surrounded the area making it difficult to see. Grace was dead. Amy was fairly certain of that.

Where was the little boy? She couldn't see him now but could clearly see his parents. They were both sobbing as was a little girl who appeared to be no more than eight years old. Amy watched as the little boy's body was lifted on a gurney by the paramedics. He was so tiny. *Please don't let him die.* The parents and the little girl were helped into the ambulance and then the door closed. Amy watched as Doug was helped to another ambulance and though he seemed shaken, he was able to walk.

He is alive! Thank God. She was weak with relief.

For a split second, their eyes connected. "Go," Doug seemed to be saying with his expression. "Now!"

He was warning her and she understood the reason when she saw the media vans approach. This will be all over the news she realized. *I've got to get out of here. Where is my car?* She couldn't remember for several seconds but then recalled that she and Doug rode to the restaurant together.

She'd left her car at Doug's hotel. *Oh no!* Her only option was a cab or Uber driver; she decided against both. The drivers might remember her or become suspicious. That was too risky. Guilt-ridden, she didn't want anyone to associate her with Grace or the shooting. She thought of Abbie and knew she could trust her best friend. *Call Abbie. Yes, that's what I'll do.* She was thankful that Marlo was out of town.

My purse. Where's my purse? She searched, frantically, and found it several feet away, almost unrecognizable. The black Coach clutch was filthy from being trampled but Amy could have cared less. Just let my phone work, she thought. She stood slowly. Her body ached but, otherwise, she was okay. After grabbing her purse, she slowly made her way from Doug and the scene of the shooting. She walked two blocks before nearly collapsing on a bench. For a period of time, she sat, unconscious of the goings-on around her; unaware of the questioning stares she received by passersby. Finally, she reached for her phone, panicked when she noticed its cracked face, then sighed with relief when it worked. *Please answer, Abbie.*

"Hello," Abbie said, breathlessly as if she had been running.

"Abbie? It's Amy. I need your help. Something terrible has happened and I need you to pick me up." Amy, afraid and traumatized, was on the verge of panic.

"Slow down, Amy. Slow down and calm down. Are you okay?"

"No—yes. Just come get me." By now, Amy was crying. "Please come get me."

Usually composed in crisis situations, Abbie was nearing a panic state herself and willed herself to remain calm. To Amy she said, "Tell me where you are."

Amy found it difficult to focus. "Uh—I don't know. Wait a minute. I'm on the corner of Main and 25th. Across from the Macy's."

"Okay. I'm leaving now. I should be there in twenty minutes. Just sit tight."

"Abbie, you can't tell Ahmad. Promise me you won't tell him. You can't tell anyone. Please promise me."

"I promise. I'm on my way."

Abbie was stunned by Amy's disheveled appearance as she helped her in the car. "What happened, Amy?"

"Let's just go. I'll tell you later," Amy said, fatigued and over-whelmed. "I just want to take a shower and get out of these clothes."

Amy appeared to be in shock. She did nothing but cry the entire ride which elevated Abbie's concern. Sensing Amy's fragile state, Abbie didn't press the issue as she drove the thirty minutes to Amy's home. Once inside, Abbie helped Amy undress and into the shower then went to the kitchen to make coffee and wait. She had grown even more concerned when she noticed Amy's injuries and torn clothing. Finally, Amy appeared dressed in pajamas and a robe. Baffled and worried, Abbie poured a cup of coffee for Amy and patiently waited until she was ready to talk.

Amy spoke in a monotone. "There was a shooting today outside of Pezazzi's. This woman...she was crazy. I saw her eyes...can still see them. I've never seen anything like it before. She was yelling at her husband and waving a gun. She accused him of having an affair. I was knocked down but managed to crawl to an alley. Everybody was running and screaming."

"Oh my God. Was her husband there?" Abbie asked.

Amy nodded. "He was there. He tried to get her to put the gun down but she wouldn't. She kept asking for his slut to come forward. I think she wanted to kill them both. It was so horrible," Amy said, shivering.

"What happened next?" Abbie asked.

"It all happened so fast. She pointed the gun at her husband and pulled the trigger just as this family walked out of the restaurant. They must not have known what was happening. I think she only fired once but I can't remember. The bullet intended for her husband hit the little boy in the chest. I saw the bullet hit him, Abbie. He fell immediately. He didn't even know what hit him. Then the police arrived and ordered the woman to put down the gun but it was like she was insane. She raised the gun again and that's when the police shot her. Dead."

Amy sobbed as she relived the horror.

"Amy, that must have been awful and scary," Abbie said while handing Amy more tissues and allowing her time to compose herself. "Did you know the woman? Her husband?"

Amy didn't answer immediately. Abbie noticed that Amy's hands were trembling as she lifted the coffee cup to the lips.

"I know the husband and know of the wife," Amy said, softly.

"Oh no. How do you know them? Do I know them?"

Amy shook her head. "I don't think so." She sipped her coffee as if it were the source of strength. "I know them because I am the slut she was referring to," Amy said not daring to look at Abbie.

"What? Amy, what are you talking about? I don't understand."

Amy sighed deeply. "I've been having an affair with Doug. You met him. He and I worked on the YMCA fundraiser. It was his wife who was killed today. She tried to kill Doug. I just can't believe it," Amy said, shaking her head.

"Doug told me she was crazy and mean but I never thought she was capable of this. Oh my God, Abbie. I'm responsible for those people being hurt. Grace is dead. Doug was shot and the little boy may be dead, too. All because of me. If Doug hadn't pushed me down, I may have been killed, too. What am I going to do? How can I live with this?"

Abbie had no answers.

Chapter Twenty-One

---❋---

Marlo sipped the vodka, grimacing slightly as he swallowed it. The taste was strong, even unpleasant, but welcomed. He seldom drank but he was worried and afraid. The two most important facets of his life were in danger of falling apart. His basketball program and his marriage.

During his recent travels to various AAU tournaments, he'd had time to think, especially about his marriage. He didn't like the distance between he and Amy but was at a loss for what to do to make things better. The more he thought, the more worried he became. He'd even been worried enough to reach out to Coach Butler, his high school coach and lifelong mentor. He'd often confided in Coach B and because he trusted him, he felt free to openly discuss the status of his marriage and his assistant coach's attempts to undermine him.

Coach Butler addressed the basketball situation first. "You have a solid reputation in the coaching ranks. Man, you're one of the most respected coaches in college basketball. Why are you worried about what Cordell is trying to do? He should be the one worrying. What have you done about it?"

"Nothing really. I'm trying to monitor the situation as best I can. Some of the players tell me things out of loyalty. Other coaches, too."

"Well, let me tell you what I'd do. I'd dismiss him from my staff immediately," Coach Butler said, emphatically. "Today. You need to surround yourself with people you can trust. If you can't trust your top assistant, you've got a major problem."

"I guess I was trying to avoid drama. Didn't want to upset the team dynamics. It could get ugly."

"It's already ugly and before it gets worse, you need to address it."

"I think part of me doesn't want to acknowledge the truth. Cordell has been with me for eight years. I considered him my right hand. It just bothers me that it has come to this. I gave him a chance. I thought—"

"I know what you thought. You thought he was a different person but he's not. Cordell is what he is and he's showing you his true colors. Now you need to man up and address it. It's not just your reputation at stake but the lives and careers of the young men in your program and those being recruited."

Marlo considered each individual player, especially Kenny, the loner. He knew he'd established a connection with Kenny because the young man was becoming more outgoing, even seeking him out at times. He'd begun confiding in Marlo sharing painful details of his experiences. Not only did Marlo enjoy talking to him but had developed a great deal of respect and appreciation for Kenny's keen insight and resilience. Marlo noticed Cordell spending more and more time with Kenny which was cause for concern.

"You're right, Coach. You're absolutely right. I will address the matter today. In fact, I know of a young man who will make a great assistant if he's ready to take on the responsibility. May shake things up a bit but shakeup is probably needed."

"Let me know how things work out," Coach B said, and as if reading Marlo's mind, he asked about Amy and the kids.

"The kids are good, loving life and breaking the bank," Marlo said. "But, things aren't too good between Amy and me. I don't know what's going on. She's distant and has no interest in the games, players or in anything I do. We hardly ever talk or see each other. I'm worried...really worried."

"Have you tried talking to her?"

"Yeah. She complained a lot about our lives being centered about basketball. Said she wanted more. Now she's very evasive...doesn't say much at all."

"I'm not an expert when it comes to women, Marlo, but I've been married for a long time. You've got to take care of home first.

A woman needs to feel as though she's number one in your life. Nothing or no one, except God, should be more important or come before your wife.

"I almost lost my wife," Coach B admitted. "A couple of years after we were married. Spent most of my time in the gym and set no boundaries when I was home. If the phone rang during dinner, I'd take the call. I did most of the scouting myself and was at every open gym or summer league game.

"I allowed basketball to interrupt many family events and dominate our home life. Well, I came home one day to find my wife standing at the door, bags packed. Said she was done and I knew she meant it. Gave me a reality check real quick and made me realize that my life was out of order. Work shouldn't come before family. You understand? Amy is a wonderful person. I hope y'all can work this out."

Of all that Coach B said, the point that resonated most with Marlo was the importance of taking care of home first. As he lay on the hotel's king-sized bed nursing his drink, he did some serious soul searching. Their lives were indeed deeply intertwined with his coaching career he admitted. In fact, he could think of few times spent with Amy that weren't basketball-related.

Ah ha! Their family trip to Hawaii last summer had nothing to do with basketball. Yes, he'd taken a few work-related calls and even scheduled a conference call for one of the days but that was it. His excitement was deflated, though, when he remembered that he'd taken film to watch and one afternoon stayed in the hotel while Amy and the kids went to the beach and then to dinner without him.

As he replayed his life with Amy, he sadly concluded that he had not taken care of home. He had provided all that money could buy, for sure. But he had not really taken care of the heart of his home: his wife.

"I've been so stupid," Marlo said out loud. He thought of the times he declined Amy's invitations to go for a walk or to the art museum. He remembered instances where she'd asked him to watch a movie with her but, more times than not, he'd said he had other things to do. Yet, until recent months, she seemed happy. "How would you know?" he asked himself. He truthfully and sadly admitted that he hadn't paid enough attention to know whether Amy was happy or not. He was caught up in his world determined to maintain his reputation as one of the best coaches of one of the most successful programs in the country.

He decided then to make things right. *I've got to fix my marriage. I love Amy and don't want to lose her.* He phoned the airline and began packing.

Marlo arrived home two days earlier than planned to find Amy in bed. Though it was noon, it appeared that she had been in bed all morning. He became concerned when he saw her red eyes and blotchy skin.

"Amy? What's wrong? Are you okay?" Marlo asked.

"I don't feel well," she responded softly.

"What is it? Do you need to see the doctor?"

"No. I'm just not having a good day. I wasn't expecting you home so I decided to stay in bed. I—I really miss Mom and Dad and it just hit me really hard today," Amy said. Tears sprang to her eyes. At least she was telling a partial truth.

"I'm sorry, Amy. I didn't know you still missed them."

"Of course I miss them," she replied angrily. "They're my parents. I will always miss them. How would you know what I feel anyway? You're never here."

"I'm sorry, Amy. I know you miss them. I just didn't know you had days like this," Marlo responded, feeling awkward and confused. He began unpacking.

"What are you doing home?" Amy asked. "I thought you were coming home Friday."

"I wanted to surprise you. I've been worried about you—about us—and wanted to be here with you." Marlo had never felt more unsure of himself.

Great. Just what I need. "I just need some time to myself. If you have something else to do, I don't mind," Amy said.

"I have nothing else to do. I'll be downstairs watching tv. Let me know if you need anything. I'll take care of dinner, too. Just relax." As an afterthought, he asked, "Do you want me to run a bath for you?"

Again, tears sprang to her eyes. He was being unusually attentive to her. *If only he knew.* "No, I may take a bath later. I just want to rest for a while. I'll be fine."

"Okay." Before he walked out of the bedroom, Marlo said, "Amy, I love you and I'm sorry you're hurting."

As soon as she was sure Marlo was downstairs, she put her face in her pillow and sobbed. Marlo's kindness hurt more than his indifference. She didn't deserve it.

Again, she listened to an internal conversation.

Moral Voice said firmly, "I warned you."

Defensive Voice responded with less conviction than before. "Yeah. Who knew Grace was crazy?"

"Crazy or not, Doug was her husband not yours. I warned you," Moral Voice repeated.

Amy put the pillow over her head, wanting to scream. Instead she cried, consumed by guilt and shame. Later, she reluctantly checked her phone. Up until now, she had ignored the numerous text message alerts. As she guessed, all of the messages were from Doug.

Was it just two days ago that her world had fallen apart? The weight of it all was overwhelming and disabling. So far, her identity had not been revealed and she was not captured in any of the footage shown on the various news broadcasts though that could not be said for Doug. Pictures of he and Grace were shown repeatedly, the story told and retold.

There was good news. Amy learned from the news updates that the little boy was alive though in critical condition. She prayed for his life and admitted that part of her motivation was selfish. How could she ever live with herself if he died?

Finally, she responded to Doug knowing that she could not continue to ignore him. She could only imagine the hell he was experiencing, his personal life exposed for all to judge. His text messages read:

"How are you?"

"Please respond. Need to know you're ok."

"Need to talk to you."

"Amy, please?"

The last message shocked her. *"Amy, I love you. Please contact me."*

Reluctantly, she typed the following: *I'm ok considering this nightmare. Think it best that we not see each other. Please don't contact me again. Sorry.*

Though she hit the send button she wasn't at all sure of her decision. In spite of the horrendous situation and her guilt, it was difficult to let Doug go. He wasn't just her lover, he was her friend. He had opened up a new world for her and filled it with joy. He'd given her the companionship that she longed to have with her husband.

Had she been thinking clearly, she would have realized that Marlo would see the news and, quite naturally, have questions since he knew that she and Doug worked on the fundraising committee together. She was not prepared for his questions as they watched the news together during dinner.

"Did you know about this? I can't believe you didn't mention it to me. This is terrible," Marlo said, waiting for an explanation, his eyes glued to the television.

"Yes, it is," Amy said, weakly. "I guess I forgot to mention it to you."

"Have you talked to Doug? How is he?" Marlo was now looking at Amy.

Avoiding his eyes, Amy said, "No, I haven't. I figured he had too much going on right now. Um-thanks for dinner. I've had enough. Think I'll take a bath."

Marlo watched Amy leave the room. How do you forget to mention major news like this? It didn't make sense.

Chapter Twenty-Two

━━━━━━━━━━ ✳ ━━━━━━━━━━

*D*oug read the text message from Amy again. *Don't do this, Amy. Please don't do this.* Desperate, he dialed her number only to get her voice mail. He left a message: *Amy, we need to talk. I love you. Please call me.*

The past two days were tortuous for Doug as he'd endured lengthy interviews by the police, unwanted media attention and his own unending guilt. Through it all he held on to the belief that he and Amy would be together. Amy was his lifeline. He loved her. He had no doubt that she loved him, too, but if that were true why end their relationship?

He finally convinced himself that she was reacting out of fear. She could have been killed; Grace wanted to kill her. He needed to give Amy time which he had in plentiful supply. Time and patience. If only he could talk to her.

Today was a relatively quiet day compared to the trauma of the past two days. The police investigators' questions were finally answered to their satisfaction and the media were becoming less of a nuisance. The worst part for Doug, aside from the shootings, was DJ's reaction. He had attacked Doug, physically and verbally, throwing punches while saying vile and hurtful things.

Doug allowed him to vent but when DJ's anger didn't subside, Doug had been forced to stronghold him. It was only when Doug inflicted pain that DJ stopped. Doug tried to reason with him but to no avail. Because of the publicity about Doug's affair, DJ blamed him for his mother's actions and death.

Before storming out, he said to Doug, "Forget that you have a son. I never want to see you again." Doug could only hope that, in time, DJ would feel differently.

The next day, Doug packed and moved back into the house that he and Grace had shared. There were several matters that needed his attention including the arrangements for Grace's funeral. Regardless of the circumstances, Grace was his wife and he had a responsibility to her. It did not surprise him that he had not heard from Irene, Grace's mother. Nor did it surprise him to find Irene in his home when he arrived. She was in the kitchen looking in the pantry. He noticed a suitcase on the floor but had no idea whether she was coming or going.

"What are you doing here?" Irene asked with open hostility.

"This is my home, Irene. What are you doing here?" Doug countered. He had never liked Irene and his patience with her was worn thin.

"I came to get some of Grace's things. I know she would want me to have them."

No doubt she had gathered Grace's most expensive jewelry and clothing.

"Have you thought about her funeral service?" Doug asked. "We need to make plans."

"I know damn well you don't plan to be at her funeral. DJ and I will make plans. You can go to hell," Irene said.

"Irene, Grace was still my wife, legally. You can't make plans without my permission, unless of course, you're willing to pay for everything."

He knew that would get Irene's attention. "So, either we do this together or we do it my way. It's your call." Doug made a mental note to cancel Grace's credit cards immediately.

Irene's words expressed the bitterness she felt. "I don't know what my daughter saw in you. You had a good woman—too good for you—and you treated her like dirt. She's dead because of you," she spewed.

"I'm sorry Grace is dead, Irene. I'm real sorry about that but I will not take responsibility for her actions."

"You'd better watch your back, you piece of scum," Irene yelled, pointing her finger in his face. "I'm warning—"

"Do not threaten me." Doug spoke in a low but deliberate voice. "It's time for you to leave. I'm proceeding with the arrangements whether we speak tomorrow or not."

Irene angrily walked to the door, yanking the huge suitcase along.

Doug's voice stopped her. "Before you leave, give me the house key. This is my house and you are welcome only by invitation."

Later that evening, Doug received an unexpected phone call.

"Hi Doug. It's Deidra. I'm not sure if you remember me."

"Of course I remember you."

"I wanted to call to offer my condolences. I was shocked when I saw the news and wanted you to know how sorry I am."

"Thanks Deidre. Your phone call means a great deal to me. It's been a difficult time to say the least but I'm taking it one day at a time. How are you?"

"I'm well. Aaron and I have been married for almost twenty years and have two kids." After a brief pause, Deidre continued. "I'm also calling to apologize. I feel badly about the way I handled things but I didn't know what to do."

"I'm not following you," Doug said. "You didn't know what to do about what?"

"The reason I suddenly cut off all communication with you was because Grace threatened me. She actually stalked and harassed me, calling at all times of the day and night at work and at home. At first, she pretended to befriend me but I realized later it was only to get information from me. The truth is I was afraid of her and I allowed her to intimidate me. Because of my fear, I requested a job transfer and moved to Atlanta which is where I met Aaron. He's the only good to come out of that situation. I know you have a lot going on and this may not be the best time but I regret not handling the situation differently and I wanted you to know."

I should have known. "I had no idea," Doug confessed. "Thanks for calling, Deidre, and for explaining. I really appreciate it and wish you well."

Six days later, Doug was awakened early by his alarm clock. The day was sunny but rain was expected to begin around noon. Doug grimaced as he nicked his chin while shaving, an indication of his nervousness and dread for what was to occur later. He sighed as he applied pressure to the bleeding wound.

This was one day he was eager to end. Fortunately, his sister and brother-in-law arrived shortly after learning of Grace's death and were a source of unconditional support, anticipating his needs while respecting his privacy. They planned to stay with him another week before returning to their home in Charleston. He hoped to persuade them to stay longer.

He found himself thinking of Amy. Again. He was in love with her and desperately missed her in spite of the circumstances. He had experienced something with Amy that he had not experienced before, certainly not with Grace. There was no selfishness, no competition, no self-promotion, no insulting or attacking behaviors. Instead, there was acceptance, respect, encouragement, affirmation, and excitement. Doug was happy when he was with Amy. Somehow, she captured his heart and, in doing so, inspired him to want more out of life than to be Grace's scapegoat for her anger and insecurities. Doug wondered about the status of Amy's marriage. Did Marlo know about them? How was she coping? If only he could talk with her...if only he could hear her voice.

Finally dressed for the occasion, Doug walked into the kitchen. Though there was an abundance of food, he had no appetite. Checking his watch, he realized it was time.

As much as Doug wanted a different outcome, Grace's funeral was a spectacle. Irene had the audacity to deviate from the agreed upon arrangements by having several persons speak who knew Grace from the old neighborhood. Their stories did not paint Grace in the most positive light, in Doug's opinion, but there was a contingent of Irene's family and friends who seemed quite entertained.

A service that should have lasted no more than ninety minutes dragged on and on. At times, Irene was loud and inconsolable in her grief at the church and gravesite. Other times, she could be heard laughing boisterously. Doug, expecting to be shunned by Grace's family, was pleasantly surprised that most were polite and cordial. Only a few of Grace's co-workers attended the service though a beautiful floral spray was sent from the company.

DJ's behavior was most peculiar and disturbing to Doug. DJ insisted upon his girlfriend sitting with him on the front row with immediate family and, at times, the two of them talked and snickered during the service. At no time did he cry or demonstrate sadness. Just another indication of DJ's immaturity or was his behavior a ploy to mask his pain, Doug wondered. Or, were DJ's problems of a more serious nature? Doug had cause to worry about his son's mental and emotional wellbeing and hoped to speak with DJ after the burial but it was not to be. DJ angrily let it be known that he had no desire to engage in a conversation with him.

Chapter Twenty-Three

————————❋————————

*T*hree weeks after the shooting resulting in Grace's death, Amy received a phone call from Abbie. They talked often but this call was different. It was early afternoon and Amy was in her customary state as of late, floundering around at a loss for direction or purpose.

Absent were the activities that before had filled her emptiness. The public and private meetings with Doug, their phone conversations and text messages. The persistent anticipation and longing went unfulfilled because of Amy's decision that Doug could no longer be a part of her life. The relationship that began as a diversion had developed into an essential part of her life and a huge source of her happiness. But, she had no choice other than to let him go. Now, she forced herself through the days as best she could so that Marlo would not be suspicious.

It was exhausting to coexist with Marlo as if all were well. The guilt was, at times, unbearable. To make matters worse, Marlo was spending a great deal of time at home. More than he ever had which meant she had little time to herself. As a result, there were few opportunities to let go of the weighty facade she carried. She wanted— needed—to mourn what she had lost and to figure out what to do with her life.

She finally picked up her ringing cellphone. "Hey Abbie."

"Have you been watching tv?" Abbie whispered loudly and urgently.

"No, I've not had it on today—"

"Something terrible has happened. Turn it on right now," Abbie ordered.

Amy turned on the television in her bedroom and, after seeing the headlines, collapsed rather than sat. She couldn't believe what she was seeing. BUSINESSMAN DOUGLAS SHIPMAN FOUND DEAD IN HIS HOME. FOUL PLAY IS SUSPECTED. She stared at the photo of Doug being displayed on the screen under the caption.

The news reporter said, "...Mr. Shipman was the husband of Grace Shipman who, you may remember, was killed by police three weeks ago as she publicly confronted her husband with a gun..."

Amy heard her name being called from a distance. She looked in the direction of the sound and realized that she had dropped the phone on the bed. She picked it up and, without thinking, disconnected the call. It rang again but she ignored it.

Amy sat, motionless, on the bed staring at the television but no longer processing the information. Her mind was in a continual spiral. *Doug is dead. It's my fault. Doug is dead. It's my fault. Doug is dead. It's all my fault. Oh my God. What have I done?*

She felt more alone, ashamed and guilt-ridden than she ever thought possible. Her parents were gone, her marriage was empty, her children had their own lives, she was an immoral woman who'd broken her marriage vows, she'd caused a woman to attack her husband, and her lover—and friend—was now dead. *This can't be my life. I can't—I can't—I can't. Too much.* Slowly, Amy stood and walked to the bathroom.

Meanwhile, Marlo sat in his home office working on a new offensive scheme while watching the news. What a tragedy, he thought, shaking his head. Poor Doug. Dead. Since Amy had been out of sorts lately, he thought he should be the one to tell her. Hopefully, she was resting and not watching television. He made a quick phone call to his new assistant, Adam, before walking upstairs to check on Amy. He found her lying across the bed, sleeping.

"Good. She's resting. I'm not going to wake her," Marlo said softly to himself. He was just about to walk out of the room when he noticed a pill bottle on the floor beside the bed. Strange. Amy was very careful about medicines and would never be so careless as to leave a bottle—

Marlo didn't finish his thought. Instead, his heart constricted with anxiety. "Amy? Amy? Wake up, Amy," he said while gently shaking her. No response. "Amy! Baby! Wake up!" Marlo shouted with panic in his voice. He shook her harder. Still, no response. *Her pulse. Check her pulse.* It was very faint—hardly detectable—and that's when he realized that his wife was in grave danger. He quickly dialed 911 and anxiously waited for the ambulance's arrival.

Please, God, don't let me lose her. Don't let her die.

Marlo watched, helplessly, as the paramedics tended to Amy in route to the hospital. She appeared to be peacefully sleeping except they couldn't wake her. After the initial panic when he had time to think, he tried to understand it all. He was beyond baffled.

Amy and suicide? The two didn't go together. Why did she want to die? He had no explanation even though Brianna and MJ—who arrived at the hospital shortly after he called them—were looking to him to provide answers to their numerous questions. They, too, were confused and traumatized by their mother's actions. He simply didn't know what to tell them or how to help them. How could he help them when he couldn't help himself?

He'd finally insisted that they go home to rest. There was nothing they could do at the hospital other than sit and wait. They were both exhausted and distraught and it agonized him to see them in such pain.

Truthfully, he couldn't cope with his wife's situation while trying to be a tower of strength for the kids. He needed to focus on only one challenge at a time so he'd called Abbie to take MJ and Brianna home. Poor Abbie. He knew he was asking a lot of her as Amy's best friend but there was no one he trusted more, especially in a crisis. When he'd informed her of the circumstances, she had said, "Oh no! I knew something was wrong."

"What do you mean you knew something was wrong?" Marlo asked.

"Uh—it's just that she hasn't been herself lately," Abbie said.

She regretted not being totally truthful with Marlo but now was not the time. In spite of her inner turmoil, she assured Marlo that she would take good care of the kids.

"Call me as soon as you have any news," she said. "Know that I'll be praying."

Marlo nodded. "Thanks Abbie."

The attending physician told him later that Amy's stomach had been pumped and she was being given liquids intravenously to help flush the toxic medication from her system. Fortunately, her internal organs and brain function were not compromised. Physically, the doctors expected a full recovery. The biggest unknown was her emotional and mental recovery.

Once she was stable physically, she would be assessed by the attending psychiatrist to determine the appropriate treatment. Based on the history Marlo provided—and the fact that Amy attempted to end her life—the doctor advised that intensive therapy would likely be necessary. After, she would be released into the care of an outpatient therapist. Those were the usual treatment options the doctor cautioned and emphasized that the psychiatrist would determine the best plan after his assessment.

The coffee was bitter and lukewarm but it served the needed purpose of keeping Marlo awake. Because Amy would likely sleep through the night, the doctors had advised him to go home but he couldn't. He looked at his wife and tears spilled from his eyes. He'd been so frightened when he realized that he might lose her and while he was grateful she was alive, he had questions that only she could answer. As he thought about the past few weeks, some things were beginning to make more sense. Her sadness, melancholia, moodiness, and lethargy. It was as if she was simply going through the motions. She had tried to convince him that she was fine but he hadn't been fooled. Something was wrong but he never imagined this outcome.

Because he worked on a college campus, he was required—along with all staff and faculty—to be trained annually in suicide prevention. As a result, he considered himself quite informed on the subject and was aware of the latest statistics, risk factors, warning signs, and high risk groups.

He knew that, often, suicide was attempted because of a feeling of hopelessness. *Did Amy feel hopeless? Did she feel as though her death was the best solution to her problem? Surely not.* Marlo could not accept that. He didn't understand why she would choose to die. *Was she suffering from depression? How did she go from being a happy and vivacious woman to one who wanted to die? What was wrong? They had a great life. Maybe not perfect but it was a good life. And if something was troubling her, why didn't she talk to me? To Abbie? Did she even think of me and the kids? Did she consider how her death would affect us? Her brothers and sisters? Oh my God,* Marlo thought. *I've got to notify her family. I've got to call Mom and Janole, too.*

He looked at his watch and decided to wait for a few hours. There was no need to awake everyone. After all, he reasoned, Amy was going to be all right. Plus, he still had no answers and he knew that their families would bombard him with questions.

Groggy and nauseated, Amy tried to open her eyelids but they felt extremely heavy. *My mouth feels so dry. If only I could have a sip of water. So thirsty.*

"Wa-wa," she moaned. She could feel herself going back to sleep and was too tired to fight it.

Marlo, who had finally fallen asleep, was startled awake by Amy's moaning. Instantly, he was at her bedside.

"Amy? Baby? Can you hear me? I'm right here, Amy. Can you hear me? Talk to me, baby." She didn't respond. Marlo held her hand and laid his head on the bed. Desperate for answers, he was forced to wait.

Chapter Twenty-Four

━━━━━━━━━━ ✳ ━━━━━━━━━━

*E*ight long agonizing weeks had passed since Amy's attempt to take her life and Marlo had few answers. The one thing he knew for sure was that Amy had been given a clean bill of health, physically. He also knew that she didn't want to see him. She made that crystal clear when she had finally awakened and remembered the circumstances. He doubted that he would ever forget their conversation. Even now as he thought of it, it caused him to relive the hurt and anger he experienced.

"Amy, it's me, honey. How are you?" he had asked when she was fully awake and lucid.

Initially, she said nothing and refused to look at him. Tears continuously rolled down her face. Finally, she made eye contact with him albeit brief.

"I'm sorry. I'm so sorry," she said before sobbing uncontrollably.

Thinking she was talking about the suicide attempt, Marlo said, "It's okay, Amy. Everything will be okay."

"Nothing will ever be okay," she said as she continued to cry. "Ever again and it's all my fault. I need you to leave. I don't want to see you right now. Please leave and don't come back."

Marlo had stood still, speechless. He expected an explanation, not rejection. In fact, he felt as though he and the kids were entitled to an explanation. As much as he wanted to be sensitive to the circumstances, he couldn't stifle his anger.

"Amy, don't you think you owe me an explanation? I've been worried sick. So have the kids—"

"I can't. I just can't," she had said and turned away from him. "Please leave me alone."

"What do I tell the kids?" Marlo asked, feeling helpless.

"Tell them I love them and I need some time," Amy said, sniffling. "And tell them I'm sorry."

Marlo had walked away feeling a range of emotions. Anger, disappointment, worry, shame, embarrassment, confusion, pain, and sadness. The overriding emotion, however, was anger. His wife—who had been acting strangely for weeks—attempted to kill herself, and then refused to talk to him. In fact, she didn't want to see him. *What the hell is going on? And, what am I supposed to tell Brianna and MJ? This is crazy and I don't know how to deal with it.*

Marlo had driven around for hours, thinking, to the point of exhaustion. Finally, he had phoned Abbie and told her about Amy's behavior. If anyone had insight as to what was going on with Amy, it was Abbie.

"Come home," Abbie had said. "Let's talk."

"Okay. But what do we tell the kids?" Marlo asked, feeling at a loss.

"I'll handle it. Just follow my lead. We'll talk to them together when you get here," Abbie said.

The conversation with Brianna and MJ had gone better than Marlo anticipated primarily because of Abbie's expertise as a mental health counselor. And, as Abbie reminded him, his "kids" were no longer children, but young adults. Abbie and Marlo were as forthright as they could possibly be without dramatizing the situation.

Abbie said, "Your mom is doing well, physically, but has asked for time to deal with the things that are bothering her and we all need to respect that, including your dad and me. We are very confident that this is the right thing to do for her even though it's difficult for us. I know that she loves us all. The best way we can help her and show her how much we love her is by respecting her desires."

"I really want to see her," Brianna had said, tearfully. "I need to know that she's all right."

"She doesn't want to see us, Bri. Weren't you listening?" MJ did not attempt to hide his anger.

Abbie thought for a few seconds. "Guys, this is no different from a physical illness, right? We would let her rest as much as possible without disturbing her because its what her body needs. Now her mind needs rest so that she can begin to handle things one at a time until she's healthy again. I know you're confused—we all are—because we don't know what's troubling her. But I know how much your mother loves all of us and it's because she loves us so much that its difficult for her to face us right now. We have to think of your mom and put her needs first. Does this make sense?"

Brianna and MJ both nodded though neither looked convinced.

Abbie continued. "I'll go to the hospital tomorrow. Mind you, she may not want to see me either so there are no guarantees. But if she does, I'll let her know how much you guys miss her and want to see her. I'll give you a complete report, I promise. Sound good?"

"Yes," they both answered in unison, their relief obvious.

It was Marlo who spoke next. "There's two things that I expect of you, Bri and MJ. One, to resume your lives as much as possible. Your mom would want that, too. Secondly, don't blame yourselves. None of us saw this coming but we are going to get through this. Understand?"

Again, they nodded. Brianna looked at her father.

"Dad, how are you? You look tired. Are you okay?"

Marlo said, "I will be."

Now he was on his way to meet Amy, having been summoned by her, and he had no idea what to expect. He was as confused as he was eight weeks ago. After being discharged from the hospital, Amy decided to stay at her parents' home in New York rather than return home. Her favorite aunt, her mother's sister, lived in the home now and Amy's youngest brother lived nearby. Though she was embarrassed and pained by her actions, she felt most secure at her parents' home. More than anything, it allowed her to distance herself from her husband, unpleasant memories and all-consuming guilt.

Marlo pulled the rental car into the familiar driveway, turned off the ignition and took a deep breath. He looked at the brick ranch home without really seeing it. Was his marriage over or was Amy coming home? What caused her to want to take her life? Had she resolved those issues? Nervous and anxious, he inhaled deeply trying to calm himself. Not only was he uncertain of the future, he resented that his well-ordered life was unsettled and out of his control. Amy was calling all the shots.

"Hi Marlo. Thanks for coming," Amy said in greeting. She and Marlo embraced, tentatively, both unsure of the other's feelings.

"How are you, Amy?" Marlo asked, his concern apparent.

"Much better. Therapy is helping a lot," she said, awkwardly. "Can I get you anything?"

"No, I'm fine," Marlo said as they settled in the small but comfortable family room.

Amy broke the awkward silence. "Aunt Betty is working today so we have complete privacy. I know you have questions and I know this has been extremely difficult for you."

"You're right on both accounts," Marlo replied.

"I'm sorry—so sorry—for all I've put you through. And our family. I never meant to hurt you and the kids," Amy said, wringing her hands. "Things spiraled out of control so quickly."

"What things?"

"Me, us...everything."

"Amy, I have no idea what you're talking about," Marlo said, his impatience rising.

"I know. I messed up big time," Amy said. "And I've also had to face some things."

She grabbed several tissues and wiped the tears from her eyes.

Marlo said nothing.

"I have been so lonely," Amy said. "For such a long, long time. You were never at home and when you were, you were either tired or consumed with basketball—"

Marlo interrupted. "So, I'm responsible for what you did?"

"No, that's not what I'm saying," Amy said, softly. "But I'm trying to explain how things spiraled out of control for me and my loneliness was a big part of it. I'm not excusing my actions, I'm trying to explain them. It's not a pretty story but what I'm about to tell you is the truth. My truth. Do you want to hear it?"

"Go ahead," Marlo said.

"I was very lonely and unfulfilled in our marriage. Not in the beginning but after a few years. Our life revolved around basketball and I wanted more than that. I wanted to talk about other things and do things with you that had nothing to do with your job as a coach. I wanted you to share in my interests.

"I didn't realize how badly I needed that...I tried to explain that to you many times but it didn't seem to make a difference and I was hurt by that. I see now that my involvement in the kids' activities was filling a void for me. Don't get me wrong. I loved being a mother and enjoyed doing things with them and for them but somewhere along the way I lost me. And, that became crystal clear when they left for college. I no longer had anything to fill the void."

She paused to take a sip of water and wipe her eyes. "I became so angry and since it seemed you weren't going to change, I decided to take matters into my own hands. That's why I stopped attending games and participating in other basketball-related activities. If you didn't care about what was important to me then I was going to stop caring about the one thing that was important to you. The truth is that our relationship was one-dimensional, Marlo."

"I knew you were unhappy, Amy, but I had no idea you felt this way," Marlo said.

"Because you didn't listen," Amy said, factually. "It seemed as if you really didn't care about me."

Marlo was becoming angry. "So you invited me here to tell me how much I am to blame for this situation. If that's the case—"

Amy interrupted quickly, her own anger rising.

"I called you here so that we could talk and so that I could be honest with you. There's plenty of blame to go around. Do I feel as though you are partly responsible for my loneliness and pain? Yes, I do. Did you cause me to do what I did? No, you didn't. I take responsibility for my actions but I cannot and will not take full responsibility for the state of our marriage. A marriage I'm not sure I want and you may not want either after you hear all I have to say."

Amy's last statement jolted Marlo. To hear Amy speak about their marriage ending was a shock and confirmation that their marriage was indeed in serious trouble. He loved Amy and wanted to spend the rest of his life with her. In fact, he couldn't imagine his life without her and told her so.

"Well, you may not feel that way in a few minutes," Amy said. She sighed heavily.

"You know about the YMCA fundraiser and how much I enjoyed my involvement. Now maybe you can understand why I enjoyed it so much. It gave me purpose and fulfillment to do something worthwhile and important. I enjoyed the people and found out that I was really good at fundraising. My talents were appreciated. I guess I felt validated and significant...things that I hadn't felt for a long, long time. We worked hard as a committee and because we spent so much time together we developed friendships. Doug and I became very good friends. We found we had things in common, worked well together as a team, and enjoyed talking to each other." Amy couldn't continue talking. She cried for several minutes.

Marlo assumed she was crying because of Doug's tragic death. "I'm so sorry about his death. He seemed like a decent guy."

"He was a decent guy. I was at the restaurant the day of the shooting," Amy said, her voice trembling. "It was horrible. The committee met at Pezazzi's that day to celebrate our success and begin planning for next year. As Doug and I walked out of the restaurant, he was confronted by Grace who was pointing a gun at him. Doug pushed me out of the way so I wouldn't get hurt. I actually fell and crawled to the nearest alley." Amy shook her head as she recalled the events.

"Everything happened so fast...there was chaos everywhere... people were screaming and running to safety. I've never been more afraid in my life. It was like a movie except it wasn't. This was real life."

Tears streamed down Amy's face. The raw pain that Marlo saw in her expression touched him deeply.

He said, "Im so sorry, Amy. Why didn't you tell me?"

Ignoring his question, Amy said, "I saw the bullet hit the little boy's chest. Poor baby. He had no idea what happened. His parents were inconsolable. It was awful. I also witnessed Grace's death. It was as if she was crazed. The police warned her but—"

Marlo was beginning to make a few connections. "So, is that what was bothering you when I came home early? The day you were in bed and said you were missing your parents? Was that the truth?"

Amy shook her head. "I do miss my parents, at times painfully so. But, no, I didn't tell you the truth that day. I had witnessed those shootings and it sickened me and scared me to death."

"That's understandable, Amy. I would have been shaken, too, but I still don't understand why you didn't tell me that you were there. Why didn't you tell me?"

Amy sighed. "Because of my guilt and shame."

Marlo's confusion was apparent. "This isn't making sense to me. The shooting wasn't your fault."

"I wish that were true. Here comes the hard part," she said, sighing deeply. "Grace was angry with Doug because he was having an affair and had moved out of their home."

There was complete silence in the room. Amy had expected Marlo to explode but when she looked at him, she saw confusion, not understanding.

Marlo said, "The news coverage mentioned that but what does that have to do with —"

"Doug and I were having an affair, Marlo." She hastily added, "It wasn't planned. Neither of us were looking to have an affair. We were both miserable and lonely. It just happened."

"You and Doug were having an affair? Sleeping together?" Marlo asked, incredulously.

Amy nodded.

"How long?" he managed to ask, feeling as if he had been punched in the guts.

"Several months."

"Months? Months?" he repeated as he envisioned all sorts of passionate scenarios which disgusted and angered him. "I can't believe this. Why would you do this?"

"I'm so sorry," Amy said. The magnitude of her actions was almost unbearable. She was responsible for so much pain and destruction. She never intended for any of this to happen.

"Did you love him? Were you planning to leave me for him?"

"I don't know. Uh-we hadn't made plans."

That was not the answer Marlo expected.

"You don't know? You don't know?" he yelled as he stood and began pacing, back and forth. Suddenly, he stopped and turned to face Amy with a rage that frightened her.

"You tried to kill yourself the same day that Doug's death was announced. You tried to kill yourself because your lover was dead, didn't you? You loved him so much that you didn't want to live without him. Unbelievable. You wanted to die because he died."

"No! That's not true," Amy stated, her voice cracking with emotion. "I wanted to die because I was deeply ashamed of myself and the terrible things that had happened. Two people were dead and a child critically wounded. It was all too much for me to handle at that moment. I felt responsible. It all happened because Doug and I were having an affair. I'm not proud of that."

Marlo was furious and battling to maintain control.

"I would think not. Do you know what you put us through? We thought you were going to die. Did you think about the kids at all? No, you only thought about yourself and your precious Doug. He got what he deserved, didn't he? If he wasn't dead, I'd kill him myself."

Amy gasped. "Marlo, you don't mean that. That's a horrible thing to say."

He looked at Amy with disgust. "I mean every word. Make no mistake about it." He stood, rigid, with his back to her for several moments then turned around to face her.

"Let me get this straight. You—my wife—were having an affair with Doug, a married man...playing me for a complete fool...for months. And, at no point did you have the decency to either end your relationship with him or end our marriage. And—"

"I didn't—"

"Shut up, Amy. I'm talking now. It's important that I get this straight," he said with sarcasm. "Rather than talk to me or Abbie or anybody, you decided to kill yourself and to hell with me and the kids? Forever, we'd be wondering why you decided to end your life, blaming ourselves."

He paused just briefly. "Who are you? You're not the woman I married because the woman I married wouldn't be whoring around pretending to be something she's not. A fake! Was Doug the only one? Is there anything else I need to know?"

"Doug was the only one," she replied. "I know this is difficult, Marlo, and I know you're angry and hurt but you need to know this. The woman you married has been lonely and hurting for a long, long time and she tried to talk to her husband about it but he never heard her. I made terrible choices and I couldn't face you. I was—am— ashamed and didn't want you to know what I'd done. I'm so very sorry for my actions and I hope you can forgive me. I hope God can forgive me, too," Amy said, with tears streaming down her face.

Marlo laughed, sarcastically. "Now you think about God. That's funny. Did you think about Him while you and Doug were screwing? Yeah, maybe He can forgive you because it will be a cold day in hell before I do. You disgust me!" Marlo said as he stomped out of the house and slammed the door.

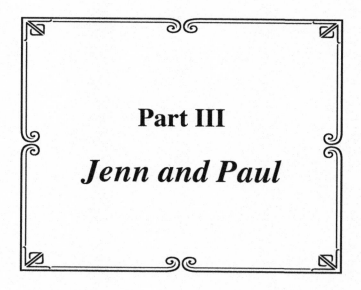

Part III

Jenn and Paul

Chapter Twenty-Five

———————✳———————

Though the events weren't planned to coincide, Jenn could not have been more pleased. The twins were away at a soccer camp at the University of Southern California at the same time that Paul was in Los Angeles attending a legal conference. The house was peaceful and quiet. The only noise was the soft hum of the refrigerator as Jenn enjoyed breakfast at her leisure. Paul would return on Friday so Jenn planned to enjoy her alone time this week. The twins were flying from camp to New York City to vacation with their grandparents there and in the Hamptons, affording she and Paul the luxury of reacquainting as a couple while disconnecting briefly from their parenting responsibilities.

Dressed in running gear, Jenn had already completed her three mile run and decided to work in her flower garden before showering and running errands. But, right now, she lingered over a second cup of chamomile honey tea and made a mental list of all she needed to get done. Take clothes to the cleaners, confirm the order with the caterer for Saturday's dinner party, restock their wine collection, get a manicure and pedicure, clean the refrigerator, have the carpet shampooed, and order flowers. Tomorrow she planned to visit the spa for a facial and massage. Her hair appointment was scheduled for Wednesday.

This was no ordinary dinner party. It was a farewell of sorts to their closest friends and most significant acquaintances. Jenn was excited about the move to Washington, DC, primarily because she would be closer to her parents and Janole. But, she was sad, too. There were many special memories for her in Seattle.

She recalled the day she and Paul coincidentally met while shopping at Angie's, one of her favorite boutiques. She had no way of knowing then that this handsome stranger was her destiny, her future, her life long partner. Their relationship amazed her still. Just this morning, they had tenderly made love and it felt like the first time. The chemistry...the magic...the desire...the love...were as strong as ever. She knew that their union was a special gift, one she didn't take for granted.

She'd almost lost him. She'd almost lost it all. Her marriage, sobriety, sanity, happiness—her life—were slipping away from her. The memories remained vivid of her unhealthy and destructive lifestyle. Even more vivid were memories of the circumstances that caused her such great pain. Her brother's death when she was a child, parents so engrossed in their pain that they ignored her for years, sexual molestation by a stranger, and her father's inappropriate behavior during her teen and adult years. Until therapy, she didn't know that her father's inappropriate behavior had a name—emotional incest. All along, she'd thought she was the problem when, in actuality, she was the victim. She had suffered greatly as a result of tragic circumstances, including a dysfunctional home environment, and was on the brink of losing everything if not for an amazing occurrence.

The turning point of her life was hearing God's voice the day after Tam's funeral. She has often shared this story for she was one, at that time, who doubted God's existence. Yet, He spoke to her. The impact and irony continued to amaze her. After paying final respects to Tam—a time of profound loss—her new life was about to begin.

God's mysterious ways.

Her arduous journey to recovery began when she left Paul to find herself. And, though it was a necessary journey, her greatest fear throughout was that Paul would not wait for her...that he would give up on her and their marriage. But, he hadn't and neither had God. It was as if God was waiting for her to take the first step of faith. And after that initial step, He revealed Himself to her—and Paul—in ways completely unexpected. He gave her the grace to forgive those who had hurt her, including herself. One of the greatest blessings, aside from her relationship with God, was the birth of their twin daughters. Two bundles of joy at the same time. Needless to say, life changed drastically.

Jenn adored her daughters but, at times, she was overwhelmed by them which is why she appreciated this week of solitude. They were energetic and precocious, especially Lynn, as little girls. Ruth was more inclined to listen and consider consequences. Lynn, on the other hand, was more inclined to act with little regard for the outcomes. Though younger by two minutes, Lynn was definitely the leader of the two and had been responsible for many of the challenges Jenn faced as a mother.

The twin's resemblance and allegiance to each other was unlike anything Jenn had witnessed. Even if Ruth—the more level-headed one—disagreed with Lynn, she never verbalized it to her parents.

They were charming girls—often described as stunningly beautiful—who had grown accustomed to being the center of attention and stealing the show. From Jenn, they inherited their slim athletic frames, cobalt blue eyes and black wavy hair that they often wore in a pony tail. Their olive complexion, which tanned deeply during summer months, was very similar to Paul's skin tone.

Most couldn't tell the twins apart. Even Jenn struggled at times from a distance but there were distinct differences. Ruth had a small mole—she referred to it as a beauty mark—on the right side of her face above the lip. Lynn did not. That is until recently. Lynn decided that she wanted a mole, too, so she had one tattooed on her face without Paul's or Jenn's permission.

When they questioned her behavior, her belligerent response was, "I did it because I wanted to. Why would I need your permission? Now I look just like Ruth. How could you be upset with that?" But Jenn was upset. She sensed a deviousness—an ulterior motive— behind Lynn's actions.

Another distinction between the two girls was their habit when concentrating. Lynn tended to bite her nails whereas Ruth twirled her hair around her finger. When disturbed or startled, Ruth responded with a questioning smile. Lynn responded with a frown. To Jenn these were subtle but significant differences.

Sitting alone in her kitchen with no distractions, Jenn was able to think freely and clearly. The truth was that Lynn's behavior worried her. Her daughter was manipulative, cunning and secretive. It pained Jenn to admit the truth even to herself. Was this normal teenage behavior? A phase? Did she, as a mother, tend to overreact as Lynn often accused?

Paul tended to agree with Lynn and faulted Jenn for being too strict. But, in Jenn's opinion, the girls had Paul wrapped around their fingers. They could convince him of almost anything.

"Dad is cool, Mom. You're such a nag." She'd heard that or similar sentiments often enough.

She and Paul agreed about most matters or, at least, understood the other's point of view. The one exception pertained to the girls. Their biggest arguments were about the girls' behavior and appropriate discipline. From Jenn's perspective, Paul refused to see the underlying motivation driving the girls' behavior and often defended them. Their behavior was never as serious to Paul as it was to her.

A perfect example occurred the previous summer while Jenn was out of town for several days. The girls invited friends over even though she and Paul had expressly forbid it. Jenn held Paul partly responsible, too. During her absence, she reminded him to check on the girls while he was at work but he felt as though they could be trusted. A week after Jenn's return, she and Paul had been furious— and embarrassed—to learn the truth in a casual conversation with another parent.

Several days during Jenn's absence, their home had been a hangout for a large group of kids. With no adult supervision, God only knew what all went on in their house with inquisitive, hormone-raging teens. Suppose someone had gotten hurt or drowned in the pool?

When the girls were questioned, Lynn maintained that their actions weren't disobedient...that Paul trusted them...that it was their home, too, and they should be able to invite friends over whenever they wanted to do so...that it was a spur of the moment decision and they didn't mean any harm...that they just wanted to have fun and thought their home was the safest place. Again, Jenn was made to feel as if she were being unreasonable and was incensed as she listened to Lynn's rationalizations. Ruth, as usual, said very little.

Jenn wanted to impose major consequences, including restriction for the remainder of the summer and no allowance, but Paul backed down, minimizing their behavior. He accepted their tearful apology and, after giving them a stern talking to, felt as though no further consequences were necessary. Jenn was not as accepting or forgiving. Time after time, she watched in amazement and frustration as the girls manipulated their father.

As Jenn saw it, her daughters—with Lynn as the leader—stopped at nothing to get what they wanted. Jenn could, at times, see Ruth's struggle in challenging their authority but Lynn was determined and headstrong. Jenn was worried. Her daughters were no longer precocious little girls. They were young women and their behavior was disturbing.

Looking at her watch now, Jenn was surprised that it was almost noon. The flower bed could wait. After a quick shower, she assembled Paul's suits and shirts before heading to the girls' room to gather their few items needing to be dry cleaned. She stood in their room, admiring its beauty and feeling like an intruder.

It was decorated tastefully in shades of lavender, gray and green. There were numerous photos of the girls from infancy to now causing memories of her daughters to flood her mind. In quick snapshots, she saw them as infants so beautiful and innocent; then they were carefree toddlers laughing and playing as they discovered the world. She recalled their first day of school and various school events, the soccer matches, holidays, vacations, church programs, and birthday parties. Before Jenn realized it, tears were in her eyes. She loved her daughters with all her heart and it saddened her that she did not completely trust them...that she sensed a deviousness.

It had been a while since Jenn felt welcomed in this room or welcomed in their lives for that matter. She missed their hugs, kisses, and talks. They no longer needed her; they had each other and were inseparable. It was the girls' decision to share a room. She and Paul encouraged their individuality and offered them the option of separate rooms but they had declined.

Jenn, who had no living siblings, thought their close bond was especially endearing. But, in spite of herself, she wondered what secrets may be hidden in this room. Janole had encouraged her to "investigate" because of her concerns about the girls' behavior but Jenn had always respected their privacy. Perhaps too much, she thought. Now — for a reason that she could not explain — she felt compelled to look around. The girls would refer to her behavior as snooping. No, I'm exploring, she thought smugly.

She found nothing suspicious or concerning in their bedroom or private bathroom. No hidden drugs, thank God. And, there were no indications of sexual activity. Jenn was relieved. Of course, they had their tablets and phones with them but, overall, she felt encouraged. *Perhaps, I have been overreacting.* She decided to strip the beds completely so that everything could be washed, including the mattress covers. Just before the girls returned, she'd put fresh flowers in their room and an assortment of their favorite chocolates. She smiled, anticipating their return.

After the beds were completely stripped, she performed a cursory check under the beds and mattresses expecting to find nothing. Instead, she found two items. Both disturbing; both under Lynn's mattress. Marijuana and a journal.

Marijuana! Jenn was heartbroken. One of her biggest fears was confirmed. The girls were smoking pot. She knew this stuff was dangerous, too. Yes, she smoked marijuana a few times while in college but from all that she'd read, today's marijuana was ten times more dangerous and addicting that the marijuana of the 70's.

As she sat on the bare mattress, many questions raced through her mind. *How long have they been smoking? Where did they get it? Who else knew? Are they using other drugs? Are they both smoking?*

She'd found nothing incriminating or suspicious among Ruth's things. Still, she knew Ruth wasn't innocent. Even if Ruth wasn't smoking, she had knowledge of Lynn's behavior; yet, she'd said nothing.

Jenn opened the turquoise journal with no reservations about reading it. Perhaps she would have ignored it had it been the only item stashed under the mattress. But, after discovering the marijuana, Jenn was no longer concerned about the girls' privacy.

At some point while reading the journal, Jenn began trembling as she attempted to reconcile the disturbing contents with the sixteen-year old author who was her daughter. The journal was laced with profanity and contained explicit information about Lynn's sexual desires and behaviors though her sexual partners were not identified.

Jenn's hopes were shattered; yet, her suspicions that something was amiss were confirmed. There was no doubt that her daughter was sexually active—but not just active. This was no narrative of one smitten with a boyfriend who had finally given in to her desires. Nor did there seem to be an indication of peer pressure. No, her daughter was promiscuous, to put it kindly. *You stupid, stupid girl. What is wrong with you? Have you not heard of AIDS? Herpes? STDs? Pregnancy? Do you have no decency or self-respect?*

Jenn was furious but at a loss for what to do with this information. Her immediate thought was to phone Paul but, because he was a featured presenter at the conference, she didn't want to ruin this opportunity for him. She persuaded herself to wait until Friday. After all, the girls were away. Good thing, too. Jenn didn't trust herself right now. At this moment, she wanted to wring Lynn's disrespectful neck for her disgusting behavior. *Poor Paul. He would be devastated.*

Though the evidence was indisputable, Jenn was having a difficult time accepting the implications about her daughter. So who was the real Lynn? The popular, well-liked girl who was an honor student and exceptional soccer player? The girl who attended church regularly and was actively involved in the church's youth activities and missions work? Or this girl with slutty behaviors who smoked pot? Everyone spoke so highly of the twins. Perhaps we've been talking to the wrong people, Jenn thought.

Where have we failed? What did we do wrong? How did we not know? Drugs and promiscuity? And, just as quickly as anger overtook her, it was replaced with overwhelming sadness, disappointment and pain. Sobs wracked Jenn's body. She cried until there were no tears left.

Finally, she looked at the journal in her lap and forced herself to continue reading and became even more troubled. Apparently, a new girl had recently enrolled in school who was challenging Lynn's starting position on the soccer team and receiving a great deal of attention from the boys. Lynn's words had a chilling affect on Jenn. *"...She thinks she's all that. Even told me that RJ asked her out on a date. She thinks we're friends. Ha! Ha! Clueless! I will ruin her. She has no idea who she's messing with. Already got a plan. Can't wait for team camp. That bitch will be so sorry she ever moved here. LOL!"*

Jenn was flabbergasted and emotionally drained, the priorities she had outlined for the day no longer important.

A couple of days later, Jenn awakened after a restless sleep with team camp on her mind. She'd received brief text messages from both girls saying that they were having fun and had little free time but, in light of her newfound knowledge, she wondered how things were really going. She decided to call the coach just to check in. While she didn't want to raise suspicions, she could not ignore Lynn's journal reference to team camp.

"Please God, let everything be all right," Jenn whispered as she dialed the coach's number.

"Hello. Coach Browning speaking."

"Good morning, Coach. This is Jenn Donaldson. How are you?"

"I'm okay. I was just about to phone you. I'm assuming the girls told you about the incident. Is that why you're calling?"

"Incident? What incident?" Jenn asked, alarmed.

"There was a situation involving the newest member of our team. I've been phoning parents this morning."

"What happened?" Jenn asked, dreading the answer.

"She became very ill shortly after lunch yesterday and had to be hospitalized. We're not sure what made her so sick but we know that it's not contagious. None of the other girls have gotten sick. Everyone else is fine."

The new girl? Sick? Hospitalized? "I'm sorry to hear about this. Is she okay now?"

"She's still very sick. Her parents are here. Out of consideration for their privacy, I don't want to share specific details but she will probably be hospitalized for a while."

"Oh my God. That's horrible. Could it possibly be food poisoning?" Jenn asked.

"We're not really sure but no one else became ill," Coach Browning said. "I have a few other calls to make but I want to reassure you that your daughters are fine. And I couldn't be more pleased about the camp itself. It was recommended to me by a colleague and it really is top notch. We're busy from sun up to sun down with matches and other activities. Great competition."

"Okay. Well, if there is anything we can do don't hesitate to contact my husband or me. You know you have our support."

"Thank you," Coach Browning said. "I really appreciate that."

"Don't forget that the girls are flying from LA to New York," Jenn said.

"I haven't forgotten. Thanks for calling and don't worry."

But Jenn couldn't help but worry. That's all she'd done since the discovery in the twins' room. *Lynn, what did you do?* As much as Jenn wanted to believe that the new girl's illness was happenstance, she knew there was more to the story. Only one girl became ill? And it just happened to be the new girl? The same girl Lynn referred to in her journal? Exactly how far would Lynn go to get what she wanted? To prove her point? Jenn didn't want to overreact; yet, she now wondered whether her daughter was capable of being malicious. Now you're going too far, Jenn, she admonished herself. *Lynn would not harm anyone. Not physically. Would she? I sure hope not. God, help me.*

Chapter Twenty-Six

---✳︎---

*J*enn waited anxiously while Paul read the journal. She had already told him about the marijuana but couldn't bring herself to tell him about the specific contents in the journal. She simply handed it to him and waited. It was Sunday afternoon.

He had returned Friday evening exhausted but excited about the conference and his presentation. Saturday, the dinner party consumed their time and attention. Looking back, Jenn had no idea how she managed to pull it off. Attending to the details while struggling with her new reality was extremely difficult. Fortunately, the party went off without a hitch; Jenn, grateful for the temporary distraction.

It was an evening of celebration and nostalgia as memories were shared and best wishes offered. Everyone was happy for them but sad that they were leaving. She and Paul were deeply touched by the warm sentiments expressed by many. One of their friends, a former law student of Paul's, attempted to make a toast but became so emotional that he was unable to finish.

Jenn almost lost it when Mary Ann, a youth pastor and good friend, referred to the Donaldsons as the "perfect" family. Jenn recalled Mary Ann's comments.

"I've always been envious of the Donaldsons. God forgive me," Mary Ann had said as others laughed. "Look at them. They're the golden family. They love each other like teenagers, they look like teenagers." More laughter. "Seriously, they're beautiful inside and out, and they have those gorgeous girls who are smart and talented. They're perfect, aren't they?" Everyone had applauded.

Jenn was jolted from her thoughts when, suddenly, Paul flung the journal across the room. It bounced off of the refrigerator before landing on the floor.

"I can't believe this. I just can't believe this!" Paul shouted. Jenn said nothing knowing that Paul needed time to process the revelations about his precious daughter. Even after a week, she continued to have difficulty accepting it all.

"She sounds like a little whore. There has to be another explanation," he said.

Jenn didn't respond.

"Lynn wrote this?" Paul asked.

"It would appear so," Jenn said. "It's her handwriting."

"How could you not know?" he asked, lashing out at Jenn.

"Wh-what?" Jenn had not expected Paul's anger to be directed at her. "How could I not know? I've asked myself that question thousands of times since reading the journal," Jenn said, defensively. "I had no idea—"

"But you should have known. You're her mother," Paul said, desperate for answers.

"Baby, let's not do this," Jenn pleaded. "Let's not attack each other. I know you're upset...and hurt...and angry. I am, too. I feel horrible about this and I am blaming myself. Believe me. I've wracked my brain for clues that I may have missed and I've come up empty," she said softly. "I was as shocked as you. I believe Lynn is very good at deceiving people and that scares me to death."

Shaking his head, Paul thought of his other daughter and fear gripped his heart. "How about Ruth? You think she's been doing the same thing? She does everything Lynn does, you know. Oh my God."

"I don't know," Jenn responded. "The journal and marijuana were both under Lynn's mattress. I found nothing incriminating among Ruth's things so I don't know what Ruth is doing but I'm pretty sure she's not innocent in all of this. At the very least, she knew of Lynn's behavior. They tell each other everything."

Paul paced back and forth, his handsome face contorted in anger.

"I'm going to get to the bottom of this," he declared. "You can count on that. Let's phone your parents right now and tell them to put the girls on the first plane out tomorrow morning."

"You think that's the best thing to do?" Jenn asked.

Paul stopped pacing and stared at Jenn. "You have a better idea?"

"Well, let's think about this. We have the journal and the marijuana. But there's a lot we don't know."

"What more do we need to know?" Paul snapped. "We know she's using drugs and sleeping around like a tramp."

"Yes, but we don't know where she's getting the drugs or when she's using. We don't know who she's having sex with. We really don't know what she is capable of. Plus, if we make them come home they'll know that something is wrong. It'll give them time to come up with a cover and—"

Paul banged the table with the palm of his hand causing Jenn to jump.

"I just can't believe they would deceive us like this. They have the world. We gave them everything. We taught them right from wrong. I am so furious! I trusted them," he said.

"You also spoiled them," Jenn said, unable to keep the agitation out of her voice.

"What are you talking about?" Paul glared at Jenn.

In exasperation, Jenn explained. "Paul, you always gave in to the girls. I laid down the law and then they appealed to you with those tears and it was all over. Honey, I tried to tell you this before. You spoiled them."

"Oh, so now you're blaming me?" he yelled. "You're here all day every day and knew nothing about our daughters' behaviors but you want to blame me for spoiling them? You've got to be kidding me!"

"Paul, please stop yelling. No, I'm not blaming you. I'm telling you the truth," Jenn said. "You giving in to the girls needs to stop. We've got to make a few changes. Both of us. Now more than ever we must be united when we impose consequences. We need to hold the girls accountable and stand by our decisions or else we'll have more serious problems on our hands."

Paul was distraught. The joy had been zapped out of his spirit by his own daughters. What he thought was an impossibility was a painful reality for him. His girls—at least, one of them—sexually active before the age of sixteen. All that he thought was true about them—their beauty and innocence—was destroyed. He loved them—nothing would change that—but this was an extremely bitter pill to swallow. What Lynn had written in the journal was down right filthy.

The words replayed themselves over and over in his mind as he ran. He had already completed his three mile route but continued, driven by anger. Never in his life had he felt like this. He thought of the day Jenn told him she was pregnant...how he'd received the news as a special gift from God. Then he thought of the day they were born...so tiny and beautiful even at birth. He thought of the times they'd sat on his lap or come to him when afraid. He was so proud of his family and it was a pride that he often couldn't hide.

He hadn't meant to undermine Jenn's authority in dealing with the girls. He, honestly and foolishly, was of the opinion that his girls could do little wrong. At times, he'd thought Jenn was somewhat jealous of his relationship with the twins as she stood by and watched their interaction.

While he knew that Jenn deeply loved the girls, he also sensed that she felt excluded by their behavior.

"We love Mom but she doesn't understand us like you do, Dad."

"Dad, can we go? You know how Mom is" or "Mom doesn't trust us but we know you do, Dad."

He recalled the clever statements and manipulative behaviors that fed his ego and probably made Jenn feel horrible. He had been duped by his daughters and was infuriated. He felt like a fool. Jenn had been right all along to be concerned about them.

Sweat was pouring off him as he continued to run. Every piece of clothing was saturated including his socks. He wanted to continue to push himself but the burning in his eyes from the dripping sweat and his accelerated heart rate caused him to slow down. He found himself near Seward Park and decided to sit for a while. It was serenely beautiful and quiet and while sitting, the hurt and disappointment surfaced, replacing his anger.

Tears formed in his eyes and ran down his face as he allowed himself to feel the pain caused by his daughters' behavior. Up until now, he had suppressed the deep hurt but now he released it, gently and slowly. His attention was drawn to birds flying overhead and when he looked up, he couldn't help but notice the sunshine and blue sky. Huge cumulus clouds, puffy and white, moved quickly across the horizon. In spite of his disappointment and pain, the view was a reminder to him of an entity bigger than he. In quiet desperation, he prayed for his daughters.

Paul sat on the bench for a long time thinking about the situation. He was not naive about young people or their behaviors. In fact, he had insisted to Jenn that they have honest conversations with the girls about the dangers that particularly targeted innocent youth including drugs, alcohol, sex, social media, on line predators. He openly explained to them that sex was created by God as an intimate expression of love between husband and wife. And, out of that love the world was procreated.

They discussed the difference between love and lust and the difference between how young men and women viewed sex. As their father, he cautioned them to be very careful and reminded them that they could always talk to him or Jenn if they had questions or needed advice. He thought they had listened...that they understood but, obviously, he was wrong judging by Lynn's behavior.

Is her behavior the norm for teens? Is there a new teen phenomenon? This was difficult because no father, including him, enjoyed thinking about his daughter's sexuality. She was only sixteen and actively pursuing sex. But his daughter's behavior disturbed him for reasons beyond the sexual acts she described.

Lynn didn't seem to care where these acts took place or with whom. Nor did she appear concerned about her reputation or health. More questions raced through his mind. *How long has she been sexually active? What method of birth control is she using? What would she do if she became pregnant? What would they do? Has her health already been compromised? Does she possess a moral conscious? Is this a form of rebellion? If so, what is she rebelling against?* Her behavior was extreme and went against their values or what he thought were their values and he was completely baffled.

There had to be a plausible explanation. As he thought about the past few years, he had the sinking feeling that Lynn needed more help than he or Jenn could provide. He wondered about Ruth again. *Is she also engaged in the same types of behavior?*

Paul phoned Jenn and asked her to pick him up from the park as he lacked the energy to retrace his steps. He was spent, exhausted more by the circumstances than his hard run. After a long talk, he and Jenn decided to allow the girls to remain with their grandparents. They also agreed on not alerting the girls to their knowledge until they were prepared. They needed time to think and develop a plan for handling this crisis.

Jenn thought of a plan though, as she explained to Paul, it was extreme and out of character for them. Paul acknowledged that the circumstances called for unusual and drastic measures. They had nothing to lose in his opinion.

Berta was a member of their social club notorious for gossiping. A wealthy widow with time on her hands, she involved herself in many activities and made it her business to know everyone else's business. Also referred to as Busy Berta, she was tolerated because of her willingness, as a volunteer, to do both the important and menial tasks. She did whatever was asked of her and did it well. Jenn knew that she volunteered at the girls' school.

Later that week, Paul and Jenn put their plan into action. Paul happened by the club when they knew Berta would be there lunching with a friend. He, innocently, struck up a brief conversation with Berta before heading to his table to meet his lunch date who would be a no-show. As planned, Jenn was seated at a table behind Berta's, within earshot but out of view and dressed in disguise. A short blond wig, cap, brown contact lenses and different clothing style did the trick. Jenn didn't have to wait long.

"Who was that handsome young man?" 70-year old Elaine asked Berta as soon as Paul left their table.

"He's a club member, an attorney. Paul Donaldson. Nicest person you ever want to meet. Beautiful family. I'm surprised you don't know them. His wife's name is Jenn. They have twin girls."

"I think I've seen them now that you mention it," Elaine said and then chuckled.

"What are you laughing at?" asked Berta.

"Just being silly. Thinking if I were about twenty years younger…"

"You are being silly. Plus, you wouldn't get to first base. He only has eyes for his wife," Berta said.

"Good for him," Elaine said. "Can't say the same for most of the men here."

"They're good people, he and his wife. Civic-minded and very involved in church but their girls—they're a different story. Now you didn't hear this from me but those girls are a bit wild. You know I volunteer at the school, right? Well, one day after school I was walking to my car which was parked in the student parking lot. As I approached a red Honda, the aroma of marijuana was so strong it made me dizzy. I kept walking to my car as if I hadn't noticed any-thing but waited for the kids to get out. One of the Donaldson twins got out of the car and guess what?"

"What?" Elaine asked, eager to hear the story.

"She was the only girl in that car. There were four boys and one girl."

"Oh my," Elaine said. "That doesn't look good at all."

"That's not all. I also volunteer at the library on Tuesdays. Well, a couple of months ago, I walked by one of the private study cubi-cles and heard a strange noise. I knocked on the door and tried to open it but a chair had been propped against it. I kept knocking and, finally, the door opened. Inside was one of the twins and the Hinson boy. He's much older than she is and has been in all sorts of trouble. They acted innocent but I know something was going on of a sexual nature. I can't tell the twins apart so I don't know which one it was."

"Have you talked to the twins' parents?" Elaine asked.

"What am I going to say? I have no proof of any wrongdoing," Berta said.

"But you have suspicions—strong suspicions."

"Well, until I have proof I'm saying nothing. I could be wrong. I didn't actually see the girl doing anything. But my granddaughter, Michelle—who goes to the same school—told me that the Donaldson girls have everyone fooled. She said they're not nice like everyone thinks. Said they're bullies and spread lies about people. She swore me to secrecy before telling me about an incident she witnessed at school one day while in the restroom.

"The twins and two other girls had cornered another girl, taunting her and making her cry. They didn't realize that Michelle was there. They called this poor girl all kinds of names and told her if she said anything they would post lies about her on Snapchat and all that other stuff they use. Michelle said the girl kept asking what she had done. Finally, when Michelle couldn't take anymore, she flushed the commode. The girls quickly left the restroom except the one being attacked. Michelle said she felt badly for her and told her she would go with her to the office to report it but the girl refused. Michelle said she never saw her again. Heard the girl transferred to another school."

Jenn had heard quite enough. Paul, who had positioned himself nearby so that he could clearly see Jenn, saw her get up and rush out. He left shortly after and followed her to his car. Color had drained from her face and she was in tears.

"What? What did you hear?" Paul asked.

"Our daughters are monsters. Please, let's get out of here," Jenn said as she ripped the wig from her head.

There was something else Jenn felt it necessary to do while the twins were away. Retrieving the list of parent contact information provided by the soccer coach, she phoned the parent of the new girl on the soccer team. The one name unfamiliar to her was Sabrina Lucas.

"Hello?"

"Mrs. Lucas, my name is Jenn Donaldson. My daughters and Sabrina are on the same soccer team. I-uh-was calling to check on Sabrina. I heard she became ill at camp. How is she?"

"She's shown some improvement and we're thankful for that. She still has a ways to go. I appreciate you calling."

"I'm glad she's better. Was it the flu or a stomach virus?"

"No, it was neither. We initially thought food poisoning but that's been ruled out," Mrs. Lucas said. "One minute she was fine, the next she was fighting for her life. Sabrina never gets sick. We're so worried. I'm sorry I've been very distracted lately. What's your daughter's name?"

"Twins. My daughters are the twins, Lynn and Ruth Donaldson."

"Oh yeah. Sabrina has mentioned them." Did Jenn detect a change in Mrs. Lucas' voice? She couldn't be sure.

"Thanks for thinking of us. I'm sorry but I need to take another call," Mrs. Lucus said before abruptly disconnecting the call.

Jenn definitely detected a change.

Chapter Twenty-Seven

---✼---

*L*ynn and Ruth returned home, tired and excited, with tales of team camp and the time spent with their grandparents. New York City and The Hamptons were two of their favorite places and, of course, their grandparents had planned many activities, doting on their only grandchildren. Shopping, broadway shows, dining at trendy restaurants, touring the city, beach parties and sailing were all accomplished during their three week stay.

At the airport, Jenn looked at her daughters and questioned her own sanity. Surely these beautiful girls did not possess the bullying, sex-craved, marijuana smoking behaviors she'd recently discovered. She wanted to believe that so desperately but her hopes were shattered when they arrived home and she followed the girls to their room.

"Mom, you've been in our room," Lynn said, disapprovingly. "You know our room is off limits."

"I wanted to surprise you," Jenn said, innocently. "I had it thoroughly cleaned, even washed the bed linens. Don't you like the flowers and candy?"

"What we'd like is for you to stay out of our room," Lynn said angrily, quickly looking at her bed.

"I just wanted to do something nice for you," Jenn said, disappointed but not surprised that the girls showed no appreciation.

"Thanks Mom," Ruth said. "That was very thoughtful but I hope you didn't rearrange things."

"Of course not," Jenn said. "I thought you would be pleased; instead, you seem irritated."

"It's just that we aren't little girls anymore," Ruth said, in an attempt to buffer Lynn's anger.

"You will always be my little girls," Jenn said. "Before you get too comfortable, be sure to put your dirty clothes in the laundry room. Dinner is at six. I made your favorites. Your dad can't wait to see you."

Jenn closed the door to the girls' bedroom and exhaled deeply. She had just gotten through one of the biggest performances of her life and the girls were none the wiser. She and Paul wanted to keep it that way for the time being though Paul would have more difficulty masking his pain.

He decided not to accompany Jenn to the airport for that very reason. He couldn't face the girls without his anguish and hurt showing. And, there was no way he could spend an entire evening with them without revealing his true feelings. He'd agonized about this all day. Finally, he called Jenn to admit the truth.

"I can't do it, Jenn. I just can't face them right now," Paul said.

Jenn could hear the unspoken plea and pain in his voice. "It's okay, honey. I understand. Just speak to them on the phone so that they won't be too disappointed or suspicious. Tell them you're a consultant for an upcoming trial and won't be home until late. I'll cover for you."

Paul exhaled a huge sigh of relief. "Thank you, Jenn. I'm so sorry."

"It's not a problem. I understand. I really do."

"I love you so much. Put the girls on the phone, please."

Paul and Jenn had not yet decided on the best course of action. Restriction of privileges? Removal from the soccer team? No allowance? Constant supervision? After considering all of their options, they were still at a loss and agreed to meet with Mary Ann, the youth pastor. They hoped to gain both insight about teenage behavior and spiritual counsel from one they trusted. They met the day after the girls' return. Mary Ann listened attentively.

Paul said, "We've just described behaviors that are very upsetting to us yet you don't seem surprised."

"There isn't much that I've not heard before. Our youth face many challenges today, more than ever. It's an unhealthy world that we, as adults, have exposed them to."

"Wait a minute," Jenn said. "Are you blaming us for our girls' behavior?"

"No," Mary Ann said. "What I'm saying is that we live in a corrupt world and it's very difficult for our young people not to be tainted by it. I was making reference to society in general which makes your job as parents extremely difficult."

After a brief pause, Mary Ann continued. "What you have described about their behavior, particularly Lynn's, is not typical teenage behavior, in my opinion. A degree of curiosity and experimentation—even belligerence—is normal but what you have described is excessive based on my experience. My advice is that you talk with them as soon as possible. You don't want to add to the atmosphere of deception in your home by being untruthful and keeping your own secrets. Confront them with the behaviors and impose what you feel are appropriate consequences. Remain consistent and united but keep the lines of communication open. I think it's also important to determine Ruth's role. Don't assume. You need to treat them as individuals, not as one entity."

"What if they deny their behaviors?" Jenn asked.

"Deal with the evidence you have and act accordingly. Be firm. You found marijuana in your home. Unacceptable, right? The journal speaks for itself and then there is the conversation that you overheard. I also think you should consider therapy."

"For us or the girls?" Paul asked, making a feeble attempt at humor.

Mary Ann offered a compassionate smile. She knew that this situation was extremely difficult for the Donaldsons. "I was referring to the girls but it may help you, too."

Paul and Jenn agreed to confront the girls the next day after dinner but the conversation did not take place as planned. While preparing dinner, Jenn was interrupted by the ringing of the doorbell and surprised to see two men at her door. The taller of the two appeared to be in his mid fifties; the other in his early forties. Both wore slacks, collared shirts, ties and lightweight jackets.

"Good evening, may I help you?" Jenn asked.

"Good evening, I'm Detective Biles. This is Detective Dunlap. Is this the Donaldson residence?"

Jenn perused the identification they offered before answering. "Yes, it is."

"We need to speak with your daughters," Detective Biles said politely but formally.

"Come in. What is this about? Is there a problem?" Jenn asked.

Detective Biles responded. "I'm afraid so, ma'am. We're following up on an incident that occurred while your daughters were at soccer camp. We need to ask them a few questions. Are they home?"

"Yes, they are but I don't understand. Why do you need to talk to them?" Jenn asked with butterflies in her stomach.

"We're speaking with all of the team members and other possible witnesses. We're hoping they can help shed light on what happened," Detective Biles said.

"What incident are you talking about?" Jenn asked, fearful and frustrated at the same time.

"One of the soccer team members became ill during camp. We're trying to determine what caused her illness," Detective Dunlap said.

"Yes, Coach Browning informed us that she became ill. Do you think someone tried to hurt her?" Jenn asked, trying to remain as calm as possible.

"We're trying to determine what happened and hope your daughters can help," Detective Biles said. "We'd like to talk with them at the station. Of course, you're more than welcome to accompany them."

Jenn looked at both detectives before speaking. "Are you arresting my daughters?"

The two detectives quickly exchanged glances.

"No ma'am. As I explained, we simply want to talk with them at the station," Detective Biles repeated. "Your cooperation is very important and greatly appreciated."

In spite of Detective Biles' polite reassurance, Jenn was extremely concerned.

She said, "I've got to call my husband. He's an attorney."

"Feel free. Ma'am, I know this is a shock for you but this is a very serious matter. Do you understand? Would you please get your daughters?"

Jenn nodded as a thousand thoughts went through her mind. Stiffly, she walked across the room and with a trembling voice yelled from the stairs, "Girls, please come here. It's very important."

"What do you want, Mom?" Lynn asked from the top of the stairs, clearly irritated at being summoned.

"Come down, please. Now," Jenn commanded.

Lynn noticed her mother's worried expression and walked downstairs with Ruth directly behind her.

During their investigation, the detectives had compiled detailed information about the Donaldson family and were aware of the identical twins. Still, they were surprised as they looked at the mirror images. Though skilled observers, the detectives could detect no physical differences. Except for different attire, the girls were indeed identical.

"Which one of you is Lynn Donaldson?" Detective Biles asked.

"I am," Lynn said, petulantly.

"And you're Ruth?" Detective Biles directed the question to the other twin.

"Yes," Ruth said.

"I'm Detective Biles and this is Detective Dunlap. We'd like for you to come to the station with us. We have questions about an incident regarding Sabrina Lucas," Detective Biles said.

Ruth looked at Jenn before speaking. "What kinds of questions?"

"Routine questions. We're speaking to all potential witnesses," Detective Biles said.

"I don't know very much," Ruth said. "I didn't go to lunch the day she got sick. I-uh-had cramps and was in my room most of the day."

"Mrs. Donaldson, we need for the girls to come to the station now so that we can take their statements," Detective Biles said.

"I'm not going anywhere, you scumbag. Who do you think you are? You can't come here and demand to speak with us," Lynn said, arrogantly.

"Lynn! Have you lost your mind?" Jenn asked, fighting hysteria.

"Have you lost yours?" Lynn retorted. "I'm not talking to these jerks. I don't have to if I don't want to. Sabrina Lucas is a whore and a liar. You can't believe a word she says," Lynn said, angrily.

Interesting. The detectives noticed Lynn's growing agitation and wanted to avoid an unpleasant situation if at all possible.

Detective Dunlap said, "Let's all calm down." After a moment, he said to Lynn, "Young lady, this is an important matter and I would advise—"

"I said I'm not going anywhere," Lynn interrupted, glaring at the detectives. "Are you deaf or just stupid?"

"Lynn please," Jenn implored, embarrassed and shocked by her daughter's behavior.

"No!" Lynn screamed as she picked up a brass figurine and threw it at Detectives Biles who was standing closer to her.

Detective Biles didn't have time to react. The figurine struck him on the right side of his face piercing his skin. Blood immediately began dripping from the wound. In an instant, Detective Dunlap grabbed Lynn, turned her around forcefully, and handcuffed her. He noticed a small red heart-shaped tattoo on the inside of her left wrist. The sudden attack was so unexpected that even the seasoned detectives were caught off guard.

Everyone began speaking at once. Lynn continued her verbal assault using a variety of choice words and profanity. A frantic Ruth begged for her sister to be released and had to be restrained by Detective Dunlap. Detective Biles requested assistance from the police officer parked outside of the Donaldson home. Jenn, with trembling hands, dialed Paul's number and watched helplessly as her handcuffed daughter was escorted from her home to the waiting vehicle.

"Where are you taking her?" Jenn asked from the sidewalk.

"To the 4th precinct," Detective Dunlap responded.

"Lynn, your dad and I will be there," Jenn yelled with tears rolling down her face. When she heard Paul's voice on the phone, she screamed. "Paul, where are you? They've taken Lynn! Where are you?"

"I'm turning on our street now. I can see the house—"

Just as Paul pulled into the driveway, the police car pulled off with Lynn sitting in the back like a criminal.

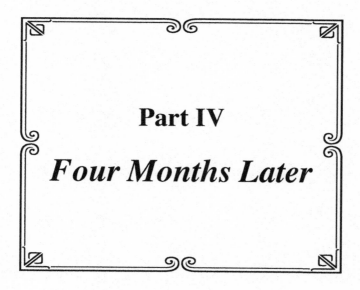

Part IV

Four Months Later

Chapter Twenty-Eight

------------------- ✳ -------------------

Janole

*J*anole, with Wallace's blessing, had decided to take an extended leave of absence from work. In fact, they had discussed the possibility of early retirement for her. Her job as the lead clinical research psychologist at the nearby public university was demanding and because her department was short-staffed, she had assumed additional responsibilities.

Though she and Wallace were back on track, Janole had been on overload for quite some time. In hindsight, she realized that it would have been wise for her to have taken a temporary break from work shortly after the pharmaceutical company ordeal. During that time, her job responsibilities kept her busy and allowed her to function throughout the day without dwelling on her situation. But the stress of it all had a cumulative effect on her especially because of recent circumstances.

For the past few months she had been dealing with critical situations of those she dearly loved. Marlon's battle with cancer, Amy's suicide attempt, Marlo's state of mind regarding his marriage, and Jenn who was devastated by Lynn's behavior and arrest. At times, it was all quite overwhelming.

Janole spent a great deal of time in prayer, thankful for her relationship with God and for the privilege to talk to Him about all of her concerns and problems. This morning she felt especially close to Him. In spite of the circumstances, she had joy in her spirit and couldn't restrain her praise. And, as she praised God and thanked Him for her journey, she felt strengthened, encouraged, and reassured. In reverence and quiet solitude, she thought about the many Bible stories of faith.

One of her favorites was the story about the woman whose faith was so great in Jesus' power that she merely wanted to touch the clothes He was wearing. She didn't need to have a conversation with Him. She didn't need to stand out in the crowd or compete for His attention. She didn't need to touch Him. She simply needed to touch a piece of His clothing knowing that it would suffice. And, in that touch her faith was communicated to Jesus. Incredible faith.

Janole thought about God's unconditional and all encompassing love. How He bestows grace not because of...but in spite of. Eric had made a similar comment about his wife. Janole understood what a precious gift she had given him. *We can neither earn God's love nor lose it. He gives freely...in spite of our weaknesses, sins and unfaithfulness. God loves us so much that nothing can separate us from Him. Nothing.* Janole was humbled, empowered and in awe.

It was clear what she needed to do. She would be the prayer warrior for her son, her brother, her sister-in-law, and her dear friend. She would fight for them each day...in prayer. She already felt victorious and in the privacy of her home she continued to praise God. And, the more she praised Him the more she received. She gained new insight, joy, increased fortitude and a divine revelation. It could only be explained as a mountaintop experience. She was no longer worried, but encouraged and inspired.

She inserted Sissy's newly released CD into the disk player and was brought to tears as she listened to the beautiful renditions of hymns and contemporary gospel songs. She sat still and allowed the music to minister to her.

Oh Lord my God
When I in awesome wonder
Consider all the worlds Thy hands have made.
I see the stars, I hear the rolling thunder.
Thy power throughout the universe displayed.

And when I think, that God, His Son not sparing;
Sent Him to die, I scarce can take it in.
That on the cross, my burden gladly bearing,
He bled and died to take away my sin.

Then sings my soul, my Savior God to Thee.
How great Thou art! How great Thou art!
Then sings my soul, my Savior God to Thee,
How great Thou art. How great Thou art!

Later, Janole assembled all of the ingredients for Wallace's favorite seafood casserole and then decided to surprise him with her fabulous peach cobbler. She'd forgotten how much pleasure she derived from cooking and experimenting with new recipes. Now that she had more time, she cooked and baked frequently. Wallace couldn't be happier. He enjoyed Janole's cooking even if it meant a longer workout to keep off the extra pounds.

Just as she was about to mix the peaches and spices, she was interrupted by a text message from Nate. He checked in with her regularly but this text had a more urgent tone. He wanted to meet with her as soon as possible about an important matter.

Janole sighed as she realized it was time to address her friendship with Nate. She was convinced that the feelings she and Nate once had for each other were in the past but Wallace had made it clear that he didn't appreciate their relationship. Because she never mentioned Nate, Wallace probably assumed that she and Nate were no longer communicating but that wasn't the case.

Janole couldn't be absolutely certain of the extent of Nate's feelings for her. Did he consider her only a friend or was he waiting for an opportune time to reveal deeper feelings and a desire for more? Janole had no answers and realized his possible feelings for her—or lack thereof—were of no consequence. The important consideration was that she was being dishonest with her husband and that shouldn't be occurring. She did not want a marriage where secrets existed. Nate had helped her during one of the most difficult times of her life and for that she was deeply grateful. But it was time for her to inform him that, out of respect for her husband, their friendship could not continue. The sooner the better. She responded to Nate's message indicating that she was free to meet with him.

His response was immediate. "Let's meet at the Panera Bread near you. Three o'clock?"

Janole was relieved that Panera Bread had few customers. She was sipping a cup of coffee when an attractive woman approached her table. "Janole?"

"Yes. I'm sorry. Have we met?" Janole asked.

"No, we haven't. But I'd like to talk with you. I'm the one who sent you the text, not Nate. I know you're confused. I promise not to take too much of your time. May I join you?"

"Okay," Janole said with reluctance. "Who are you and what is your relationship to Nate?"

"My name is Ellen. I'm Nate's ex-wife."

Janole's surprise was evident. "Does Nate know about this meeting?"

"No, he has no idea. This is difficult for me in more ways than one," Ellen said.

Guarded, Janole said nothing as she assessed Ellen, wondering about her motives. She silently prayed for discernment and asked God to direct her thoughts and words.

Ellen said, "I owe you an apology."

"For what?" Janole asked, baffled. None of this was making sense.

"For the note I left in your mailbox and on your car."

"You left those notes?" Janole asked in astonishment. "Why would you do that?"

"Because I was jealous of you and your relationship with Nate," Ellen confessed. "I've been very foolish and I'm sorry."

"Nate and I don't have a relationship. We're nothing more than friends. What did you think was going on between us?"

"I didn't really know. What I did know was that he was very concerned about you. One day months ago I overheard him talking on the phone. He referred to you as someone extremely important to him. He said you were in trouble and would be his priority for as long as necessary.

"It was how he spoke about you that bothered me. He sounded as if he held you in such high esteem...as if you were very special to him. When I asked him about you, he didn't offer much information but I persisted. Finally, he told me the entire story. We were married for years and not once did he mention you."

"And because of that you decided to leave me anonymous notes?"

"I thought he was still in love with you. I'm not sure that he isn't. Our marriage was always missing something and when Nate told me about you, I decided that you were the reason. Though we divorced, we continued to see each other and because I had access to his phone, I was able to keep tabs on him. So I knew of the times you and Nate met and I left a note shortly after. I couldn't let you threaten our chance for a reconciliation. Some times I followed him without him knowing. He never suspected. Some times I followed you," Ellen confessed.

Understanding dawned for Janole. "I never associated the notes with Nate." She remembered her worry and fear, thinking that the pharmaceutical company wanted to exact revenge. *God give me grace.*

"You must love him very much," Janole said.

"I do but that doesn't excuse my behavior. I loved Nate so much that I made him a god. I, literally, worshiped him."

"But now?"

"I still love him but I can't continue like this. My daughter made me realize how stupid I've been when she told me about one of her friends who is obsessed with a man.

"My daughter said, 'Mom, I keep telling her that she can't make him love her. She's driving herself crazy over this man...' She described her friend as desperate and pathetic. During our conversation, I was in the middle of writing another note and realized how desperate and pathetic I'd become."

"The things we go through for our men and because of our men," Janole said, with empathy.

Tears rolled down Ellen's face. "I'm sorry. I don't mean to cry," she said as she swiped at the tears. "It's just that I expected you to be furious with me. You have every right but, instead, you've been so kind. I didn't want to like you. You were supposed to cuss me out so I could feel better."

Janole smiled. "You caught me on a good day. How do you think Nate will react when you tell him?"

Ellen sighed heavily. "I have no idea. Well, that's not true. I'm sure he will be very upset. Livid. I've probably ruined any chance of us getting back together but I think I'm okay with that. I'm tired and I don't like the person I've become. I'm so ashamed of myself and I've wasted precious time."

Janole nodded. "It sounds like you've suffered enough. I accept your apology and I hope things work out. I'll pray for you—"

"What's going on here?" Nate asked, angrily. Ellen and Janole were so engrossed in their conversation that they hadn't noticed him. He looked at Janole briefly then stared at Ellen. "What the hell is going on? Ellen? I saw the text message on my phone. You need to explain this. Right now."

Janole watched as Ellen's facial expression conveyed shock, fear, embarrassment and regret. "I think I need to leave and let the two of you talk," Janole said.

Ellen said, "No, please stay for a moment. I want you both to hear this."

"Are you sure?" Janole directed her question to both Ellen and Nate.

Nate shrugged, in response. Ellen nodded her head.

Janole slid over so that Nate could face Ellen. "Sit down, Nate. Please," Janole said.

Ellen spoke. "I've done some things that I shouldn't have and I owe both of you an explanation and apology. That's why I sent Janole a text message from your phone. I've already apologized to her and—"

"Apologized for what?" Nate asked, still angry.

"I was jealous of your relationship with her so I began checking your phone and following you. I also left notes for Janole."

"Notes? What are you talking about?" Nate was confused.

Janole responded. "The notes I mentioned to you. The ones that prompted us to contact the FBI."

Nate was furious. "Notes? You told me about one note," he said to Janole.

"There were two," Janole said.

He looked at Ellen. "Are you telling me you left those notes? Ellen, that's a federal offense! You could go to prison. What in the world would possess you to do something so stupid? And checking my phone?"

The color drained from Ellen's face. "I didn't think it was...I didn't think." She began to cry. "I'm sorry. I'm very sorry."

After an awkward pause, Janole said, "Nate, I agreed to come today because I thought I was meeting you. There's something I need to say to you. You helped me during the biggest crisis of my life and I'm eternally grateful to you. I will never forget what you did to help me find Wallace. You were a Godsend and I mean that literally. Wallace is grateful, too, but—because of our past—our friendship makes him uncomfortable. So, out of respect for my husband, its best that we not communicate. I hope you understand."

Nate said, "I meant no disrespect. I was just concerned."

"I know," Janole said, reaching for her purse. "You two need to talk. Ellen, I wish for you the very best. No matter what happens, I think you'll be okay. Nate, take good care. Wallace and I are forever indebted to you. Be blessed."

Chapter Twenty-Nine

---*---

Marlon

*M*arlon stretched his long body and looked at the clock. He couldn't believe it was almost noon. He'd slept close to twelve hours. Usually he heard Nick bustling around in the mornings but this morning he'd heard nothing. He grabbed his phone to check for messages. Sure enough there were several texts—one from Nick, his mom, Zo and Brandy.

Nick wanted him to know he had a date and would be late getting home. *Good for you, Bruh.* His mom sent her love. *Love you, too, Mom.* Zo wanted him to know that he and the team were thinking of him. *I'll send them an email real soon.* Brandy confirmed their dinner plans and, of course, sent her love. Marlon smiled, his heart filled with love.

Tears leaked out of his eyes as he thought about the past months. Chemo and radiation were no joke. The life-saving combo zapped his energy and made him nauseated at times. He developed a dry mouth and lost his appetite. The foods that he usually craved didn't appeal to him or tasted different. At times, he felt he had little to no control over his body. He reminded himself that these side effects were only temporary. He hoped and prayed that was the case.

Tomorrow was an important day. He was being tested to determine whether he was cancer-free or needed to continue treatment. He was accustomed to playing in a sport where the higher the total score, the better. But what he needed now was a count of zero. If his PSA level was at zero, he'd won.

He now had such a great appreciation for those who were diagnosed with cancer. Before, he'd never been directly impacted by cancer—or other life-threatening illnesses—and hadn't considered what it meant to live with the disease day in and day out.

Over a span of months, he'd met incredibly strong and courageous people. Whenever he had a mind to complain, he thought of their struggles and victories. Some of them had been battling cancer for years, bravely enduring a variety of treatments, drugs, surgeries and pain. Their stories were incredible and inspired him when he was at his lowest. When word got out that he had prostate cancer, he began hearing from many men who were prostate cancer survivors. Some of these men he knew quite well but had no idea they'd once had prostate cancer. They included fathers, brothers and uncles of some of his friends; even coaches he admired. Others were complete strangers.

So far, he had only experienced one of the two side effects he most dreaded. There was sporadic urine leakage that was, at times, frustrating but manageable. If it was determined that he was cancer-free and leakage was the only residual problem, he could definitely live with that. He knew that erectile dysfunction was still a possibility but he'd been given a gift from the other cancer patients he'd encountered. He'd learned to take one day at a time. It was a priceless gift. Live in the present and don't anticipate tomorrow's problems. The last few months had been tough, no doubt about it. But his tears weren't due to sadness. This wasn't a pity party. He'd grown and gained too much, his life forever changed.

His phone rang and he wasn't surprised to see Eric's name on the screen. They talked frequently.

"Hello Eric," Marlon said.

"Just calling to check in. How are you?" Eric asked.

"No complaints. Feeling good. Not too long woke up. I slept for almost twelve hours."

"Nothing wrong with that. Your body needed the rest. Guess where I'm headed?" Eric asked.

"Uh-to lunch? That's my best guess."

"Nope. Headed to the gym to work out, man. I'm so excited. When Dr. Bowers referred me to his doctor friend here in Phoenix, I had no idea it would be life-changing. I'm walking without a cane and hardly have any pain. Lost thirty pounds, too."

"That's incredible. I'm happy for you—real happy," Marlon said, sincerely.

"Before long, I'll be ready for you on the courts. You'd better work on your game," Eric teased.

Marlon laughed. "On your best day you couldn't handle me but keep dreaming."

Eric laughed in his loud baritone voice. "What time is your appointment tomorrow?"

"One o'clock. I'll keep you posted on the results."

"You do that. I'm praying."

Shortly after they disconnected, Brandy phoned.

"Hi Gorgeous," Marlon said.

"Hey! Did you get my message?" she asked.

"I sure did. Looking forward to it. You're cooking, right?"

"Yeah. I need a guinea pig and you're it."

"So if the cancer doesn't kill me, your cooking will," Marlon said, chuckling.

"You're going to pay for that," Brandy said with laughter in her voice. "Seriously, how are you feeling today?"

"I'm feeling good—real good. Feel rested and ready."

"I'm happy to hear that, baby. I've got a meeting but I'll see you later. I love you."

"Love you more," Marlon said.

Marlon had just showered and was in the process of heating one of his mom's dishes, when the doorbell rang. Their freezer was stocked with foods she had prepared which he enjoyed now that his appetite was returning. He opened the front door and was surprised to see his uncle.

"Uncle Marlo! What a surprise," he said, as he embraced his uncle. "I didn't know you were in town."

"I decided to take a few days off and hang out with my peeps," Marlo said. "You look good. How're you feeling?"

"Feel great. I hope the worse is over...depends on my test results. You hungry? Mom stocked us with a wide variety of her cooking. You've got your choice. Chicken broccoli casserole, mac and cheese, lasagna, spaghetti, or your choice of soups: chicken noodle or beef vegetable or fifteen bean with ham. What's your pleasure?" Marlon asked.

"Good Lord! You're not kidding. I'll take the fifteen bean soup. I love that stuff."

While the food was thawing in the microwave, Marlon asked, "Does Mom know you're in town?"

"No, I'm going to surprise her later. I plan to spend a few days with her and Wallace."

"She'll be happy to see you," Marlon said. "She told me that you and Aunt Amy had separated. I'm sorry."

"Thanks, man."

"How're MJ and Brianna coping? I haven't talked to them in a while."

"They're doing okay. They're confused and hurt, of course, but doing okay."

"You want to talk about it? Mom only told me that the two of you were separated."

"I'd rather not go into all the details. Not today. Why don't you tell me what all has been going on with you. It's been a while since we've talked. How's Brandy?"

Marlon and his uncle talked for hours. Marlon filled him in on the past few months. He shared details about he and Brandy's relationship, his growing friendship with Eric, and the incredible people he'd met who were also diagnosed with cancer. He also talked about his spiritual growth and connection with God.

"I always knew about God and believed in Him but I didn't really know Him. It's like I'm a new person," Marlon said. "When I was first diagnosed with cancer, I thought it was the end of the world. But it wasn't. In many ways, it's the best thing that ever happened to me. Don't get me wrong. I would never choose to have cancer. I don't think anyone would. But I can't say that I regret having it because of all the good to come out of it. You know what I'm saying?"

Marlo nodded. "I think I do, nephew."

Marlon continued. "You know what's amazing? Checking PSA levels is not a routine part of our physical exams. It was a fluke that my PSA level was checked. A fluke that saved my life."

"Hmmmm. That's powerful. Sounds like you've got a story to share."

"You think so?"

"No doubt about it. You would be a perfect ambassador for the importance of men being tested. Tell your story, man," Marlo said, helping himself to more soup. "I couldn't be more proud of you."

Marlon smiled. After his parents, the person whose opinion mattered the most to him was his uncle's. "I just might do that. I'm eager to get back into basketball. If I don't need any more treatments, I'll be good to go. I'm still hoping—and praying—a coaching position will open up soon."

"That's one of the reasons I stopped by," Marlo said, smiling. "There's an opening at GW. I happen to be good friends with Coach Swann and the position is yours if you want it."

Marlon looked at his uncle. "Are you kidding?"

"I never joke when it comes to basketball," Marlo said, smiling. "Coach has followed your career and said he would be happy to have you. Of course, my recommendation didn't hurt. He's a good brother, too. Christian man."

"I don't know what to say. Coach Swann is a great coach. It's perfect because I won't have to relocate," Marlon said, excitedly.

"You'd be learning from one of the best," Marlo said. "He expects to hear from you later in the week. In fact, let me know when you plan to meet with him and I'll go with you. That is, if you don't mind."

Marlon was too excited to sit still. His uncle had been gone for half an hour and, after washing the dishes, Marlon had done nothing but pace. He found the space in his brother's condo too confining so he decided to take a walk. He felt like skipping. Many thoughts were running through his mind. Just a few short months ago, he didn't know whether he would live or die. In fact, he thought he'd received a death sentence.

In addition, he lost the one thing he loved...that defined him. Basketball. One day he was a professional basketball player on top of his game, the next he was a bystander. He recalled the depression and sadness; how he ignored his team mates and sulked while watching games.

On top of that he found out that Wallace, the man he most revered, wasn't his biological father. His parents had deceived him...another painful blow at a time when he felt off balance and needed them most. He recalled the hurt and anger he experienced because of their deception. But he discovered an important truth. Several truths. Wallace would always be his father, blood or no blood. Nothing and no one could change that. Just as nothing could alter the love he had for his incredible mother. They were family, forever bonded by love. And, he'd gained a friend in Eric, his biological father, who had shown nothing but support for him. In fact, Eric had done all he could possibly do to help him. Marlon was happy that he was a part of his life.

Then along came Brandy, the only girl he had loved. He knew she was special the first time he met her. No other women compared though many, unknowingly, competed. Brandy had given him strength and encouraged him in his faith. She convinced him that he was an answer to her prayers and assured him that she would stay with him through thick and thin. She demonstrated her love for him each day. He remembered their initial conversation about his diagnosis when she urged him to have his prostate removed. She wanted the best chance for him to live and was unconcerned about his sexual performance or impotence. *Crazy woman! She didn't realize what she was giving up.* He couldn't help but smile now. He wasn't smiling then.

He was going to marry Brandy—his queen—and couldn't wait to ask her but he had to make it a special occasion. If the cancer was gone, he'd go ring shopping and propose this weekend. If he needed more treatments, he'd delay the proposal until he was cancer free. *God, please let me be cancer free. Please!* In just a few days he'd know the answer.

One of his life long goals was to be a basketball coach and it could happen...if he were cancer-free. Sure, he could assume the coaching responsibilities while having cancer but It wouldn't be fair to Coach Swann for him to accept the position knowing that he couldn't give it his all. Everything—his marriage and career—was contingent upon him being cancer free.

He'd been walking for a while with no destination in mind. He looked around and saw that he was standing in front of a small church surrounded by a white picket fence. On impulse, he entered the quaint, white framed edifice and was enveloped immediately in peace.

From his seat in the rear, he took in his surroundings noticing the stained glass windows, polished wooden pews and blue carpet that complemented the windows. It was a beautiful sanctuary. He took note of the piano, organ, and small choir loft. For a long time, he stared at the pictures depicting The Last Supper and Jesus' death on the cross. He'd seen these before but now he looked at them with a different perspective.

He realized then that the most important and significant gift he had acquired in recent months was his relationship with Christ. Marlon now understood and appreciated that there was a never ending source of strength and love and grace—through Him. Before, Marlon felt in control of his destiny but realized he was in control of very little. He knew only too well that circumstances can change quickly and drastically with no forewarning. He learned that in spite of disappointments, pain, tragedies, illness, and unpredictable circumstances, there is a loving power bigger than humankind.

Marlon had seen beauty personified in Brandy who loved him not because of what he could give her. She, simply and purely, loved him the person. And, not only that...through his cancer experience, he'd gained his purpose, a divine calling to help others.

"Thank You, God," Marlon whispered, overcome with emotion. "Thank You for Your game plan for my life."

As Marlon walked out of the sanctuary, the voice of a person he did not see said, ***"Walk in faith, My son."***

Chapter Thirty

—————— ✳ ——————

Marlo

Marlo knew one thing, unequivocally. Something had to change. He couldn't continue as he had for the past few months. He'd become a shell of a man, hollow and empty, robbed of all joy, laughter, even purpose. Amy destroyed their marriage, betrayed him and ruined his capacity to trust. If not for the anger that consumed him, he would be devoid of all capacity to feel like a human being.

As an athlete, he had experienced the power of adrenalin to push him beyond his limits...to allow him to accomplish feats he thought impossible...to keep him going when his body was depleted. Anger— not adrenalin—had been his inescapable driving force in recent months, allowing him to be a functional, if not likable, person. But, the weight of such intense anger was tiring, debilitating and scary in its power to overtake him without warning. It was all-consuming and he, more often than not, lost the battle to control it.

The kind, even-tempered Marlo had been replaced with an angry, sullen, moody and cynical Marlo. One evening, as he foraged in the refrigerator for something to eat and came up empty, the anger hit him suddenly and forcefully. His life was not the life he wanted, having been cruelly snatched from him by the woman who professed to love him, the only woman he loved.

He grabbed the can of beer he'd just placed on the counter and hurled it across the room. "Damn it!" he yelled over and over. He watched the ruin as the liquid splattered the wall and floor but he had no regrets. With a festering anger, he walked to his work out room and began violently pounding the punching bag. He called Amy every name, profane and otherwise, that entered his mind and when he could not throw another punch, he sat on the floor and cried.

For hours he remained on the floor with only his thoughts to keep him company. He took no notice of his swelling hands and bleeding knuckles. Finally, he was overcome with exhaustion. The next morning, awakened by the throbbing pain in his hands and stiff from sleeping on the floor, he slowly walked to the kitchen for ice. The beer stench greeted him immediately causing him to be nauseated. He noticed the stains and dent in the wall. It can all be repaired, he thought. Unlike my marriage.

Lately, though, it wasn't so much anger he felt but a deep, unrelenting hurt. Amy had given herself to another. His wife had allowed another man to possess her, caress and kiss her, make love to her. To do those things to her that were reserved for him because of their vows years ago. Did Doug pleasure her in a way that he couldn't? When he thought of Amy and Doug in the throes of passion he experienced a pain unlike any he had ever experienced. The images conjured in his overactive imagination were brutally detailed and vivid. Did she think of Doug when they made love? Such an insulting thought. Even more insulting was the realization that, for a period of time, Amy had slept with him and Doug. He'd suspected something was going on but it had not occurred to him that Amy was capable of committing adultery. In fact, he remembered her saying that sleeping with a man other than her husband was something she could never do. She considered it the ultimate breach in morality; nevertheless, she had done it and, at the same time, become an expert in deception.

He couldn't determine which was worse. The anger or pain. He did know that he wanted to release their control over his life. He was ready to talk…he needed to talk…to gain some type of healthy perspective so that eventually he could resume living. And, he needed advice. As of yet, he hadn't filed for divorce. Neither had Amy.

Janole and Wallace were ecstatic to see him and he knew he'd made the right decision by coming to them. At a time when he most needed it, he felt supported and comforted simply by being in their home, surrounded by their love for him. He ate plenty and slept more than he had in the past few months. He and Wallace spent time together—mostly talking sports and watching television—and, in spite of his pain, he found himself laughing from time to time. He didn't realize it then but his soul was being nurtured and strengthened. At no other time in his life had he been more grateful for family.

After dinner, one evening, he confided in them. He told of Amy's affair, the shooting, her suicide attempt, and their separation.

"Oh my God," Janole said. "I'm so sorry. This is awful."

"It's been a living hell that's for sure," Marlo said.

"You had no idea she was having an affair?" Janole asked.

"I knew something was different about her. She'd changed. Become distant but at the same time she was happier than I'd seen her in a while. An affair never occurred to me."

"I'm sorry, man," Wallace said. "What did Amy say when you talked?"

"She said she was very lonely and had been for a long time. Said she didn't intend to have an affair...that it just happened. That she wanted things from our marriage that I wasn't providing. That basketball had completely taken over our lives and she needed more."

"She never told you how she felt before this conversation?" Wallace asked.

"According to her, she'd tried to talk to me but I didn't listen. To let her tell it, I'm the one responsible for the big mess that she's made of our lives," Marlo said, angrily.

"Is that what she actually said, Marlo?" Janole asked. "That doesn't sound like Amy."

Marlo took a deep breath. "Not exactly. If I remember correctly, she said I was responsible for her loneliness but not responsible for her actions. Something like that."

"And how did she explain her suicide attempt? Why would she do that?"

"She said if she and Doug weren't having an affair, the shooting would not have happened. She tried to kill herself the day Doug's death was publicized. Said she was overcome with guilt and shame."

"I can only imagine. My heart bleeds for you both," Janole said, tears rolling down her face.

The next day, Wallace and Marlo had a private, man to man talk.

"Have you decided what you're going to do?" Wallace asked.

"No, not yet. I'm sure we'll get a divorce but I haven't contacted a lawyer. Neither has she to my knowledge."

"I sure hope it doesn't come to that," Wallace said.

"Hope on, bruh. Our marriage is over. It's just a matter of the legalities. I'll never be able to trust her again and there's no way in hell I can forgive her sleeping with Doug."

"Yeah, that's tough," Wallace said with empathy. "But it doesn't have to be a death sentence for a marriage. Many marriages survive infidelity. It's not easy but it can be done."

Marlo didn't respond.

"Can I ask you something?" Wallace asked.

"Shoot."

"Was what Amy said true? About basketball taking over your lives?"

Marlo didn't answer immediately. "I've thought a lot about that. Before I knew about the affair, I realized that I was losing her and needed to do something. I even talked with Coach B about it. When Amy didn't come to Janole's birthday party, that was a wake up call. To answer your question, I did allow basketball to take over and I shouldn't have done that. Amy is right. Basketball had become our lives and that's my fault. And, she did try to talk to me about it. On more than one occasion. I won't deny that. I'm not saying I'm blameless but, still, that doesn't justify her sleeping with another man."

"But weren't you having an affair?" Wallace asked.

Marlo looked at Wallace as if he had two heads. "What did you say? I've never had an affair," Marlo said, indignantly.

"Maybe not with a woman," Wallace said, qently.

"I don't need to listen to this," Marlo said, his anger rising. "I can't believe you're taking Amy's side."

"I'm not taking Amy's side. I'm not taking anyone's side. You know how important you are to Janole and me. We love you but I want to be real with you. Man to man. We can talk later if you want."

Marlo settled down. He wanted to hear Wallace's opinion. "Go ahead," he said. "I'm listening."

"I hurt your sister very badly in spite of the best intentions. You saw her when I left. I thought I was protecting her by not telling her about the pharmaceutical company but really I disrespected her and our marriage, our partnership. I made a decision to exclude her and that decision almost destroyed us. I'm her husband and I almost destroyed her. And guess who came to the rescue? Nate, her old boyfriend. And I really couldn't blame him. After all, I was gone and she was hurting because of me.

"Nate was an issue in our marriage long after the ordeal with the pharmaceutical company was over. It was so bad between us that I thought she and Nate were having an affair or on the verge. She told me that he was there for her when I wasn't and that was a painful thing to hear. But I couldn't deny it. What I'm saying is there are times when our decisions are very hurtful to those we love.

"We get caught up in circumstances and before we know it, the damage is done. It's unintentional but still permanent. I couldn't understand Janole's anger at first but then I got it. I was wrong, Marlo. Dead wrong and it almost cost me my marriage. In that way, you and I have a lot in common. You understand what I'm saying?" Marlo nodded.

Wallace continued. "I know you don't want to hear this but you've had a mistress for years and her name was basketball. Imagine how Amy felt wanting and hoping for something different...for years. Hoping you'd hear her and acknowledge her feelings—"

"I know you're not comparing my 'affair with basketball' as you put it to Amy sleeping with another man," Marlo said, indignantly.

"Yes, I am. You can hurt people in more ways than one. You think Amy's pain is less than yours? If you think that, you're wrong."

Chapter Thirty-One

---✳---

Amy

Marlo awakened early after a restless sleep. For the first time since learning of Amy's affair, he was forced by Wallace to think of the circumstances differently. He was certain that his marriage was over but he wasn't yet ready to take the necessary step to put the divorce in motion. He wanted to walk away without regret and he'd only be able to do that when he understood and came to terms with what had gotten them to this sad place. He was now willing to admit that the answer was more complicated than Amy's affair with Doug.

With his blessing, Wallace and Janole kept their appointment with a real estate agent in Charlotte, North Carolina. They had arranged months ago to view several vacation properties there. He expected them to return in a day or two. Out of concern for him, they offered to change their plans but he wouldn't hear of it. He had the house to himself, plenty of Janole's home cooking and cable television. After his intense conversation with Wallace, he appreciated this time to himself.

While heating a healthy plate of food, he checked his phone. There was a photo from Janole of one of the properties they were considering. It was beautiful. The Charlotte area appealed to him, too. Perhaps, he'd move there himself one day. A new start may be in order. If he remained in East Lansing, he would definitely sell the house unless, of course, Amy wanted it. He couldn't imagine living in their current home without her. Again, he had the unsettling feeling that his life was out of his control with many decisions pending.

Not surprisingly, he had voice messages from Brianna and MJ. Rather than call them back, he texted them. He and the kids checked on each other regularly. Their resilience surprised him. In spite of the ugly facts, they seemed to be coping better than he...perhaps because they had finally spoken to their mother.

He didn't inquire about their conversation nor did they volunteer information. Regardless of Amy's actions, Marlo hoped—for the kids' sake—that they mended their relationship. Amy deserved their respect; he would be the first to acknowledge that she was an incredible mother. She, almost singlehandedly, raised them and did an outstanding job. He'd weighed in on the big decisions but Amy handled the everyday, routine matters. Because of Amy, their children had developed into mature, intelligent, respectful and accomplished young people. They were also kind and considerate. He was extremely proud of them.

Marlo thought about his conversation with Wallace. He never considered basketball his mistress but, without a doubt, it was his passion. For years it consumed most of his waking hours but now it wasn't as important. The responsibilities associated with being a collegiate coach had become more burden than passion probably because he needed a break. He was tapped out....drained. Ironically, now that he was ready for a different lifestyle, he had no one with whom to share it.

With a full plate and large glass of tea, he relaxed in his sister's media room with the mega sized television. He channel surfed for a while before choosing the animal channel. Later, he was awakened by the doorbell. Glancing at his watch, he was surprised to discover that he'd slept for three hours. He was even more surprised when he opened the door. He couldn't hide his shock.

"Amy, what are you doing here?" he asked. She was dressed casually in jeans, a pink top and flats. A sweater draped her shoulders and sunglasses were propped on top of her head. He hadn't seen her in months and was taken aback by her appearance. She was beautiful.

"Marlo," Amy said, equally shocked. "I didn't know you were here."

"What are you doing here?" Marlo repeated, sounding harsher than he intended.

"I-uh-came to visit Janole. I didn't know you were here," she said, apologetically.

"Did Janole know you were coming?" Marlo asked, suspiciously.

"No, it was a surprise. Obviously, it was a bad idea. Just tell Janole that I stopped by. I'll call her some other time," Amy said, turning to leave.

"Amy, you don't need to leave. Come in. You've come this far."

"Is Janole here?" Amy asked, hesitantly stepping into the foyer.

"No, she and Wallace are out of town. They'll be back in a couple of days."

Amy looked at Marlo. "I'm surprised to see you," she said.

"I needed a change and decided to hang out with family for a while."

There was an awkward silence.

"Let's sit in here," Marlo said, indicating the family room. "Do you want water or tea? Janole cooked a ton of food."

"No thanks," Amy said, nervously sliding her hands over her jeans. "I'm fine."

"The kids told me they talked to you. They were happy about that."

She smiled. "Yes, we've had several long talks. They were difficult but necessary. They're good kids."

"Yes, they are. I was thinking about them earlier today. You did an exceptional job with them."

Amy's eyes registered surprise. "Thank you for saying that. They made my job easy."

"Have you-um-seen an attorney yet? About the divorce?" Marlo asked.

"Not yet. You?"

"No, but I've been thinking about it. I don't see how we can overcome this but there's still a lot I don't understand."

Amy said nothing.

"Did you love him?" Marlo blurted out.

Amy sighed. "You asked me that at my parents' home. No, I didn't but—"

"But what?" Marlo asked.

"I don't know what my feelings could have developed into. I certainly liked how I felt when we were together. We enjoyed each other's company and shared similar interests. He was good to me," Amy said, truthfully.

"And what was I? A monster?" Marlo asked, facetiously.

"I don't want to argue, Marlo. You said there were things you don't understand and I'm answering your questions. Can we talk honestly without you getting angry?" Amy asked.

"I'll do my best," he responded.

"To answer your question, you were never a monster. Ever. You were a great provider and trusted me with decisions. In some ways, it was very easy living with you. You gave me free rein of the finances and because of your salary we enjoyed a very comfortable lifestyle. More than most. But, you were physically and emotionally unavailable and somewhat uncompromising. I always felt as though I was competing for your time and attention. There were times I felt you considered me a nuisance.

"We wanted different things I guess. I yearned for more out of life and from our marriage. I needed more of you the husband and less of you the coach. I tried to make it work because I loved you so much but I felt as if you weren't too interested in my desires and needs."

"I'm sorry, Amy. I didn't intend to make you feel that way."

"But you did...over and over," Amy said gently. "I realized we were a lost cause the week after my parents' death. I begged you to stay with me but you left for a scrimmage. Remember that?" Tears ran down her face.

"I needed you to hold me, talk to me, just to be near and available for me. I was utterly devastated by their deaths. To lose Mom and Dad at the same time and so suddenly was an unimaginable pain," Amy said, wiping her eyes and nose. "I wondered how you could be so insensitive. You had to know how much I was hurting but it didn't seem to matter. That's when I knew, without a doubt, that I couldn't compete with your job and your love of basketball and I was tired of trying."

Amy excused herself before walking hurriedly out of the room. When she returned, Marlo noticed her red eyes. Truth be told, he wanted to cry, too.

After a few moments, he spoke. "For some reason I was driven when it came to my job. I wanted to be regarded as one of the best coaches of one of the best programs in the country. That's why I worked so much. I don't know why that was important to me but it was. I wanted—needed—that recognition. And, some of the young men were in desperate need of a mentor. They looked to me as more than a coach and when they needed me I tried to be available. I wanted to be for them what Coach B was for me.

"When your parents died, I was going through a tough time. Cordell wanted my position and was trying to undermine me so that I'd be fired. That's why I felt the need to be at the scrimmage. Damage control. Eventually, I fired him."

"You never told me about that," Amy said.

"I know. You had made it clear that you weren't too interested in basketball matters," Marlo said.

"There's something else that baffles me," he admitted. "I've asked myself this question many times. Why didn't you tell me you wanted a divorce? Why continue to see Doug in secret? Why the deception?"

"Because I wasn't sure what I wanted. I was afraid and confused. Obviously, I wasn't thinking clearly. I wasn't happy with our life together but I wasn't ready for it to end either. Now that I've had time to think about it, I realize I was grieving and not just the loss of my parents. I was also grieving the loss of our marriage—the marriage I'd hoped for. No matter what I did, I couldn't make our relationship better and had to let go of my dream. Plus, MJ and Brianna were gone and that was a loss for me, too. And, I was very angry at you because you had the power to make everything right; yet, you didn't. In hindsight, I realize how empty and vulnerable I was at that time."

Amy hesitated before continuing. "I know my affair with Doug was wrong and I know I hurt you. I regret that more than I can say. In spite of my pain and disappointment—and my anger at you—I should have handled things differently. I expected more of myself."

"I'm sorry for all the pain I've caused you, too. It's been real tough for me to accept my failures as a husband. I didn't have a very good example in my father but that's no excuse," Marlo said. "God, I wish none of this had happened. Sometimes I want to put it all behind us but when I think of you and Doug together…having sex…I get so angry. I don't think I can ever forgive you for that—"

Amy's loud sigh caused Marlo to pause. "Marlo, I've apologized for having an affair. It was wrong. But please don't be self-righteous. We've both made mistakes. As I see it, you were no more faithful to me than I was to you. Whether or not you can forgive me is up to you. I'm doing my best to forgive you because I don't want to be consumed with hate and anger. I can accept that our marriage is over. Truthfully, the marriage I wanted hasn't existed for years and I've wasted enough time begging and pleading and hoping. I deserve to be happy. We both do. Hopefully, we can learn from our mistakes."

Amy glanced at her watch. "I didn't realize it was so late. I'm going to check into a hotel. It's been a long day and I'm tired."

"There's plenty of room in this huge house, Amy. You're welcome to stay here. Janole will be back soon."

"Thanks but I think I'll be more comfortable in a hotel. I'll catch up with Janole another time. I don't want to interfere with your visit but I'm glad we had a chance to talk."

"Yeah, me too," Marlo said, as he walked her to the door.

Janole phoned Amy as soon as she received the text from Marlo about Amy's visit. She suggested that they meet at Eddie's, a new establishment owned by one of her friends. The two women embraced tightly.

"How are you?" Janole asked. "I've missed you so."

"I've missed you, too, but before we get into my life, tell me about Marlon. Is he okay?"

"I'm trusting and believing that he will be completely cured. He expects to get the results soon. Marlon is strong. Stronger than he realized before this experience. And, he's seriously involved with a lovely girl. Her name is Brandy. I expect to hear wedding bells soon. I'll keep you posted on his health status. As soon as I hear, I'll let you know."

"That would be great. Thank you for not excluding me."

"You're family, Amy. Regardless of what you and Marlo decide, you are family. Don't ever think otherwise. Now tell me how you are."

"Better than I was a few months ago for sure. I'm sorry I didn't return your calls. I needed time."

"I understand. Marlo finally shared the details a couple of days ago. I can't imagine..."

"He told you about the affair?"

Janole nodded. "He told us everything. Do you want to talk about it? I assure you I will not sit in judgment."

Amy felt safe confiding in Janole even though she was Marlo's sister. Janole listened patiently, interrupting only if she lacked clarity.

After telling the entire story, Amy said, "Janole, I'm so ashamed. How did I ever let things get out of control?"

"It sounds as if you were angry, hurt and disappointed and had been for quite some time. You're only human, Amy."

"I tried to talk to Marlo so many times but at some point I should have just let him know that I wanted out or insisted that we see a marriage counselor. I can't believe I allowed myself to stoop so low. It all seems so dirty and degrading now. People are dead because of my actions," Amy said, her voice thick with emotion.

"Amy, listen to me. People are dead because of Grace's actions. You didn't pull the trigger. She did. She certainly had other options and shooting her husband should not have been one of them. You need to take responsibility for your actions, not Grace's actions. Neither Grace nor Doug is dead because of you. You need to release that guilt. Do you hear me?" Janole asked, gently.

Amy nodded. "I do but it's not easy. You sound like my therapist but somehow it means more coming from you. Thank you."

"I'm only telling you the truth," Janole said, offering a reassuring smile. "Have the police determined who killed Doug? He was murdered, right?"

"Yes, he was murdered but no arrests have been made to my knowledge. His sister has promised to keep me informed. Apparently, Doug told her about me. She's very nice and, understandably, broken up about Doug's death. The detectives have assured her that they're actively following leads but they don't tell her too much. They even questioned me but I had very little information. I do have good news though," Amy said, smiling for the first time. "The little boy who was shot by Grace was released from the hospital last week. He's expected to make a complete recovery. Thank God."

"That is good news," Janole said. "Very good news. Thank God for that." Hesitating briefly, Janole spoke again. "Can I ask you something?"

"Sure. You can ask me anything."

"Is there any hope for you and my brother?"

Amy considered Janole's question before answering. "I don't think so. Too much has happened."

"Do you still love him?"

"I honestly don't know, Janole. But even if I do, I cannot and will not go back to a one-sided relationship."

Chapter Thirty-Two

───────────✳───────────

Jenn and Paul

*S*eated at her writing desk, Jenn was so intently focused that she didn't hear Paul enter their bedroom.

"What are you doing, babe?" he asked as he sat on the bed and fell backward, enjoying the feel of their comfortable mattress.

"Just reading," Jenn said, minimizing the computer screen.

She studied her husband. Paul looked exhausted and older than just a few months ago. There were fine wrinkles around his eyes and more gray in his hair. His eyes no longer had the twinkle that communicated his zest for life. His entire affect was different. Jenn hated how their lives had changed. She knew all too well that recent events had taken a toll on her, too, but not to the extent that Paul was affected. He was heartbroken and discouraged. It was unimaginable to him that his family could ever be in such a distressing predicament.

Jenn lay beside him on the bed and tenderly caressed his face. "How are you, honey?"

"I'm okay," he said, wearily, as he loosened his tie. "I called my brothers today to fill them in. I'd been putting it off but decided that I couldn't delay any longer. It was a painfully exhausting conversation. They had so many questions."

"I'm sure they did. They adore Lynn and Ruth."

"They offered to help in any way they could including coming to stay with us for a while to lend support but I convinced them now wasn't the best time. It took a lot of talking for me to change their minds. They both sent their love to you."

"I love them, too," Jenn said. "You look tired. Why don't you take a nap. You need to rest."

"I am tired," Paul admitted. His fatigue was another indication of how drastically their lives had changed.

Jenn slipped Paul's shoes off, helped him remove his shirt and pants, and pulled the bedding back. She kissed him on his forehead and said, "I'll wake you when dinner is ready."

Paul's eyes were already closing. Jenn grabbed her computer and his cell phone so that he wouldn't be disturbed. Situating herself at the kitchen table, she immediately opened the computer and resumed reading.

Lynn was recently diagnosed with histrionic personality disorder, a condition unknown to Paul and Jenn.

Jenn read aloud, "HPD is characterized by a pattern of excessive attention-seeking emotions, usually beginning in early adulthood... including inappropriate seductive behavior...histrionic people are lively, dramatic...and flirtatious. They have a high need for attention...exaggerate their behaviors and emotions...exhibit sexually provocative behavior. Other associated features include egocentrism, self-indulgence...and persistent manipulative behavior to achieve their own needs..."

That describes Lynn to a tee, Jenn thought. She continued reading.

"People with HPD are usually high-functioning with good social skills. They use their social skills to manipulate others into making them the center of attention...related conditions include antisocial and narcissistic personality disorders."

Jenn could no longer read because of the tears that blurred her eyes. Though she refused to admit it, she'd known for quite some time that Lynn was different...in a socially inappropriate way. Jenn now had an answer but that knowledge offered little comfort; similar to not knowing the cause of a loved one's death. When provided with the answer, it can offer a degree of closure but still the loved one is gone. Lynn suffered from a mental disorder and the diagnosis helped in understanding the cause of her behavior; it did nothing to lessen the pain of her actions.

Jenn relived the events of recent months. The day of Lynn's arrest for assaulting the detective, Paul followed the police cruiser to the 4th Precinct where Lynn was taken. She and Ruth, in tears, urged him to drive faster. Upon arriving, they were forced to wait while Lynn was processed for the assault on Detective Biles. Then Lynn and Ruth were each questioned separately about the Sabrina Lucas situation. Paul was with Lynn during her interview while she remained with Ruth.

According to Paul, Lynn berated the detectives and rudely responded to their questions. Her language and disrespectful tone, though not directed at Paul, were insulting to him. He was astonished by Lynn's uncooperative and combative behavior and couldn't believe her rantings and ravings. Finally, he'd had enough and demanded that she stop. He was furious and made it clear to her that her behavior was unacceptable. Perhaps Lynn saw something in Paul's eyes that she had not seen before because she immediately quieted down.

As the interview progressed, Paul's concern for Lynn escalated as did his fear. Her answers to the detectives' questions were inconsistent and she expressed extreme hostility towards the Lucus girl. In the other room Jenn had watched, sympathetically, as Ruth answered all questions calmly though, at times, tearfully. It appeared to Jenn that she was telling the truth but Jenn couldn't help but wonder whether Ruth knew more than she was revealing.

Finally, the interviews were complete and the assault matter handled. They arrived home close to three o'clock the next morning. Not one word was uttered during the ride home. Everyone was exhausted but rest did not come easy for Paul and Jenn. They talked for several hours before finally giving in to a restless slumber.

Seven days later, the detectives returned with an arrest warrant for Lynn as well as a search warrant. The charge — attempted murder.

Again, Lynn resorted to loud and belligerent rantings while the detectives read her Miranda rights. Paul telephoned a friend, Jason Bryson, who was also a successful and highly regarded criminal attorney. Paul explained the situation and asked Jason to represent Lynn. Built like a linebacker, Jason was physically intimidating with a no nonsense personality. He met with Lynn, bluntly explained to her the implications of her behavior, informed her that she would be tried as an adult since she was sixteen years old, and made it clear that if she continued with her theatrics she would foolishly turn a bad situation into a living nightmare.

"This isn't high school drama," he sternly advised. "This is a legal matter with serious consequences so you'd better pull it together quickly. Do you realize that you're looking at a prison sentence if you're convicted? Unless you think you know more than me, you need to listen to me and be quiet." Lynn calmed down though her indignation was apparent.

Jenn stared out of the window as she recalled the unbelievable events that occurred after Lynn's arrest. Never in her wildest dreams — or worst nightmares — did she imagine her family would be in the center of this horrible and embarrassing predicament.

Their home had been thoroughly searched from top to bottom. Lynn's computer, phone and several pill bottles were among the items confiscated.

Jenn and Paul posted bail which allowed Lynn to be released into their custody. They were forced to face painful realities about Lynn but nothing prepared them for the devastation she was capable of inflicting. Lynn acknowledged that though there was an attempt to hurt Sabrina, she was not involved. Without blinking an eye, she calmly informed them that Ruth was the guilty party.

"She planned it all and put the drug in Sabrina's soda. It was her, not me. You've got the wrong one," Lynn said, then laughed in a way that was alarming. "You don't even know if I'm Lynn. Are you sure the right twin was arrested?"

It was a rude awakening for Ruth when Lynn shifted the blame to her. Throughout the ordeal of Lynn's arrest, Ruth was so consumed with worry that she felt ill. From the time the detectives had arrived, she'd alternated between crying and fighting nausea. She was also guilt-ridden because she had knowledge about some of Lynn's secrets and, though she sometimes disapproved of Lynn's actions, she always protected her sister — always.

Initially, Ruth believed Lynn to be joking when she accused her of hurting Sabrina. Jenn recalled the shock and disbelief on Ruth's face. But Lynn persisted in her accusations and her intentions became painfully clear to Ruth.

"Lynn, why would you say that? I have no idea what you're talking about. You're lying! Stop it!" Ruth pleaded with her sister but Lynn did not change her story.

Ruth desperately tried to convince every one of her innocence but, because of her bond with Lynn, it was not an easy sell.

It took a while to sort out the facts. It was confirmed that, due to menstrual cramps, it was Ruth who had skipped lunch the day that Sabrina became ill. This was verified by the assistant coach who, being a twin herself, had no difficulty in differentiating between Ruth and Lynn. In addition, two teammates who were eyewitnesses identified Lynn as the one who dropped pills in Sabrina's drink during lunch and several others reported that Lynn bragged about fixing things so that Sabrina wouldn't be a part of the team or ever able to play soccer again.

How did they know for certain that it was Lynn and not Ruth who put the pills in Sabrina's drink? Because just before leaving Seattle for camp, a group of them had gone together to get tattoos. Ruth, who suffers severe cramping before and during her menstrual cycle, stayed at home. Lynn chose to have a small red heart tattooed on the inside of her wrist. On the day that Sabrina was taken ill, the girls remembered seeing Lynn's tattoo during lunch.

Ruth maintained that she had no knowledge of Lynn's plan and wanted her name cleared. To be as sure as possible, the girls were asked to take a polygraph test. Ruth passed with flying colors. Lynn took the test with bravado but failed. *Poor Ruth*. Jenn was worried about both daughters but for different reasons. Being in the same house with Lynn, forced to relive the pain of her accusations, devastated by her betrayal, and facing their friends and teammates were extreme hardships for Ruth. Hardships that she didn't deserve; hardships that she found incapable of handling. Ruth was so traumatized that Paul and Jenn made the tough decision to send her for an indefinite stay with Paul's parents who now lived in Florida.

Their anticipated move to the District of Columbia was on hold indefinitely which necessitated Paul having a tough conversation with many, including his new partner, Nigel. Paul was encouraged when, after hearing the entire story, Nigel agreed to delay their time-line. What was most meaningful to Paul during their conversation was Nigel's prayer for Paul and his family.

Paul had shared with Jenn that after talking with Nigel, he felt a level of gratitude that he couldn't express. He had convinced himself that Nigel may renege on their plans after being made aware of the details but that wasn't the case. Paul's relief was monumental; at least one problem was removed from the long list. Still, the uncertainty about their future was troubling at best. All plans were on hold.

Lynn was in therapy, a desperate need for her mental health and her legal case. The trial was scheduled to begin in eight months pending no continuances. After being arrested, Lynn's behaviors became more disturbing. Jenn and Paul were at a loss for what more they could do. They'd hired one of the best attorneys, sent Ruth to family where she would be nurtured and cared for, and secured the services of a top psychiatrist; yet, they'd never felt more helpless.

This was magnified for Paul. A lawyer and teacher of the law, he understood that there were two sides to a legal case. He knew that facts could be distorted and twisted by both the defense and prosecution. He also knew that mental illness was difficult to prove and, often, juries were skeptical. And, if Lynn's outbursts and narcissistic behavior didn't change, she would—perhaps singlehandedly—seal her own fate.

As a child, Jenn witnessed the death of her two year old brother. As an adult, she witnessed her own daughter's arrest for attempted murder. Both events were painfully and permanently etched in her mind. One, a tragic accident; the other, a horrible premeditated and devious scheme. And, the mastermind was her own daughter. *Lynn, how could you?*

Thanks to Lynn, life for the Donaldson family was anything but happy. They were in survival mode; each day requiring its own strength.

Sitting at her kitchen table oblivious to her surroundings, Jenn released unrelenting pain and anguish, her shoulders heaving as she quietly sobbed.

EPILOGUE

─────────── ✳ ───────────

*J*anole, dressed in a sleeveless tee-shirt and shorts, looked up at the blue sky decorated by clouds that reminded her of cotton balls. She enjoyed the feel of her face being caressed by the misty breeze and the warm sun as she stood on the cruise ship's deck. The view was breathtaking.

The luxury liner was massive—offering many attractions, delicious food, and every possible amenity—and one of the most beautiful Janole had seen. Even more impressive was the vast ocean which made the ship appear miniscule. She looked in all directions and as far as she could see, there was only water. No land in sight. She was humbled as she watched the ship slice through the deep water like a knife through softened butter.

Her mind immediately thought of the beginning as described in Genesis. *"In the beginning, God created the heavens and the earth... Let the waters beneath the sky flow together into one place, so dry ground may appear...and that is what happened. God called the dry ground 'land' and the waters 'seas.' And God saw that it was good."* Janole continued to stare out at the waters, enthralled. *Yes, Lord, it is good. It is magnificent!*

Amazingly, an entire year had passed; her birthday was less than two weeks away. She recalled the events of the past twelve months with mixed feelings and searched for the one word that could best describe their experiences. Convoluted, complex, overwhelming, challenging, painful, distresssing. She quickly gave up, realizing that she was at a loss to identify one word or even one phrase to capture what they had collectively endured.

In a year's time, life had presented unexpected challenges and significant changes. Some of the challenges, though extremely difficult and painful, brought about positive outcomes. Lessons were learned, wisdom gained and lives enriched. There were also regrettable—even tragic—circumstances with a great deal of suffering and pain attached. Again, lessons were learned and wisdom gained but at an astronomical price. And, in some instances, lives were in limbo—hanging in the balance—with outcomes yet to be determined.

The best news was that Marlon was cancer-free. Janole smiled as she recalled that special day. Marlon had come to their home to share the news and without saying a word, Janole knew. As soon as she opened the door, he picked her up and twirled her around. She laughed and cried at the same time. They both did.

When Wallace walked in and witnessed their joy, he grabbed Marlon and held him tightly. They celebrated that evening with an impromptu party, inviting family and friends. They celebrated again the following weekend when Janole's mother, Corie, and Eric arrived. Sunday, they all went to church together: Janole and Wallace, Brandy and Marlon, Marlo, Nick, Corie and Bernard, and Eric.

Of course, Marlon would be tested regularly. They all knew that there was a chance of the cancer returning but for now he was well and they were all remaining prayerful. Marlon couldn't be happier or more excited. He was coaching at GW and engaged to Brandy. He also took every opportunity to speak about his cancer experience and the importance of being tested. Janole looked to the heavens. *Thank You, Lord, for answering our prayers.*

Sadly, Marlo and Amy were making plans to divorce, both of the mindset that their marriage was irreparable. Janole refused to give up hope and continued to pray for them daily. Interestingly, they were unclear as to how they felt about each other. When asked the question, they avoided answering it. But, they both expressed that too much had happened to overcome. At least, they weren't enemies, Janole thought. They were resolving the necessary issues rather amicably but it was apparent to all who knew them that they both were hurting. And, they both had regrets. From Janole's perspective, Marlo and Amy were made for each other but perhaps the pain was too great. Relationships can be destroyed. Janole knew that only too well. But, she would continue to pray for their marriage. She would not give up on them...not yet.

Janole had been disappointed to learn that her best friend's move to D.C. was delayed but when Jenn shared the full story, Janole forgot her own disappointment. Instead, she was devastated for Jenn and Paul. Janole was familiar with personality disorders but not the specifics of Lynn's disorder.

Jenn's description of Lynn's behavior, however, painted a disturbingly vivid picture and the impact to their family was heartbreaking. Janole could only imagine Jenn and Paul's plight as they waited anxiously for the trial to begin. Regardless of the jury's verdict, they would continue to face difficult challenges because Lynn's condition was permanent. Poor Ruth. She, too, was in therapy as she attempted to cope with the circumstances and deal with her own pain.

Even now, Janole whispered a prayer. As Jenn's confidante and sounding board, she was determined to be available for her friend. She took every opportunity to remind Jenn that, as with Marlon's cancer, Lynn's disorder was out of Jenn's hands. She knew that Jenn— as a mother—blamed herself for Lynn's behavior, at least in part. She empathized with Jenn's pain but as Janole took in the view of the heavenly skies and the massive ocean, she was reassured that Jenn's problems—all problems—could easily be handled by the Creator of this magnificent universe.

The Donaldsons were the only invited guests unable to join Wallace and Janole on the cruise. And, of course, Amy decided it best that she not attend under the circumstances. Janole missed her dear friends but was happy—and grateful—that everyone else important to them was sharing in this special celebration of life.

There was much to celebrate. On the advice of their attorney months ago, Janole and Wallace decided to sue the pharmaceutical company. The case was settled out of court, quickly and quietly, with the pharmaceutical company offering an amount that surpassed their expectations. As a result, Janole and Wallace were millionaires, many times over. Janole pinched herself at times to convince herself that she wasn't dreaming.

Janole had never felt a greater sense of peace—and joy—and it was unrelated to their new financial status. She knew that no amount of money could buy a happy marriage, health, mental stability or peace of mind. Money couldn't buy family...and love. And, she would be the first to acknowledge that the acquisition of money had nothing to do with the growth she had experienced for it was priceless.

In a year's time, she had gained a deeper appreciation of forgiveness, compassion, faith, hope and purpose. And, not only that—in a year's time—she came to more fully understand God's unwavering faithfulness and His unconditional love.

She sensed her husband's presence before she felt his warm arms embrace her. She and Wallace stood together—joined in spirit and love—thankful for the blessing of one another as they watched the setting sun.

Unlike her last birthday, she was eagerly anticipating this one and celebrating it with those she loved, especially Wallace.

Do you think anyone is going to be able to drive a wedge between us and Christ's love for us? There is no way! Not trouble, not hard times, not hatred, not hunger, not homelessness, not bullying threats, not backstabbing, not even the worst sins listed in Scripture...I'm absolutely convinced that nothing— nothing living or dead, angelic or demonic, today or tomorrow, high or low, thinkable or unthinkable— absolutely nothing can get between us and God's love because of the way that Jesus our Master has embraced us.

Romans 8: 37-39 The New Message

Discussion Questions

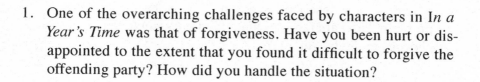

1. One of the overarching challenges faced by characters in *In a Year's Time* was that of forgiveness. Have you been hurt or disappointed to the extent that you found it difficult to forgive the offending party? How did you handle the situation?

2. Are there "unforgivable" actions? If so, what are they? What advice would you offer to one who is the victim of an "unforgivable" act? Likewise, what advice would you offer to one who is the perpetrator of an "unforgivable" act?

3. With what female character or circumstance can you most identify? Why? Conversely, which female character was most disturbing to you? Why?

4. With what male character or circumstance can you most identify? Why? Conversely, which male character was most disturbing to you? Why?

5. Divorce statistics in the United States are higher than ever. What, in your opinion, are the contributing and causal factors? What advice would you offer a young couple contemplating divorce?

6. Janole and Jenn make reference to God "speaking" to them. Has God spoken to you? In what ways does God communicate with us?

7. Wallace prohibited Janole from having further contact with Nate. Janole refused to end her friendship with Nate. Which of the two, do you feel, were justified in their actions? Why? How are relationships impacted by a spouse's or partner's friends of the opposite sex?

8. Amy accused her husband, Marlo, of being as guilty of unfaithfulness to her (referring to his involvement with basketball) as she was to him (referring to her affair with Doug). What are your thoughts? Do you believe their marriage is salvageable?

9. Suicide can be described as a permanent solution to a temporary problem. How are families and loved ones impacted by one who chooses to die by suicide?

10. Grace decided to kill Doug rather than accept that their relationship was over. Ellen chose to threaten Janole whom she considered a rival for Nate's affections. What do these women have in common? What might be underlying causes of their behaviors?

CHERYL M. ROBINSON

A story of betrayal, regret, and human frailty
that test the capacity to forgive.

ABOUT THE AUTHOR

Cheryl M. Robinson is a graduate of the University of Virginia and
George Mason University. She is also the author of And, Not Only That
which was nominated for the 2016 Christian Literary Henri Award. She
enjoys writing novels that inspire, encourage, inform and uplift. She
has worked in corporate America and public eduction. A recent retiree,
her twenty-five year career in Education included the positions of
professional school counselor, career and college counselor, guidance
director and school counseling program manager. A native of Charles
City, Virginia, she currently lives in Charlotte, North Carolina with her
husband, Will. Together, they have four children and four
grandchildren. Hobbies include playing tennis and reading.

Feel free to connect with Cheryl at **www.cherylmrobinson.com**
or cherylmrob@yahoo.com.

* * * * *

And, Not Only That is available at Amazon.com.

Book Cover Design:
Doug James | The D. James Group, Houston, TX
www.thedjamesgroup.com

Copyright 2016 © Cheryl M. Robinson

CPSIA information can be obtained
at www.ICGtesting.com
Printed in the USA
BVOW03s2307130117
473483BV00001B/1/P